The Cymry Ring

Michael Allen Dymmoch

DIVERSIONBOOKS

Also by Michael Allen Dymmoch

The Fall
M.I.A.
Death in West Wheeling

Caleb & Thinnes Mysteries
The Man Who Understood Cats
The Death of Blue Mountain Cat
Incendiary Designs
The Feline Friendship
White Tiger

Diversion Books
A Division of Diversion Publishing Corp.
443 Park Avenue South, Suite 1008
New York, New York 10016
www.DiversionBooks.com

This is a work of fiction. Names, characters, places and incidents either are the
product of the author's imagination or are used fictitiously. Any resemblance to
actual persons, living or dead, events or locales is entirely coincidental.

For more information, email info@diversionbooks.com

First Diversion Books edition June 2015.
Print ISBN: 978-1-68230-047-3
eBook ISBN: 978-1-62681-820-0

For
Ruth Rauter,
Mary Ann Rosberg
and Marilee Luttig
Romantics in the finest sense of the word.

Thanks to Mary Harris for her good advice.

March 21

I

Sunday. Pale edges of dawn defined the horizon above the eastern shore of Cymry reservoir, sketching naked trees to the north and south as the first splinters of sunlight spilled across water steaming in the frigid air. Ian Carreg pulled his small sports car to the verge of the cliff that formed the reservoir's western edge. He emerged, gray and balding. He disrobed and walked, naked, to the edge of sky. Poising momentarily, in shivering parody of the classic diver's pose, he described a perfect parabola diving into the icy water.

He cut the surface with little splash, bracing himself for the heart-stopping shock, plunging far below. The numbing, cramping cold gripped his whole being, and for a moment he was frozen. *Shattering!* he thought as he descended. *So easy to give up...*

But as a cold-induced tetany seized his extremities, he fought it. *Tempering!* he told himself, *Bracing!*

In-vig-or-a-ting. He forced his cold-numbed will to oppose his momentum. He forced his anguished muscles to resist. When he resurfaced, spraying steaming breath and water into the March air, he let out a whoop of delight at having survived what had become— since his university days, when he'd first dived on a dare—an annual ritual. It was the vernal equinox, the first day of spring.

"Marjory was right," he told himself as he began the long swim to the water's edge. "I'm getting too old for this."

Marjory!

It'd been weeks since he'd last thought of her. No. Longer. Thinking of her still brought pain. *But Marjory was right. Life goes on.* Tomorrow he'd wear his swimming costume. Tomorrow he'd go down to the road-entrance of the reservoir and climb to a sane distance from the water before diving in. Tomorrow his swim would be purely exercise. *Oh Marjory, love!*

He reached the western wall and treaded water as he groped for a handhold along the frosted stone. Stiffened by cold, his hands obeyed reluctantly. Steam poured from his mouth and boiled from his skin as he heaved himself onto the ledge that formed the first step of his climb back to the car. His lungs burned. His limbs grew rubbery with fatigue. His feet became scalding weights that answered clumsily and with deadened sensation, but as he considered the alternative, he kept on climbing.

When he'd hauled himself onto the cliff top, he didn't pause to contemplate the sunrise, but hot-footed it across the frosted grass. He dried off quickly, scraping the water off with a thick terry towel, then he shivered into his clothes. He combed his thinning hair with numb fingers and smoothed his mustache to make himself presentable before climbing into the car and starting the motor.

With the heater turned on full, Ian backed away from the verge and turned the small red vehicle toward home. He drove fast, but with the conditioned expertise of practice, changing up and down without thought or grinding. He took no real chances, although he exceeded the limits by an extensive amount until the more regular recurrence of houses signaled the town boundary. He parked in front of his block and got out, picked up the *Times* from near the front door, then climbed to the second floor.

II

The drawing room into which he let himself was conventionally furnished save that one entire wall was covered by bookshelves. An orderly office area with desk, computer terminal, and file cabinet occupied a corner. On the wall behind the desk hung a framed citation for exceptional police work. Marjory's portrait—her lovely, younger self—smiled at him from the desk, flanked by the smaller, family photos. Except for the citation and the wall of books, the decor reflected Marjory's tastes more than his own, but as he could not have said how he'd have gone about re-doing the flat, he was content with her arrangements, and comforted—as if her presence lingered in the room.

The large cat perched on the back of an armchair by the door greeted him with a personable "Yee-oow."

Ian said, "Good morning, Charles."

He crossed to the desk and lifted the portrait. As he gazed at the cherished face, he probed for remnants of the pain he'd once felt, gingerly, the way one probes for toothache. He found only mild regret. They had wanted to grow old together. He sighed.

"Not this year, Luv."

Marjory smiled back as if to say, "I'm glad."

"You were right, Luv. Life goes on."

Shivering, he put the portrait back and hurried along the hallway to the loo. He undressed while he ran up the hot water. It took almost all there was to warm him, but by the time he emerged from the steam, he was whistling, and he grinned at the fogged mirror.

"Count Dracula, I presume."

He turned on the fan and wiped the mirror. With Charles looking on from a perch on the basin, Ian stared at his face, examining the wrinkles, thrusting his chin out to make the lines disappear. "Not bad for fifty-five," he told the unimpressed Charles. Ian was not himself impressed. In his mind, he was still thirty. The face that looked back at him was older than he felt. The thinning thatch, the grizzled brows, mustache and sideburns, the lines, and the gray stubble were incongruous. Only the eyes were still right. Hunter's eyes. Charles rubbed his face against Ian's shoulder, and Ian ran a knuckle along the cat's jaw line. He reached for his electric shaver. His steam-softened whiskers resisted the rotary blades, so he took his time.

When he'd finished in the loo—it being Sunday—he adhered to tradition, laying out a dress shirt and a suitable-for-church suit and, though he had no intention of leaving the flat for hours, he selected his best tie and knotted it round his neck.

In the cheerful yellow kitchen, equipped with the gadgets that make life tolerable—microwave, Cuisinart, digital coffee machine—he put his suit coat on a chair back, tucked a tea towel around his waist for an apron, then rolled up his sleeves. He fried sausages and eggs while he squeezed juice from fresh oranges. And he brewed Darjeeling in a Wedgwood pot his grandmother had owned, warming a croissant in the microwave while the tea steeped. Charles supervised.

Ian lay the table with a place mat, silverware and cloth serviette and put a second place mat on the floor for Charles. He emptied a tin of cat food onto a plate that matched the teapot and set it down for the cat before serving his own meal.

"*Bon appetit*, Charles."

Ian ate slowly, savoring every taste and texture, even the aroma of the tea. He felt clean and pleasantly tired, completely relaxed, and—as his hunger abated—totally satisfied. Only the real, physical presence of Marjory could have improved on his feeling of well-being. Only the flesh and blood woman, for she was still with him in the sense that her hand was everywhere. She had decorated the flat and, over the years, had helped him to establish the routines that had eased him through his grief. Like Sunday breakfast. And midnight Mass at Easter and Christmas. Ian sighed and watched Charles finish his breakfast and begin his wash.

Later, Charles watched Ian wash up, using the tea towel, again tucked into his waistband, to protect his suit. When he'd rinsed the last plate and put it in the rack to drain, he used the sprayer to water the potted herbs that sat on the windowsill behind the sink. Parsley, sage, rosemary—*that's for remembrance*—thyme and basil, as well as tarragon and oregano. He brushed the rosemary gently and breathed in the piney scent he'd liberated. "You don't get that from a tin, Charles," he told the cat as he wiped his hands on the cloth and draped it over a chair back to dry.

Charles followed him into the drawing room and perched on

the back of his recliner when he sat down. Ian put on his reading glasses and had just settled himself comfortably with the *Times* when the phone rang. He regarded it with irritation. He let it ring several times before getting up to answer—phone calls on Sunday were bound to mean trouble. He said "Hello" cautiously.

His daughter-in-law's voice answered. "Hello, Dad. How've you been?" Susannah seemed more than averagely cheerful.

"Well enough, thank you. Has something come up?"

"No, dinner's still on. Margaret's still coming. In fact, she's bringing a friend."

As Ian waited for her to get to the point, he said, cautiously, "Anyone I know?"

"Someone she met in New York. The problem is the drains are blocked."

Aha! he thought. "Have you tried calling a plumber?"

Susannah ignored the sarcasm, or didn't notice. "Of course I have, but you know how difficult it is to get someone on Sunday."

Ian sighed. He could beg off dinner, but it'd been six months since he'd seen Margaret. He said, "Very well, I'll come early and see what I can do."

"Thanks, Dad."

She rang off, and Ian shook his head as he looked around at Charles. "What I get for sending my son to university."

III

Ian descended the stair wearing only a vest above his trousers. He threw the rag he was wiping his hands on over his shoulder and took a gold ring and a Rolex out of his pocket, putting the ring on his right ring finger and the watch on his left wrist. It seemed to him that Susannah looked radiant as she waited at the foot with his shirt.

"It's fixed," he told her. "Someone flushed a rag down."

She held the shirt up for him. "Oops. I can't imagine where my mind's been lately." She was blond, and pretty in a modern sort of way. Rather too thin, he thought. Fit, she said. Built much like the actress Cher, with long, tanned legs. She was wearing one of those modern things, which left too little to the imagination, and she had an alluring rosy glow.

He shoved an arm into the shirt without comment beyond a raised eyebrow.

Susannah didn't notice. "Have a cuppa with Peter while I clean up. He has something to tell you…" She gave him a smile that would've made him catch his breath if she hadn't been his son's wife.

Ian nodded and shrugged himself into his shirt.

"…And thanks, Dad."

Peter was in the kitchen, on the phone. He was twenty-five and active, though he made his living with his mind. He waved to acknowledge Ian's entrance, but kept his attention on the call. Ian hung his jacket on a chair back, poured himself tea, then took his reading glasses from his pocket. He had just started on the *Times* when Peter put down the phone.

"Brace yourself, Dad."

Reluctantly, Ian put the paper down. He took off his glasses with resignation.

"You're going to be a grandfather."

It was unexpected, though certainly not unwelcome news, and Ian stood to offer Peter his hand. "Peter, that's wonderful! When?"

"Late September."

"Well," Ian said, "Well!" The handshake developed into a heartfelt hug. "This certainly calls for a toast!"

Just then, Susannah came in, and Ian swept her up to kiss her warmly.

"You'd think it was *his* first child!" she told Peter as he got out glasses and a bottle of old scotch.

Peter poured drinks for Ian and himself, but didn't offer Susannah one, nor did she seem to expect it.

Ian held up his glass and told Susannah, "Grandchildren are much better. More fun, less work."

They toasted grandchildren. And children. And a number of other things. Susannah poured herself the last of the tea. The afternoon passed swimmingly. Just past three, it started to snow. Peter was indignant.

"Do you believe this weather? The first day of spring!"

"I find it rather invigorating," Ian said.

"I suppose you ran your five kilometers this morning?"

"Swam. In the spring and summer I *swim.*"

Peter shook his head. "In the reservoir, I suppose? Mum was right. Someday you're going to kill yourself pulling that old trick and they'll find your remains in August, floating, or on the bottom with the dead soldiers and the victims of those nasty pagan rites."

"Dead soldiers?" Susannah asked, bewildered. "Pagan rites?"

Ian told her, "Before Cymry was a reservoir, it was a flooded quarry—some say back beyond Roman times. And legend has it the druids used to throw virgins in the spring there, as gifts to the local gods."

"Virgin soldiers?" she said, dryly.

"'Dead soldiers' is American slang for empty beer bottles," Peter told her. "I'll wager there're a few of those…"

Just then, Susannah heard something and went to the window. "Here's Margaret."

Ian stood up to look. Through the window he could see an unfamiliar car. And through its passenger window, he could see his daughter. The dark-haired man driving was a stranger. "Who's that with her?" He took his jacket from the chair back as he spoke and put it on as he started for the door.

"Must be her friend from New York," Susannah said. She followed Ian's example and pulled on her jumper as they hurried outside.

Margaret didn't seem to notice the weather as she got out of the car. She wasn't wearing a coat. Her father's daughter, Ian thought as she ran up to hug him. He held her at arm's length. At twenty-three, she looked like a younger version of Marjory, gray-eyed and gold-haired.

He said, "Let me look at you!" Margaret beamed.

He paid scant attention to the young man who got quietly out of the driving seat.

"Well, New York agrees with you," Ian told his daughter.

"Michael agrees with me."

Ian took this in with some dismay, turning to inspect Michael, who'd stepped to one side with Peter and Susannah and was waiting deferentially for an introduction. He was as tall as Ian— six-one, dark-haired and gray-eyed, about thirteen stone with no distinguishing marks visible.

Margaret realized that she'd temporarily forgotten him and hurriedly made introductions. "Da, Peter, Susannah, this is Michael. Michael Gwaed. Michael, my father—Ian Carreg, and Peter and Susannah."

Michael offered Ian his hand. "How do you do, sir?"

Ian was subtly alarmed, but he was careful to remain cordial. He said, "Gwaed. Welsh, isn't it?"

"My parents emigrated after the War."

Ian watched him thoughtfully as he shook hands with Peter and Susannah. The young man was reserved and alert, and seemed unperturbed by the scrutiny. And he had eyes like a police inspector. Ian wondered what he did for a living, but before he had a chance to ask, Peter reminded them of the weather.

"Let's get in out of this. We've time for a drink before we go. Our booking is for half past seven."

"Where did you meet?" Ian asked when they were installed again around the kitchen table. Peter had fetched glasses, and Susannah was making more tea.

Margaret's eyes shone with mischief, and Ian intercepted the look she shot Michael's way. "Oh, Michael came to my rescue when my apartment—that's American for flat—was burglarized." She smiled.

"You didn't tell me about *that*," Ian said, feeling further alarm.

"In New York, it's like getting roaches. Only in this case, they took *everything*—every pot and pan, every stick of furniture, even the fruit crates I was using for end tables. All they left were my books and photographs. Thank God they left the photos!

"Anyway, Michael came to my rescue, loaned me some dishes and a bed…"

Ian felt his eyes widening—Margaret made the loan of a bed sound as inconsequential as the loan of a few pence. Even as he hoped she meant it only literally, he knew it was stupid, antediluvian really, to suppose she was still a virgin, or that her loss of naiveté was anything more than a symbol that she was her own woman and no longer his little girl.

"…and he put some *real* locks on my doors, which seems to have taken care of the problem." She shot Michael a patently adoring look.

Ian cringed. She hadn't mentioned Michael in her letters, and that was a telling omission. He stared at the man as if to coerce some sign of guilt or a confession from him; Michael returned a look that was politely attentive. Peter and Susannah didn't seem to have noticed anything.

"Tell us all about America," Peter said.

And so, over the balance of the scotch, Margaret filled them in on New York.

The pub had a bar that was contiguous with the restaurant, and most of its patrons were old acquaintances. The landlord greeted Ian, Peter and Susannah by name, and nodded sociably to Michael and Margaret. He seated them on the restaurant side, with Ian between his children.

It was an old place, carefully renovated—with oak beams and the like—to preserve the tourist trade. Ian watched Michael study it and waited for his verdict.

With a wink at Margaret, he announced dryly, "An authentic English pub."

All the Carregs laughed.

"Regulation, you mean," Ian said. "Everything the guidebooks promise. The *real* authentic's in the back—billiard-saloon, video games, goggle-box…"

"Don't spoil our fun, Da," Margaret insisted.

The waitress stopped in front of the table. "What'll it be, then?"

"Guinness all right?" Ian asked. "Susannah? A half won't hurt." Susannah shrugged. The others nodded. Ian told the waitress, "Guinness," and, indicating Susannah, said, "Just a half for her."

After she'd departed, Margaret asked, "What's it you're into this time, Da?"

"Goldsmithing."

"Yeah," Peter said, "show them your ring, Dad." He leaned over the table to tell Margaret, "It's really something!"

Ian took off his ring and handed it to her. "The style's Celtic—late first century B.C.—but the design's my own."

Margaret passed the ring to Michael, who studied it, then passed it to Susannah.

When it got to Peter, he told Ian, "I wouldn't mind if you left it to me."

Ian took back the ring and said, with thinly veiled affection, "What makes you think I've left you anything?"

Margaret ignored the two of them to tell Michael, "Since Mum died, my father's become the most accomplished amateur in Britain. He's always studying something or other at evening classes…" She turned to Ian. "…How many has it been, Da? Cabinet-making, cooking, conversational Welsh, local history and horseshoeing that I know of. What else?"

Ian looked at Peter and said, dryly, "Plumbing."

Peter grinned. "Ouch."

As the waitress arrived with their pints, Susannah asked, "Are you planning to start a second career when you retire, Dad?"

"Actually, it's a great way to meet girls." He raised his glass. "To continuing education!"

They all laughed and drank.

The waitress asked, "Are you ready to order?"

"Fish'n chips," Michael said, with a wink at Margaret.

Susannah, Peter and Ian groaned in unison. Ian said, "Why don't you give us a chance to prove English cooking's not as bad as it's reputed?" He realized, suddenly, that Michael was having him on. He gave Margaret a questioning look. "What sort of fellow have you got here?"

Margaret took his arm and smiled disarmingly. "Oh, one who's almost as sharp as my Da."

They'd nearly finished eating when the landlord approached. "Phone for you, sir. Are you here?"

"That depends on who it is."

"A man who says he's your boss. Someone from the Criminal Investigation Department?"

"I'd better take it."

"How did CID find you *here?*" Susannah asked.

"They're detectives."

Ian walked to the bar and took the phone from the barman, moving as far down the bar as the cord would permit. He recognized Andrew Blemming's voice as soon as he said, "Ian!"

Ian listened to what he wanted, then said, "Can't it wait?" Andrew thought it couldn't and said so vociferously. "I'm painfully aware I'm on the scene, Andrew," Ian told him. "This is my only day off. I haven't had a day off in three weeks. Tomorrow, Andrew. Tomorrow morning. I'll have the advantage of surprise. No one expects to be taken in charge before breakfast." He rang off while he had the last word and gave the phone back to the barman.

As Ian returned to the table, he heard Susannah tell Margaret, "I wish your father would meet someone nice. Sometimes I think he must be dreadfully lonely."

"I heard that!" he said sharply. He looked at Margaret and Michael, though chiefly at Michael. "Susannah's a wonderful daughter-in-law but a bit of a butt-in-ski." He looked at Susannah with mock severity. "I'm *not* lonely. I'm perfectly satisfied with my life, especially now that you and Peter are deigning to give me a grandchild."

This news must have been known to Margaret for she merely smiled.

Susannah said, "Don't change the subject, Dad. Whatever happened to that Irish girl from the BBC?"

Ian smiled wryly. "I found out her idea of the good life is a cottage with a white picket fence and fifteen children. So I introduced her to a nice fellow in forensics with similar delusions."

"So you *are* alone again!"

"You make it sound like a disease. I'm alone as much as I care to be, thank you."

"Da, what happened to Claire?" Margaret asked.

"Nothing happened to Claire," he said stiffly. "We see each other from time to time." He looked at his family members. "I wish the lot of you would let me manage my own love life."

Michael seemed, suddenly, to find his plate fascinating.

Margaret took Ian's arm and rested her head against his shoulder. "Don't be sore, Da. We just worry about you, living alone."

Ian softened. "I'm not living alone."

"Yeah," Peter said, "don't forget Charles."

"Who's Charles?" Margaret demanded. "Da, you haven't gone faggy in your old age?"

Ian scowled at Peter. "Charles is my cat."

Peter grinned.

"So, Dad," Susannah asked, "what was the phone call? Are you going to drop everything and go running off to catch a crook?"

"Not this time."

They brought the warmth kindled over supper back with them to Peter's drawing room, and made themselves comfortable around the fire Peter had laid out earlier. When Peter handed the brandy around, Ian felt a stab of regret that Marjory wasn't there to share his pride and delight in these grown-up children. He fought the feeling. Perhaps Marjory had anticipated all of this. Certainly she'd seen ahead. She'd recognized Margaret's beauty when she was still a gawky teenager in teeth-braces and seen Peter's intelligence when he was flunking math. And of what use was regret? Sipping his brandy, he banished it and, as he soaked up the warmth from within and without, he told himself he couldn't fault his life. He'd had twenty-six good years. He had the happy memories...

Peter emptied his glass and said, "I'm for a refill. Anyone else?"

Susannah, who'd been drinking milk, said, "Yes, please."

Michael held up his still nearly half-full glass and said, "No, thanks."

Ian nodded; Margaret shook her head. Peter left to get the refills.

Margaret said, "Da, I brought you something from New York. It's in my suitcase." She asked Susannah, "How 'bout showing me where you put it?"

"Surely."

"Da, perhaps you could entertain Michael for a few minutes?" Margaret said. "He's fascinated by stories about police work."

She winked at Michael, giving Ian the impression there was conspiracy afoot, and she and Susannah departed, leaving the two men alone. Michael seemed coolly amused and waited for Ian to take the initiative.

"Margaret tells me you're a civil servant."

"In a manner of speaking."

"What manner of speaking?" Ian asked uneasily.

"I'm a police officer."

"But why...?"

"She said you told her never to marry a policeman."

"Marry? She never said..."

Michael seemed unperturbed. "I think she's just chickened out and left me to say. We're planning to marry." He paused, slightly less sure of himself. "With your blessing, I hope."

"This is rather sudden, isn't it?"

"Five months, three days, six hours," Michael said matter-of-factly, "allowing for the time change."

Ian opened his mouth to speak, then closed it.

"I don't mean to be personal, sir, but how long was it after you met your wife before you knew your mind?"

"About sixty seconds. *Touché*."

Michael grinned—the first slackening of his unnerving reserve all evening. "I assure you, sir, she'll be well cared for…"

"Call me Ian. And never mind that. Margaret's always had good sense about such things. I have just one question."

"Shoot."

"How do you feel about children?"

"Margaret wouldn't have asked me if I didn't like children and tolerate cats."

Ian shook his head. "*She* asked you?"

"I'd have waited at least another month."

The lad had a sense of humor. And decent manners. Margaret could do worse. Ian decided to accept the inevitable. He stood and offered Michael his hand. "Well then, let me congratulate you."

Michael stood. They performed the ritual handshake and sat down.

"This calls for a toast," Ian said. "Where's Peter with those drinks?" He raised his voice to call, "Peter!"

On this cue, Peter entered, carrying a tray with glasses and champagne.

Ian looked the tray over. "I seem to be the last to know."

Peter laughed. "There's a first. The Yard's best brain stymied. Congratulations, Michael."

Michael let it pass. Peter filled the glasses, then walked to the doorway to call Margaret and Susannah. They were back before he returned to his seat, with Margaret carrying a bumper sticker she presented to Ian.

"Here you are, Da. A souvenir from New York."

The sticker said, "SEXY SENIOR CITIZEN," and Ian wasn't sure whether to be amused or insulted. He *was* pleased that she still had a sense of humor. He sneaked a glance at Michael, who contained his amusement admirably.

Susannah smiled, and Peter laughed outright. "As if he needs a notice with that hot car of his." He distributed the glasses, then raised his for a toast—"To Margaret and Michael!"

They raised their glasses with a "Hear, hear!" and drank. Then Ian proposed, "To grandchildren!" and they drank again.

Shortly afterward, he took leave of them, kissing his daughter and daughter-in-law, hugging Peter. Michael shook his hand with surprising cordiality. Then the two couples stood watching, arms intertwined, while he climbed into his car, to which Margaret had affixed the bumper sticker.

As he put it in gear, Peter took care to raise his voice so Ian could hear, "God! Do you s'pose he'll ever grow up?"

Margaret answered over the screech of his tyres. "I hope not."

IV

Charles observed from the top of the fridge as Ian opened the frosted foods compartment, and a mist of condensation cascaded floorward. He removed the carton of ice cream and scooped a quarter of its contents—with great satisfaction—into a waiting bowl. Then he put away the carton, picked up a spoon and his unfinished *Times* and took paper and bowl out of the room. Charles followed.

Ian put on his glasses and settled himself in the reclining chair Peter had given him the previous Christmas; Charles perched on the chair back, near his left ear, and they prepared to read the paper together. They'd just finished the front page when there was a rap on the door. Ian glanced at the clock. Eleven forty-five p.m. There was only Charles to see his irritation. By the time he reached the door, he'd removed his glasses and disguised his annoyance.

The woman who stood in the hall was late-middle aged and plump, his landlady, who lived in the flat below.

Ian said, "Come in, Mrs. West."

She entered like melodrama, wringing her hands. "Oh Mr. Carreg, Betty Ann's been struck by a car!"

"You'd better sit down."

"Oh no. I can't stay. I've got the grandkids and I can't take my eyes off 'em a minute. The police constable took her to the hospital, you see. Said it looked like she'd need surgery, and he'd have 'em call me. But they didn't. So I called 'em. They told me she was in surgery. Said they'd call back, only they haven't."

Ian sighed inwardly. "Would you like me to go 'round and see how she is?"

"Oh, would you?"

"Certainly."

"Oh, God bless you, Mr. Carreg! You're an answer to prayer!"

The surgery was a modern, one-story brick with plate-glass entry doors, next to which only the lower half of a sign—HOSPITAL—was legible in the poor light. Next to the sign, about shoulder level, was a doorbell with a smaller sign: RING BELL FOR NIGHT SURGERY.

Ian rang the bell, and when a sister appeared and tried to tell him through the glass that the surgery was closed, he produced his police ID. He muttered, "*Open sesame*," under his breath.

She opened the door.

"I'm here to inquire about Betty Ann West," he told her.

She gave him a rueful smile. "I'm sorry, we don't have any details. You'll have to speak to the police constable…"

He shook his head impatiently. "I'm not inquiring into the accident, Sister. Mrs. West is my neighbor. She asked me to look in."

The sister brightened immediately. "I see. Well she's just in recovery. Would you like to see her?"

Ian considered facing Mrs. West without a first-hand report and said, "Er, yes."

"Come along, then."

She led him down a long passage—smelling enough of disinfectant to accentuate the cleanliness of the place—with bright, sterile strip lighting overhead, of the sort designed to suggest illumination, the light of reason, even the omniscience of God Himself, as if the doctors were His special agents. They hadn't helped Marjory—struck down by a reckless homicide in a fast car. The bright, empty corridor only brought back the dismay, the building panic, dread, anxiety, the feeling he was falling...Well, perhaps they kept the staff awake.

They passed doors labeled RADIOLOGY, PHARMA-COLOGY and LABORATORY. The door marked RECOVERY was open. He followed the sister in and spotted machines...

The machines had kept her heart beating, had kept air entering and leaving her lungs, but couldn't hold her soul, couldn't delay the departure of her spirit. He had let the machines go on until Margaret and Peter arrived to make their hasty good-byes.

The room was familiar. Dimly lit in deference to its recovering occupants, it had the hushed and awed ambiance of a cathedral or a grail castle. But *Whom did it serve?* Green cylinders of oxygen stood at attention against the wall, waiting to be called into action. A resuscitator, with its ominous black paddles, waited to shock the stutter from a faltering heart. Green lightning flashed predictably from left to right across monitor screens facing the sisters' duty station, where the surgeon—a young knight armored to do battle with the ultimate foe—sat in his vest and surgery-green trousers, watching the monitor and making notes on a clip-board, his surgical mask hanging round his neck like a talisman.

The sister said, "Inspector Carreg is here to see Betty Ann."

The doctor smiled at Ian. "Er...yes. Nasty fracture, you know. We had to pin it, but she's doing famously. She'll be free of the anesthetic shortly, and with any luck, she can go home Wednesday." Ian nodded. "Go ahead and talk to her, but don't get her too excited."

At first Ian couldn't *see* Betty Ann. When he finally spotted her, swathed in bandages and surrounded by therapeutic gadgetry, he tried to marshal some enthusiasm. He edged closer. He patted her shoulder with a squeamish sigh. He said, "Easy does it old girl," and stroked her face gently.

Still groggy from the anesthetic and immobilized by straps and dressings, Betty Ann wagged her tail gamely. And Ian thanked God she was a tough little collie dog.

March 22

I

The next morning, Ian dressed in a conservative suit and tie. To save time, he made his breakfast in the blender, which he rinsed out before he fed Charles, and took his glass to the table. He looked longingly at the unfinished front-page section of yesterday's *Times*, then glanced at his watch. Five forty-five a.m. He shook his head, but sat and opened the paper, sipping his breakfast as he read it.

A caption on page two stood out—PHYSICIST'S DAUGHTER SOUGHT—and the accompanying photo arrested his attention. The name was familiar and the woman depicted was blond and lovely. He licked the breakfast drink from his mustache and read the story aloud.

"Listen to this, Charles: 'American officials are seeking the extradition of Dr. Jemma Henderson, M.D., daughter of renowned British physicist, Dr. Matthew Henderson, Ph.D. Dr. Jemma Henderson was convicted last month in the US of murdering her lover, Dr. John Waite, M.D. Henderson fled to the UK while free on bond pending appeal of her conviction. The UK has an extradition treaty with the US, and British authorities are expected to grant extradition as soon as the requisite paperwork is completed.'"

Ian glanced at his watch. "There's more, but I have to go." He gulped down the rest of his drink and rinsed the glass, putting it in the dish rack. Then he scratched Charles under the chin, and took the paper and his leave.

• • •

Once beyond the village boundary, Ian guided the car along a road old when the Romans invaded as it cut through a countryside divided into numerous small farm fields bordered by hedges and stone fences. Twenty minutes after leaving his flat, he wheeled the car between a pair of massive gateposts, and made his way along a graveled drive between acres of pale carpet lawn, to a house that had the air, on a smaller scale, of a stately home.

He parked in front of the door and got out to ring the bell, looking around as he waited. No one answered, so he ambled around to the back.

At the rear of the house, on the verge of a vast expanse of gardens, an elderly man was mulching the flowerbeds with rotted manure from a battered wheelbarrow. He was clad in old clothes and gardening gloves, and looked like the gardener's granddad. He said, "Good morning. May I be of service?"

"I'd like to speak with Professor Henderson, or his daughter."

"Who are *you*, sir?"

Ian produced his ID, and the old man nodded as if he'd been expecting him. "Perhaps you'd better come inside."

He laid his spade on top of the barrow and took off his gloves, then led Ian through a rose garden, with roses still mulched for winter, through tall French doors.

Ian found himself inside a small, exquisitely appointed sitting room with a fireplace burning cheerfully, with antique desk and chairs, and with a covered breakfast tray on a stand, cozied teapot and all. The old man gestured for Ian to be seated and sat down himself, looking uncomfortable.

"I am Professor Henderson," he said. "Would you like some tea, Inspector Carreg?"

"This isn't a social call, sir. I'm sorry, but I'll have to take your daughter in charge. The Americans have received authorization to extradite her."

Henderson shook his head just once, then uncovered the teapot. "You won't mind if I have some?"

Ian let it seem as if he had all day.

Henderson poured his tea out and began to add sugar. "I'm afraid you're too late, Inspector. My daughter has gone."

"Where is she?"

Henderson smiled gently. "She's escaped your jurisdiction."

"Do you know the penalties for helping a fugitive evade the police?"

Henderson stirred his tea and smiled again. "My daughter, sir…" He looked up at Ian without malice or triumph. "No jury would convict me. No one will even believe where she's gone."

"Where *has* she gone, sir?"

Henderson gave him another of his smiles before crossing to the desk to remove a letter, which he handed to Ian. "She asked me to give this to the police, when they arrived. It's a copy of a letter she lodged with her solicitor."

Ian read it.

> March 22. If I cannot practice medicine, there is no point
> in continuing in this life. When you read this, I will be long
> dead. Dr. Jemma Henderson, M.D.

"This is a suicide note!"

Henderson nodded. "I believe she intended it to be interpreted that way."

"Where *is* she, sir?"

Henderson looked at his watch. "I suppose it's safe to tell you. It's too late to stop her leaving…"

"Where?!"

"…In five minutes she'll be gone. Even with a helicopter, you can't get there in five minutes."

"Get *where*, sir?"

The old man looked at Ian as if the answer was obvious. "The henge, of course. She had to choose a landmark that wasn't under water or something, and geological evidence suggests…"

Ian didn't hear the rest because he was halfway through the doors. Thirty seconds later—still carrying the letter—he was yanking open his car door; he threw the letter on the passenger's seat as he climbed in.

• • •

He could see the landmark in the distance, at the top of a small hill, long before he arrived. A circle of huge, rectangular stones stood all but buried in the lawn and surrounded by the faintest suggestion of the concentric ditch and bank that formed the actual henge. As he sped closer, through the patchwork of farm fields, he could see the stumps of many large trees dotting the hilltop, interrupting the circles of stone, bank and ditch. A fence around the site was decorated with information signs. Near a gravel parking area stood the single building—a temporary shed in major disrepair—with an electric cable connecting it to mains that could have supplied power to a small block of flats.

Ian skidded to a halt on the gravel and jumped out, making for the henge, which was the high ground, searching in every direction as he ran. From the hilltop he could see that there was no one in the area. He was too late. He relaxed. He let himself appreciate the scenery, which was lovely, and he read the largest of the information signs.

CYMRY HENGE, DISCOVERED AFTER AN OAK BLIGHT EPIDEMIC KILLED THE SMALL STAND OF VIRGIN OAKS COVERING THE HENGE FROM ANCIENT TIMES. THE MONUMENT IS THOUGHT TO HAVE BEEN COMPLETED EARLY IN THE SECOND MILLENNIUM B.C.E., BUT DERIVES ITS NAME FROM A ROMAN INSCRIPTION FOUND...

Ian gave it up and walked slowly back toward the shed.

It was just an old wooden storage building, with a rusting galvanized steel roof, but its door had a new, shiny hasp above a conventional doorknob. The hasp was open; the lock used to keep it closed, nowhere in sight. As Ian circled the structure, trying to peer inside through cracks and boarded-up windows, he became aware of a loud whining sound. He looked up to where the oversized electric cable entered the roof. It puzzled him. The noise suddenly became louder and higher pitched.

He circled around to the door and surreptitiously tried the doorknob. The handle turned, but the door wouldn't open. He pulled harder on the knob, and the door moved slightly as if something was holding it from inside. He abandoned caution and pulled with all his strength, managing to work the door open a few centimeters. The noise from inside the shed became much louder and even higher pitched. Then the door slammed shut. He put a foot against the jamb and used the strength of his leg to muscle the door open a foot. He shifted his grip to the edge of the door and gained ten centimeters more. Finally, he threw himself against the jamb with a thud and a grunt, losing ground as he did so, but he was able to force the door open wide enough to gain admittance by bench-pressing it. For a moment he was caught between the door and jamb and was crushed there. The whining noise became unbearably loud.

He took a deep breath and heaved with all his strength, and when the door gave, he dived into the shed. The door slammed shut behind him. For a moment, he was in complete darkness. The noise had become deafening. He felt himself drawn rapidly away from the door by an unseen force, in a tunnel of darkness, toward a dim light at its end.

For the first time, he felt fear. Nothing he had ever experienced prepared him for the feeling. He seemed to be falling sideways as he was pulled into the light. Falling without a parachute. Without a safety net. Without a map.

Then he reached the mouth of the tunnel, and it widened, and he could see a woman standing in the tunnel mouth, between two gray horses whose bridles she held, next to a pile of luggage. She stared at him with seeming horror as he flew past, into the sunlight beyond. Then he could see a tree flying at him, and he felt it strike...

II

The shed door flew open. Inside the shed was emptiness. And darkness. Total darkness. Outside, no creature stirred in the landscape. The shed and all around the henge was silent.

Suddenly, the peace was shattered. Bright yellow-orange billows of hot gas and light blossomed and blasted outward, scattering the shed over the henge. Bits of debris showered down on Ian's car and its environs. The car cast an early morning shadow.

Much later, when the car cast its violet shadow the other way, a police car pulled up on the gravel verge. A constable emerged and cautiously approached the car. The PC didn't touch anything, but walked around and noted the number plate, and the letter and newspaper on the seat. He looked about the explosion site with a serious and puzzled expression on his face. Then he returned to his car and reached grimly for his radio.

22 mawrth

The woman looking down at him seemed to Ian a little out of focus. In order to see her against the sun, he had to put his hand up and shade his eyes, and as they adjusted, it became obvious she was very beautiful—oval faced with clear blue eyes and delicate, regular features, silver-gold hair tied back with a leather thong.

He had seen her before.

"Your picture doesn't do you justice," he said. Even to himself, he sounded slightly incoherent, but he felt himself sharpening as the conversation continued.

"You obviously know who I am," she said. "Who are you?" She was kneeling beside him, holding a roll of gauze down at her side as if she'd forgotten it.

He turned his head and discovered he was lying beneath a huge oak tree. He was quite disheveled—his suit crumpled, his tie loosened. A large medical bag lay open on the ground next to him. Trying to sit up made him wince, and he discovered—when he put his hand up to feel—there was a bandage around his head through which blood had seeped. He said, "Detective Inspector Ian Carreg, CID…"

He noticed she was wearing a white, embroidered linen tunic gathered at the waist by a leather belt with a bronze buckle, a long wool skirt and leather sandals. The incongruity of her dress confused him.

"Don't move," she said. "You've a concussion."

He reached for his ID and couldn't hide his surprise on finding it in his pocket. He showed her the badge. "I was sent to take you in charge."

She seemed subtly offended, though she said nothing, and in the gap in the conversation, he noticed the distant whisper of water rushing over stones. He glanced around and noticed—as men do after a close brush with death—how beautiful the place was, all gold light and deep, unpolluted sky. There was something familiar about the landscape, but it was much changed. The henge still stood at the top of its hill, but its stones seemed a good meter taller, and its bank and ditch were deep and fully formed. The spring shoots on which Jemma Henderson's gray horses grazed—looking silver in the bright sunlight—poked through winter grass that was yellow and matted like the fur on an old dog. The fence, signs, shed, utility pole, car park and his car were gone. The land around the hill was no longer a crazy-quilt of small farm fields, but was blanketed by ominously deep forest. He could hear crows cawing. He said, "What happened?"

"You blundered into my escape...I suppose you had a wife and family."

"Had? Are you going to kill me, too?"

She seemed astonished at this assumption, then annoyed. "Of course not!"

"No? Well, after murder, I suppose kidnapping is no great thing."

"You haven't been kidnapped."

"Then how'd I get here? *Where are we?*"

She thought a moment. "I don't know how to explain...!"

"Try English. We both seem to have a fair grasp."

"I'm sorry—God that seems so inadequate! I'm *so* sorry. I didn't mean to involve anyone else." She paused, then watched him carefully as she added, "You can't go back."

He felt a sudden alarm. "Where *are* we? Russia? One of the Eastern Bloc countries?"

"Geographically, we're exactly where we were before. The pertinent question is when."

"What?"

"We're nearly one thousand seven hundred years earlier than

an hour ago…"

He wondered if perhaps he *was* concussed.

"…Early in the third century A.D."

A time machine! A wishful-thinking device. Don't like history? Change it. No! Such things could not exist. Or you'd go back before the crime occurred and prevent it, change circumstances so that a different event happened, a completely different crime. Go back to the time when Marjory was well and whole, prevent her venturing out that dreadful day.

Or might one not, like Laius, by trying to prevent one's fate, insure it? Might not the house catch fire? Or a plane fall on it from the heavens had that fateful accident not occurred? Ian's head throbbed.

He said, "Right! You know, Miss Henderson, your attorneys—that's what you call barristers in America?—erred seriously. They should have pled you not guilty by reason of insanity."

"There's no point in trying to explain, then, is there?" She stood up and turned away.

He tried to get up and follow, but a white flash of pain lightninged through his skull. He grimaced as he asked, "Where are you going?"

She came hurrying back and knelt beside him. "You can't…"

She was interrupted by a scream. Both of them jerked toward the sound, toward the direction of the henge. The scene *looked* peaceful enough, but the horses had stopped grazing and were staring at the trees beyond the stone circle. In the anticlimax that followed, only the distant rush of water could be heard.

Jemma snapped her medical bag shut and snatched it up, then she was off across the open space, through the ankle-high grass. Ian got to his feet with some difficulty and dizziness and followed her, pressing his head to squelch the pain. As he walked, he studied the ground. It didn't need an expert tracker to see that the bent grass pointed in the direction taken by whomever they were following, and that horses hoofs had cut the sod and trampled the grass. And there was a splash of fresh blood.

Intent on the signs, he didn't notice when Jemma stopped

abruptly with a soft cry that sent a shudder through him. He ran into her with enough momentum to send them both stumbling forward and send pain searing through his head. He looked to see why she'd stopped and followed her gaze to where a man lay in a great blood-pudding in the dirt, with his skull split open, spilling gray matter onto the grass roots.

None of the grisliest murders he'd investigated made his hair stand up as it did now, and he looked around almost involuntarily for a glimpse of the murderer. When he looked back at Jemma, he shuddered again, for her expression displayed none of the horror *he* felt or expected of her. Then her face registered puzzlement, and she started toward the corpse.

He moved closer and saw a second man pinned in the grass beneath the legs of the first. Both had long hair and full mustaches but clean-shaven chins, and were clad in short wool tunics and wool trousers, with leather belts and soft-soled shoes. The top man wore a bronze torc around his neck and a sheath knife on his belt, and had died with a sword in his hand. Jemma bent over them.

"What do you think you're doing?"

She froze. Almost timidly, she said, "The bottom one may be alive."

Ian found he was trembling with emotion. *The incredible strangeness!* He willed himself to relax a little. "Try to disturb as little as possible."

He took in details while she felt the man's neck for a carotid pulse. The man underneath was a Caucasian, medium complected, slightly balding. Ian wasn't surprised when Jemma shook her head. The man's brown eyes were fixed—fixed forever, undisturbed by the flies crawling over them. The body was so covered with blood that the cause of his death was indiscernible.

Jemma noticed something else nearby and started toward it like a pointer after a bird. Ian was about to protest when he saw what she was after. The third corpse, also a man, was dressed and coifed like the others. Ian didn't need her diagnosis to know that he, too, was beyond help, and she didn't report on this victim, but hurried on.

The fourth body was alive, male, about fourteen years old, dressed like the others, and barely conscious. He had blood on his head and a deep gash—baring the white bone—running diagonally across the side of one leg. Beneath the leg, blood had jelled in lumps of dark crimson. When the boy's eyes fixed on Jemma, they widened with fear that became full panic when he spotted Ian. He fainted.

Jemma acted decisively, checking the boy's pulse and opening his eyes to check his pupils. She put down her bag and opened it.

"What the bloody hell do you think you're doing?"

She kept working as she answered, laying things out on a cloth on the grass. "I'm a doctor. What do you think I'm doing?"

"You're not licensed to practice here."

"You don't have Samaritan laws?"

"Well, yes."

"Then shut up and give me a hand." She parted the boy's hair to expose a nasty gash. "Superficial. I'll put a compress on it, while I deal with the other, and stitch it later."

"This is absurd! This boy belongs in a trauma center. Where's the nearest phone?"

She was bandaging the head wound, paying him no attention. "About seventeen hundred years away."

He grabbed her arm. "Stop it!"

She jerked his hand away. "Whatever you think of me or the situation, the fact remains I'm a surgeon. And if this boy doesn't get immediate attention, he'll surely die. He's in shock already."

"Then we'd better call for an ambulance."

"*You* go call for an ambulance; I'll apply first aid. If you're not going to help, at least get out of the way."

Ian hesitated. He suspected she was right about the boy's needs, and certainly, from the look of their surroundings, it would take more than a few minutes to get help. And criminal or not, she was indisputably better qualified to deal with this than he. He hesitated, then stepped aside, but he kept trying to think of a better plan as he put his tie in his coat pocket and removed the coat.

Jemma seemed to forget him as soon as he moved, devoting

her complete attention to the boy. She cut away his trouser-leg, exposing a limb that resembled a freshly butchered leg of mutton save that bright blood still oozed from the cut edges. She covered the area around the wound with clean cloths and pulled on a pair of surgical gloves and a mask, from sterile packages. She was completely unfazed by the terrible damage, using gauze to scrub dirt and grass from the wound, setting it bleeding again. Profusely. She rinsed it with a solution labeled saline from a rectangular plastic pouch like those from which blood is dispensed. The wash turned the white cloths pink and leached pink into Jemma's skirt. She tore open a packet of fine suture material and worked with quick, deft movements to tie off oozing blood vessels. The sun reflected off the cloths and off her tunic, making her face glow. She seemed oblivious to Ian, her surroundings, and the uncomfortable position in which she had to crouch to work.

Hospital personnel had kept him at bay while they raced with death for Marjory; so apart from bits in the odd movie, he'd never seen a surgeon working. But he *had* watched artists. Jemma's intensity, as she worked, was the same. Without knowing the first rule of medicine, he could tell that she was good. The insight surprised him, though it shouldn't have. He wondered if Marjory'd have made it if someone like Jemma had chanced along. A murderess, he recalled suddenly.

Jemma seemed to forget who and what Ian was, and was soon giving him orders. "Put on a pair of those gloves and hand me that scissors." Ian did so. "Thanks. Now, there's a little packet there that says 'OO gut'. Tear the top off and stand by."

He did as he was told, but not without reservations. Flies started to gather. He waved them away. "Aren't you supposed to do all this under sterile conditions?"

She took up the suture—heavier stuff than she'd used on the vessels—and kept working, closing the crevasse. "This is the best we can do under the circumstances. He's in greater danger from hemorrhage at the moment than infection."

The boy began to stir and emit a little bleating sound.

"Damn!" Jemma said. "Carreg, there's a clear glass bottle, labeled chloroform, in my bag. Get it, quickly!"

"What?"

"STAT! I can't stop and play anesthesiologist right now, you're going to have to do it."

"Oh, no!"

"It's that or watch while I sew him up without anesthetic."

The boy moaned softly and began to writhe. Ian decided to cooperate. He took the bottle from the bag. "Now what?"

"Take one of those cloths…" She pointed. "…and dampen it well, then hold it over his mouth and nose until he relaxes. Don't get any in his eyes. And be sure you don't breathe any of it yourself."

She crouched over the leg as Ian put chloroform on the cloth and moved it toward the boy's face. The boy moaned again, but the sound trailed away as he breathed in the anesthetic.

Jemma glanced up, then went back to work. "Now take it away. You don't want to kill him."

Ian was forgotten. Except occasionally, when she asked him to reach up under the cloths and squeeze the severed edges of muscle close enough together for her needle to connect them, or when she demanded that he wipe the copious sweat from her face before it splashed onto the patient, she didn't speak. Ian was left to draw his own conclusions about what he was observing. Time or adrenaline seemed to have mitigated his own injury—his head no longer hurt, and after the first wave of shock-induced nausea, he found the operation mesmerizing. Jemma made neat, rapid stitches without apparent doubt or hesitation. She'd finished mending the muscle and was closing the skin when the boy began to stir again.

"More chloroform?" Ian asked without thinking.

"Please." She looked up and seemed to notice he was a police inspector, not an O.R. assistant. She gave him a puzzling, shy smile and looked back at what she was doing. "This your first assist?"

"Yes, thank God."

"Not bad."

He had the impression, as she spoke, that she'd forgotten him already and had focused everything on finishing the operation. When she was tying the last knot on the long seam in the boy's leg, she asked, "How are your woodsman skills?"

"I beg your pardon?"

"This leg will need to be splinted so he doesn't thrash around and tear it open, but the most sophisticated tool I have is an ax. Think you could manage a few splints?"

"Well…"

She let her breath out deeply and slowly, giving Ian an impression of fatigue. For the first time, he realized that hours must have passed since they'd started, and Jemma—murderess or not—must be exhausted. He said, "Surely."

"Thanks." She held her hands apart over the boy's leg, at the approximate places the ends of the splints would have to be, and said, "Two about this long." Then she looked the boy up and down as if gauging his entire length and added, "And one about eighteen inches longer, for the side."

"Where's the ax?"

She had to think a minute, absentmindedly blowing away silver-gold wisps that had fallen in her face.

"There's a red, oiled-leather tool case. Rolled up. Somewhere over there."

She paused, before she started bandaging the leg, as if recalling with difficulty what to do next. While Ian fetched the ax and split two saplings into passably flat-edged boards, she closed her patient's head wound with three stitches, cradling his head in her lap as she worked.

Around them, the grass and trees glowed as in a backlit photo, and the bright, sunlit side of the tent they'd erected to shade the patient reflected the afternoon sun. The boy was asleep under a bright wool blanket, with his head and leg whitely bandaged. They made several trips to move Jemma's baggage into the tent, and she checked on the patient every time she came back.

As he walked back to get another load, Ian paused to have a closer look at the corpses. The chilling fact of death cooled the warm-for-March air of the clearing. The hacked remains and the trampled grasses around them gave evidence of a bloody nasty fight and the rapid exodus of three or four horsemen with unburdened horses trailing behind. He read it all with a macabre sense of unreality—what skills he had in deciphering the signs had been acquired in childhood, in the relative peace of his grandparents' farm in Wales, trailing strayed animals. He went back to where he'd left his jacket and retrieved his pen and jotter. He noted the particulars as best he could, and his impressions, but could draw no conclusion. There was nothing for it but to call in the experts. Forensic scientists would be able to determine a great deal more about the victims, their strange clothes, and the bizarre circumstances. With luck, the deceased's fingerprints were on file somewhere…He gave it up and went back to where the last of Jemma's baggage rested. He brought the remaining things to the tent and put everything down except a bridle.

"Now I think we should see about getting an ambulance," he told Jemma.

"We can't."

"Miss Henderson, if he dies from lack of adequate follow-up care…"

"Look, there's no way I can convince you, so why don't you just go look for a phone." She circled with her finger. "Choose any direction. You won't find one. Or a phone line, or a highway sign. But go look. Convince yourself."

"You'd like me to do that. And as soon as I'm out of sight, you'll disappear."

"You could always tie me up."

"There's a thought."

"But then if our patient starts to vomit or to bleed again…"

"We seem to have a stalemate."

Jemma shrugged and dismissed him by starting to rummage

through her luggage, extracting a white linen cloth, a bar of soap, a clean tunic and another skirt. Ian stared daggers at her, but when she took no notice, he walked over to one of the horses, a beautifully conformed gray mare, and put the bridle on her. He led the mare back to where Jemma was standing. She looked concerned.

"You're not going off exploring without a weapon, are you? What if you meet with whoever did in those men?"

"You don't happen to have a spare pistol?"

"Sorry." She put down what she was holding and reached a sheathed knife from her luggage. "How about this?"

"It's a start," he said as he took it. "I don't suppose you have a saddle?"

"No."

"Not invented yet?"

As he threaded the sheath onto his belt, she scowled and threw a blanket at him. He folded the blanket and put it on the back of the horse, then used the tether rope to tie it in place. He led the mare to where the second horse, which was identical to the first, was tethered and untied her. He led them both into the henge ditch to mount the blanketed mare, then led the extra horse back to the tent.

"Hey!" Jemma said. "What if you don't come back?"

"You'll have to walk wherever you were going." He urged the horses into motion.

"Hey, wait!" He stopped, and she threw him a leather bag with a shoulder strap.

"What's this?"

"Lunch."

"Why?"

"If you starve to death, I won't get my horses back, will I?"

Ian thought about that as he rode away.

• • •

He had learned to ride as a boy, on the broad backs of his grandfather's draft horses. He'd ridden only occasionally since—hacks for hire. The mare was a spirited creature, ready to race, and she danced under him uneasily, as if insecure beneath his rusty hand and flaccid muscles. Though her gait was smooth enough, just staying up was work, and Ian was sweating by the time they'd reached the forest.

The forest was very old. Immense, mature trees stretched sixty and seventy feet upward. The understory was dense with brush and snags and deadfalls—unlike forests he had seen before which had been gleaned, for firewood and fire protection, and pruned to uniform shapes. Though the oak leaves were still only bronzed-green thickenings on the branch tips, the forest was impenetrable to the eye. There were no signs of wildlife, though the horses seemed aware of creatures silent and invisible.

The immediate difficulty—getting the animals through the dense underbrush—drove theoretical problems from the forefront of his attention, but they kept returning. He considered Jemma Henderson.

She'd been convicted. That meant evidence had been presented, testimony given, and detectives like himself had satisfied themselves that she was guilty. Why should he presume to doubt their judgment just because she was beautiful and intelligent?

Other questions simmered, the distillate of which was *Why? Why me? Why bother?* No case he was on warranted such a serious course. Nor was he privy to any secrets—private or governmental—that might lead to his abduction.

That left something he *wasn't* working on. Yet. Or something he might have discovered—to someone's peril—if he had been left to explore the shed at the henge site. Apparently someone felt the need to stop him discovering Miss Henderson's escape route. That, obviously, was whoever had arranged her escape. What he recalled of what had occurred after he'd entered the utility shed was not so easy to explain—actually was impossible, but when he'd unearthed the parties responsible, no doubt he could shake an explanation from them.

Having resolved the important questions, he turned his attention to the job at hand. The small, grassy clearing into which he finally dragged the spare horse, was surrounded by the dense underbrush through which he'd been having heavy going. Although he'd been gone from the henge nearly an hour, he estimated he had traveled less than a mile. Estimated. At the slow rate of start, stop, untangle the lead, he might have gone less than half a kilometer. With no landmarks visible and no horizon to fix on, it was impossible to tell. And just the effort of staying on the horse without a proper saddle or stirrups exhausted him. His suit was soaking and torn in a dozen places where thorns and tree limbs caught it. His skin had more than a few tears as well. The tiny clearing that had formed next to a small spring, where a forest giant had fallen and lime and oak saplings vied with grasses for the sun, was a godsend. Cursing Jemma Henderson and all her ancestors, he dismounted and tethered the spare horse where it could graze. Then he remounted, took a last look around, and left the clearing.

In another clearing, larger this time, Ian discovered a little brook. Paths led away from the clearing in several directions. Only the crackling of brush, as the horse struggled through, and the faint buzz of a few early insects interrupted the awesome silence. The quiet amplified his feeling that this was all a dream. He let the horse drink while he puzzled over which way to go, then used his knife to mark a tree near one of the paths before proceeding.

Perhaps an hour later, he rode into the same clearing from a different direction and was dismayed to find his mark. He dismounted and took his coat off while he let the horse drink from the brook, then he washed his face in the cold, clear water. When he'd remounted, he left the clearing by a different path.

It was almost too dark to see when he rode into the clearing the third time. So stiff he could scarcely move, he dismounted with difficulty. He untied the blanket he'd been using for a saddle and spread it on the ground before he put his coat on. He and the horse drank together from the brook, then he tethered her to a tree and inventoried Jemma's lunch bag. Dried fruits—apples, apricots and raisins—and nuts and sunflower seeds were not his idea of nourishment. He fed the horse a piece of apple. When she looked for more, he said, "Enough. You can eat grass."

Finally, after relieving himself at the edge of the clearing, he wrapped himself in the blanket and lay down, shivering.

March 22

III

The site had been roped off with police-barricade tape and was surrounded by police cars with flashing lights, and by other official vehicles, including a bomb squad lorry. TV reporters, with minicam, stood beyond the barrier taping their reports.

"…the disappearance of Detective Inspector Ian Carreg, CID…"

From the west, silhouetted in the last of the sunset, a car approached the site with head lamps lit.

"…who had been assigned to take Dr. Jemma Henderson in charge…"

The car came nearer, until the white glare of its lights became like sunlight in the cameras' lenses. The lights went off.

"…Inspector Carreg's car was found near the site of a recent, powerful explosion. Bomb and arson experts are investigating…"

Cameras closed in on two men silhouetted in the faint glow of the sunset as they got out of the car. Their doors slammed. As the reporters rushed forward with cameras and flooded the men with lights, Peter Carreg emerged with a police official whose long, beefy face looked white in the artificial light. They walked briskly toward the police line, and reporters bombarded them with questions. Peter Carreg ducked with Andrew Blemming beneath the barrier tape and disappeared among the official vehicles. The TV lights went off, leaving the scene in darkness.

23 mawrth

I

Ian couldn't have said whether it was cold that crept in, solidifying his flesh, or the cacophony of bird sounds that woke him. He found himself conscious but immobilized, the movement of any limb causing hideous discomfort, though not to move was torture as well. His face was numb, and when he poked a hand from beneath the blanket to feel it, he found his hair and mustache were as wet with dew as the sodden blanket. It was Tuesday already. Margaret and Peter must be half mad with worry. One more thing to be laid to the account of his abductors. He looked around. It didn't surprise him to discover snowflakes scattered about, though a second look showed them to be snowdrops. He took a deep breath. The air was a distillate of spring. Intoxicating. The sun had cleared the horizon but was, as yet, nowhere near the tree tops, though it gilded the bronze-green oak buds on the upper branches around the clearing. Overhead the sky was deeper than the Mediterranean. A second day of sun and brilliant sky. This, surely, wasn't Britain. Not far away, he could hear the swish and soft grass-tearing sounds of the horse as she mowed her way across the clearing—she hadn't vanished overnight. It was comforting to know there was some consistency in this looking-glass world. He closed his eyes and willed it all to disappear. It did.

The horse woke him the second time. He'd been dreaming he was in his own warm bed when she whinnied, and he discovered that the warmth came from the near-noon sun soaking into his blanket. The mare was so close, he could hear the rubbery flapping of her ears when she shook her head, and the ground thudded dully as she stamped. Then her call was repeated from across the clearing, her stomping was echoed by the soft swish-thudding footfalls of several approaching horses. Ian was reluctant to give them reality by looking. He kept his eyes closed and followed their progress by ear. He had no fear. One didn't die in nightmares, one merely woke in a cold sweat. And from this dream, he would be delighted to awaken.

He felt the blanket flip off his chest and the sun pour down on it. He opened his eyes and got a worm's-eye view of a small horse's head. The animal was dun-colored and shaggy, with unclipped fetlocks, and wasn't a half-hand taller than a Welsh pony. It wore an ornate bridle with a Celtic-patterned bit and bronze-studded headstall, and faced Ian despite an obvious desire to ogle his horse. The small horse finally shifted, and Ian found himself staring at the sharp metal point of a spear. He followed the shaft up to the hand of the man holding it, as he sat solemnly astride the horse in a saddle without stirrups.

The man looked about twenty-five and was decked out in full Celtic regalia, from brown wool pants and orange and brown tartan tunic, to a bronze torc round his neck. He had both a knife and a short sword on his belt. His eyes were blue, and his long hair—strands of which hung braided in front of his ears like elongated sideburns—auburn. His cheeks and chin were smooth-shaven, but he sported an impressive Fu Manchu mustache. When he saw he had Ian's attention, he spoke in a tongue that was at once strange and familiar—like Welsh and yet unlike it. Ian realized the man was addressing someone else. He raised himself up on his elbows—not without discomfort—and saw two other riders.

The foremost looked to be about forty, and was costumed and accoutered like the first. He also sat a saddle without stirrups and carried a spear. Beyond him, a younger man, beardless but dressed and armed like the others, rode his horse bareback.

A movie set! Ian decided. *Arthurian method actors.* Surely they were movie extras costumed for the latest version of *Excalibur* or some other drama set in Celtic times.

Celts! Ian hadn't heard the word, even, for years. One memorized, in school, that they were tribal people inhabiting Gaul and Britain—among other places—during Roman times. The Romans conquered them, and history left them there. They were occasionally mentioned in historical novels—particularly of Arthurian times, some that even made the bestseller lists.

The redhead prodded Ian with his spear point, demonstrating it was an authentic prop.

Ian did his best to ignore him. "I don't suppose any of you speaks English?"

Red made a gesture clearly indicating Ian was to get up, and after further prodding, Ian complied with great difficulty. When Red grew impatient and poked him again, Ian demanded, "Be nice!" Then without warning, he grabbed the spear and yanked it away from Red, nearly unseating him, and sending the horse scuttling backward.

The other men instantly urged their horses forward and pointed their spears at Ian.

Not wishing to take on all three, he turned the captured spear point upward and shook it with a feigned ferocity that made the reinforcements halt abruptly and regard him as if he were quite mad. All to the good! If they thought him crazy, perhaps they'd leave him alone. He turned the spear around and drove it into the ground, where it stuck. He looked them over and, having made his point, nodded with satisfaction. He asked, in Welsh, "Does any of you speak Welsh?" He got no response. "*Parlez vous français? Sprechen sie deutsch? ¿Habla espanol?*"

The two older men looked at each other and shrugged. Ian gave up and ignored the ensuing discussion as he headed to the edge of the clearing to relieve himself. Returning to his sleeping place, he picked up his lunch bag and put it over his shoulder. As he folded the blanket back into a saddle, the conversation among the three actors was illustrated by gestures and much pointing in his direction. The older man appeared to comment about Ian's horse, then pointed at Ian. Red nodded, apparently agreeing. He threw his leg over his own horse's head and slid off. The horse backed away, reins trailing. Red advanced on Ian, staring at his suit coat.

Ian, who'd been giving the men as much notice as he might three drunks, was suddenly alert. Red's interest in his clothing made him look down to see if his zip was closed. Red reached out, cautiously, to feel the material of Ian's suit. He seemed awestruck.

Ian looked at his jacket—torn, wrinkled and dirty—and decided the actor was a bit of a ham. He said, "That's enough!"

Red seemed to find this threatening, for he backed up quickly and drew his sword. When he got close enough with it to constitute an unequivocal threat, Ian swung the lunch bag at his left side, to create a diversion, and simultaneously kicked at his sword hand. The kick connected squarely, and the sword flew in a glittering arc toward Ian's mare, narrowly missing her and sending her skittering to the far end of her tether.

Ian relaxed. "Had enough?"

Red was enraged. The flippant tone and Ian's careless demeanor, or perhaps the second disarmament, were too great a blow to his pride, for he was suddenly in deadly earnest. He jerked the knife from his belt and attacked in a rage, tackling like an American football player.

As they fell to the ground together, Ian grabbed Red's knife arm with both hands. Red landed on top, and Ian heard the others shout encouragement. He was vaguely aware that they'd dismounted to watch.

As he and his assailant rolled about, grunting and gouging and kicking, Ian felt every stick and rock beneath him through his suit coat; he heard the coat rip.

He saw an opening, finally, and used a judo trick to rid his opponent of the knife, and then a second quick maneuver to pin him. Shaking with rage, he grabbed the knife and dug its point into Red's throat. He was too winded to get up and he trembled with shock as he realized how close he'd come to cutting a man's throat. A total stranger's throat! For a long moment, while he sucked in great gulps of air, he held knife point to flesh. He took two deep breaths as he glared down at Red.

"Don't you *ever* point a weapon at me again!"

If the words were unintelligible, the meaning must have been crystalline. Red didn't move except to make a strange gesture with his fingers.

Then Ian shifted his grip on the knife and stabbed it, hilt deep, into the ground beside Red's head. He got slowly and stiffly to his feet, checking to be sure the reading glasses in his inside jacket pocket were intact. He looked carefully at all three men to be sure they'd give him no more trouble, then he went to his horse and began to saddle her with the folded blanket. He was ready to mount when he noticed his opponent hadn't moved. He walked over and offered him a hand up. Red took it, but once on his feet, he stood watching Ian with his hand frozen in the gesture Ian decided was a sign against the evil eye. Ian retrieved Red's knife, wiped it on the grass and put it in its sheath on Red's belt. "Don't take it so hard," he said. He picked up Red's sword and placed it in its scabbard. Red was still immobile.

"Perhaps we should introduce ourselves," Ian said. "I'm Ian." He thrust his hand at Red, who reacted as if he'd had a gun pointed at him. Ian slapped his chest and said, "Ian." He pointed at the older man and raised his eyebrows.

"Owain," the man said, beaming as he caught on, slapping his chest.

"Ah. Owain." Ian pointed at Red again.

"Rolf," Owain said. He pointed to the younger man. "Evan."

Ian repeated "Rolf" and "Evan," nodding to each in turn. He went back to his horse, saying, "I don't suppose you could point me toward the nearest henge?"

They stared. Apparently they weren't going to make it easy. It was going to be charades.

He shrugged and walked to the edge of the spring where he pocketed a handful of pebbles. Returning, he scooped dirt into a small heap that he crowned with a circle of the stones. He stood up to watch enlightenment dawn on their faces. To a man, they pointed west.

Ian nodded. "Rolf, how about a leg up?"

Rolf gave him a cautious, expectant look but nothing else. Ian sighed. He led his horse over to Rolf and demonstrated how to lace one's fingers together to make a foothold. With a little prodding, he got Rolf to do the same, but when Ian tried to put his foot in, Rolf dropped his hands. Ian scowled. Rolf appeared terrified, twisting his fingers against the evil eye.

"Let's try it again," Ian told him.

This time, when Rolf tried to drop his hands, Ian grabbed them and shook his head. Rolf froze. Nodding, Ian put his foot in the "cradle" and vaulted astride. Rolf seemed astounded. Ian nodded and patted him on the shoulder. "Good man!"

He collected the mare and turned her westward, glancing back to see the three mount their horses and Rolf retrieve his spear. As Ian kicked the mare forward, and three shadows followed suit, it occurred to him, with a shock and a little surge of indignation, that he'd forgotten—for the duration of the little drama—that he'd been abducted and abused. He'd been tricked into joining the charade. He'd been easy meat...

They were all very good, he decided grimly. *Very* good.

II

From the summit, he could see why he'd been lost. The track they were following lay along the crest of a ridge running south of the hill on which the henge stood. And the lower flanks of both hill and ridge were covered with the same dense growth that had bedeviled him since he set out. Forest—skeletal gray deciduous below and nearly black evergreen at the higher elevations—covered all the surrounding hills stretching to the horizon. As they sat their horses in a clearing formed by the fall of several forest giants, he could see no sign of a paved road, a settlement, rail or power lines, or aircraft.

So where are we? How far to the horizon?

Ian couldn't remember. There wouldn't be many places in

the northern hemisphere with so much wilderness. Only North America. Or Russia.

He was startled to see the other gray horse back in the clearing below, like a toy in the distant meadow. Jemma must have followed him and retrieved it. He could see that she'd rigged a collar for it and was leading the animal as it dragged something through the grass toward an impressive pile of logs and tree branches she must have collected with its aid. She stopped the horse, when its unseen burden drew even with the woodpile, and disconnected the towrope, tossing the free end over the top of the pile. Then she led the horse around behind it and, apparently, reattached the animal to its burden, because they could see what she'd been towing as the tiny figure of a man—one of the murder victims, he supposed— was dragged upward. Jemma's head appeared from behind the top of the pile, and as the body neared her position, she pulled herself up and hauled the body onto the summit. She slipped the towrope from the body and stretched the corpse out, straightening limbs and smoothing clothing.

Ian's companions seemed fascinated by the little drama. Jabbering and pointing, they urged their horses toward the scene, undaunted by the lack of any track or by the dense underbrush. Ian followed more slowly. It took them a good hour to cover the intervening ground.

When they entered the meadow, Ian's horse whinnied, and Jemma's answered it. The four men spread out and stopped halfway between the forest and the henge, from which position the others were content to watch silently as Ian dismounted and approached the horse tethered, again, to graze. He let his own mare's reins trail while he inspected the other gray, feeling through her mane and tail for a transmitter. He found nothing, but it might have been removed, or it could be something so small he'd overlooked it. He'd heard there were bugs tiny enough to masquerade as one match in a box. The mare shook her head with a rubbery flap of her ears and resumed her grazing. The distant rush of water sounded like a great wind pushing through the trees. Ian didn't hear Jemma until she was right behind him.

"Lose something?"

She had just bathed. She smelled of flowers, and her hair clumped damply in platinum ropes. Where had she found a bath in this wilderness? She'd changed to a cobalt blue tunic with gold embroidery. He wondered if she had always been beautiful, or if she'd gone through acne and braces as Margaret had. That he'd even think of such a question annoyed him and he answered sharply.

"I was looking for the transmitter."

She stared blankly for a second, then laughed. "There isn't one. I followed you." He must have looked skeptical because she added, "You made enough noise to wake the…er…as a troop of cavalry."

As she spoke, Rolf, Owain and Evan walked their horses up behind him and sat staring at her.

Jemma looked them over. "The local constabulary, I presume."

"I believe they actually escaped from Monty Python's troupe." He felt rage replace the astonishing unreality. He pointed to the pyre. "Just what do you think you're doing?"

She shrugged. "I was about to burn the evidence." She turned to watch as Evan guided his horse toward the tent.

Ian was sore and exhausted, and desperately wanted a bath. He didn't want to deal with murder or conspiracy to conceal homicide—just with soap and hot water, and maybe a good pint after. Wearily, he said, "You can't…!"

She whirled to face him. "The medical examiner didn't show, and you can't just leave dead bodies lying around. It teaches the local wildlife nasty habits."

Revolting thought! Less obvious and more probable was that cremation would destroy the evidence, end the possibility of any future autopsy, and prevent discovery of the *actual* cause of death. And what might that be? Perhaps they'd died of natural causes, their corpses mutilated afterward. Macabre, but not beyond the scope of his experience. Probably, they'd been cadavers. The thought left him slightly nauseated. He wouldn't consider—without evidence—that three men had actually been killed, and the boy hacked to pieces, for effect. Or it could have been the work of a demonic cult—some nouveau-druid, neo-pagan devil worship nonsense. A post-mortem might tell.

But she was right about the animals. He said, "They ought to be buried."

"You want to dig the holes?" When he didn't answer immediately, she added, "You can report me from the first call box we come to." The undercurrent of anger beneath her flippancy puzzled him. Surely she didn't expect him to accept the charade or to forget he had a duty to the law simply because he'd become a kidnap victim.

Ian watched as Rolf wandered over to the pyre, but the anger Jemma had kindled in him knotted his innards, to the distraction of his interpretive faculties. He kept his attention on Jemma as Rolf began to climb.

"What's that half-wit up to?" Jemma demanded.

Ian strode over to the pyre—atop which Rolf stood staring in obvious horror at the corpses—and climbed high enough to see that the murder victims had been arranged on beds of pine and green oak branches. The blood had been rinsed from their hands and faces. Flowers were laid on their chests. He noticed a sword in the hand of one, an iron tipped spear next to another. All three victims had silver coins placed over their blank eyes, and there was a dead rabbit and a small wooden bowl of grain next to each of them. Ian glared down at Jemma who'd followed him to the base of the pile.

Before he could say anything, Rolf let out a scream and leapt off the pyre with the dead man's sword, smashing Jemma to the ground. He grabbed her tunic with one hand and brandished the sword with the other. Jemma didn't speak or cry out and made no attempt to defend herself. Before Ian could intervene, Rolf had the blade at her throat. Ian rushed forward with Owain, but both stopped as Rolf threatened to sever Jemma's windpipe. Even Ian clearly understood his intention.

Rolf demanded something unintelligible.

Owain seemed astonished, then angered. He took the sword

from Rolf's hand, but Rolf drew his own. Owain held the dead man's blade in front of Jemma's face and asked something Ian couldn't understand. He looked at Ian, as if for an explanation.

Jemma answered in what sounded like Gaelic. There was no fear in her voice, and Owain hesitated, looking puzzled. Jemma rolled her eyes sideways at Ian. "They don't speak Gaelic. Can you make them understand I didn't do it?"

Ian looked at Rolf, who was obviously ready to have off with her head and wouldn't be dissuaded. Before he could speak, Evan charged up on his horse and slid off. The horse skidded into Rolf, nearly trampling Jemma. The bone skittered away as Evan dragged at Rolf's arm, pleading in his Babel tongue and, all the while, looking at Jemma with terror.

Ian could only understand two words: Rolf and Epona. But the intent was clear—Rolf was to desist immediately and come along.

Evan repeated his plea, and Owain took it up with a quiet command that seemed to penetrate Rolf's rage. He reluctantly let Jemma go. At Owain's further insistence, he followed Evan to the tent, from where the injured boy had been watching. The others followed.

The boy—Alf, Ian gathered as events progressed—told his story propped on his elbow, with much gesturing of the other hand. The three newcomers crowded around him. Ian and Jemma stood back a little, though not together. Alf pointed at her from time to time and once at Ian.

Rolf's belligerence ebbed with the story's telling and his fingers formed the sign against the evil eye. He began to look horrified.

When Alf fell silent, Jemma said, dryly, "Well, that seems to have set the record straight."

Ian stared at her. "What did he say?"

"I have no idea."

Rolf went to Jemma, fell to his knees and grabbed at her skirt like a small child who expects terrible punishment. He kept repeating something in terrified gibberish.

Jemma stepped backward, startled, and pulled her skirt away.

"Stop that! Get up and stop groveling." She accompanied her words with a gesture commanding Rolf to rise and back off.

He did so, but stood waiting for her next command.

"What was that all about?" Ian demanded.

"I'm sure he's mistaken me for someone else, but I don't intend to argue the point." She looked at the others. "Come on. We've got a service to conduct." She strode over to take the dead man's sword from Owain's unresisting hand and started back toward the woodpile, pausing only to grab a small brand from the little fire smoldering before the tent. They followed.

At the foot of the pyre, she handed the sword to Rolf, pointing, and Rolf fearfully scrambled up to replace it in the hand of the corpse. She offered Rolf the light, but he shook his head and stepped away. Owain and Evan also refused to take it. She glanced at Ian, but obviously thought better of asking him to do the honors.

He started to say, "You can't..." but gave it up. She could and obviously would.

She stood silently a moment, then held the fire up to the four compass points, raising her voice. "Into Thy hands I commend these souls, Oh Gods of the Brython, Gods of the Cymry. Let their untimely deaths repay what harm they've done in this life. Let them enter free-born to the next." Then she thrust the torch into the base of the pyre and stood back.

The fire had been well laid; the wood was dry and caught quickly. Fingers, then bright arms and sprightly bodies of flame played up through the woodpile, feeling along from twig to branch, crackling through the pine boughs, caressing the corpses and blessing the funeral offerings. As smoke rose like incense from the green oak and flamed in the searing convection currents, it hid the evidence of the grisly dead.

Ian began to doubt their very existence. It was an elaborate god-game whose purpose he could not imagine. "Lord help them," was all the prayer he could manage. He had lost faith—not in God, but in His power or willingness to intervene.

Marjory's funeral was suddenly brought back to him. Margaret's face twisted by pain. Peter's arms folded tightly around himself; Peter pressing his hand over his mouth to keep the pain from escaping. Ian had been dry-eyed. Petrified by the enormity of it. Frozen by shock. Scarcely able to appreciate the irony of the gloriously sun-filled day.

The Celts—as Ian found himself thinking of them—began to chant in a minor key. He recognized a dirge, though he didn't understand the words. It was not what he'd expected. The chant was irresistibly moving. And Jemma's words had had a strange aptness. He looked sideways at her and was surprised to see tears wetting her cheeks.

III

Maggots of flame scoured flesh from the bone, and bone glowed charcoal red, then white, disintegrating as the fire subsided. The dead man's sword, heated to the fiery color of its birth, slagged earthward and settled gravely among the coals.

As he watched the mortal remains of three human beings disappear, Ian was overwhelmed by anger, focused hot enough to fuse gold or cast-iron. Never in his life had he felt so helpless—not even at Marjory's death, which had come as an end to dreadful suffering and could be seen as natural in a way.

He wasn't a violent man. Of all the felons he'd taken in charge, he'd had to physically restrain only two. He had never served in combat, nor lost a friend to murder. He had never killed anyone, and only child-batterers had ever engendered such a murderous rage in him. Words—clichés—filled his mind trying to define it. The fury of his reaction startled and frightened him, until he found himself shaking with the intensity of it. He felt a strong desire to sit down until the sensation passed, or to throw himself on the grass and pound the earth, or pound the four watchers beside him.

But when he looked at Rolf, he saw tears. Rolf cried unashamedly, his anguish pouring out in sobs and curses in his strange tongue. The corpses had been living men once, and Rolf—whether the tears were for grief or remorse—had the humanity to weep for them. Ian found the thought powerfully moving. Anxiety undermined his rage. He felt uncertain. Could such great grief be feigned? Could Gielgud have turned in so convincing a performance? And what of Owain, so grimly reserved? Or Evan, shocked and glazed?

But Jemma was by far the best of the four. Her detached sadness was the perfect touch. And she was so exquisitely beautiful it seemed an obscenity that she should also be a killer. A kidnapper. He wished he'd been able to finish the *Times* article. It would be nice to know what one was up against, what she was really like. Perhaps it had been a crime of passion? He thought it unlikely. She was too cool and competent. He couldn't imagine her being flustered.

It was obviously a conspiracy to drive a lowly civil servant mad, a poor sod who wasn't privy to any state secrets. He supposed, when one looked at it a certain way, it made no less sense than someone holding a plane full of airline passengers hostage for obscure causes and indefinite periods of time.

But the question remained: *Why me?* Unless this was a test case—a dry run for the cuckoo-fication of a *real* VIP—the whole plot seemed senseless. Might as well give up and accept the time-machine idea.

And what would they do with him if he *did* crack? Surely they'd have to kill him. If they sent him back, he'd queer their chances of working the game on the actual target. The only incontrovertible fact he had was that he'd allowed a suspect to destroy evidence in a murder investigation.

Long before the fire collapsed in a furnace of red embers, sending shooting-star sparks aloft and its human elements to their ancestral ash, Jemma turned her glowing face from the heat and sighed and said, "Excuse me," and walked away.

Some time later, Ian followed her back to the tent and found her sorting through a pile of nested, cast-iron kettles near the small fire from which she'd lit the funeral pyre.

"How's the boy?"

"Fine. I gave him something for the pain, and it's made him sleep. That's the best thing for him."

He nodded and pointed to a covered pot she'd balanced over the fire. "Where did you get the water?" His voice sounded surly even to himself.

She pointed north, then held the largest of the kettles out to him. "Would you please bring some back?" He nodded. She walked over and withdrew from her luggage something that she wrapped in a towel and tossed at him. "Catch."

He unwrapped it. Soap! He felt a surge of gratitude, then resentment as he remembered how he'd come to be in need of it. He said, "Thank you," sullenly.

She didn't seem to notice his bad humor. She nodded and pointed to the pot on the fire. "Half an hour."

It was impossible to judge from which direction came the soft shush of rushing water. He took Jemma at her word and headed north, following her occasional small footprints in the soft earth. He noticed none of the usual evidence of "civilized" man—no cigarette ends, no discarded bottles—only, here and there, a strand of gold hair caught by overhanging branches. Something—habit, he supposed—made him collect several of these, looping them as carefully as if they were gold chains, to put into his wallet. Evidence, he told himself.

Of what? Insanity? Infatuation? The idea, like the icy water at the foot of the hill, was shocking.

Fattened by melting snow, the stream tumbled shallowly between banks of soft limestone, over a wide bed of cobbles rounded by the constant play of water. A few early bluebells bloomed where the trees thinned out on the near bank, and new green shoots poked up through grass dried and flattened by winter.

He took the keys and wallet, pen and jotter, and reading glasses from his pockets and put them with his tie and Rolex on a flat rock on the bank. Then he stripped to his underwear and plunged down to the stream. The cold so numbed his flesh that he could scarcely feel the stones beneath his feet. It made his bones ache fiercely. He had to sit down on the streambed to submerge himself, and the icy water brought back Cymry Reservoir. Was it only thirty-six hours ago he'd showered in scalding water? Or three days? Or three weeks? He had no way of knowing.

He stood up to soap himself and his remaining clothing, then sat again, gasping at the cold as he bounced and splashed to rinse the soap off. Back on the shingle, his bare feet seemed to find every sharp edge and pebble. He took off his streaming vest and pants to wring the water out, then shivered back into them. Wash and wear. He used Jemma's cloth to dry his face and hair, and he saturated it trying to blot more of the water from his undergarments. He then washed his stockings and shirt, hanging them on a tree branch to drip while he scrubbed the dried mud off his trousers and beat them against a large rock to shake out the remaining dust. He carefully repeated the procedure for his coat.

When he'd filled the kettle upstream from his impromptu laundry, he dressed himself. Damp or not, he felt better. He scrambled up the bank, retrieved his property from the rock, knotted his tie around his neck, buttoned his coat and straightened his hair and mustache. He felt more presentable. More in control of things.

Jemma smiled when he gave her back the soap. "Dinner's ready. Maybe you could ask the others to come?"

On a picnic cloth, she'd laid a meal out that was worthy of an Irish wake, with bread—baked in a pot—and butter, stewed prunes and reconstituted dried apples, lentil soup with meat, fresh rabbit—spitted and roasted over the fire—and some sort of greens. The spread made Ian realize he was starving, having had nothing substantial to eat since Sunday's dinner. Nothing he could remember, anyway. Was it forty-eight hours ago? Or longer?

He hung the damp towel over a bush and said, "I don't speak their language." He wondered where civility left off and collaboration began. But then, you couldn't go against the rules until you knew them.

She said, "But they seem to respect you. And I have only Gaelic, which they obviously don't get."

He shrugged. He went back to where the men were still watching the embers and touched all three on the shoulder, gesturing, once he had their attention, for them to follow. Evan and Owain did. Rolf brooded on.

Ian signaled the men to sit and asked Jemma, "Do you know these fellows?"

"Of course not."

He didn't believe her, but he pointed. "Owain and Evan. And that sociable fellow over there is Rolf."

"It must have been his friend or a relative."

"Brother," he said without knowing how he knew.

"How do you know?"

Rolf had screamed something like *brawd*, the Welsh word for brother, just before he'd leaped on Jemma. Or was it some kind of post-hypnotic suggestion they'd planted in his head while he was unconscious? The damned uncertainty *was* going to drive him mad.

Jemma persisted. "You speak Welsh?"

He nodded. He had the feeling she knew he did, in fact, knew everything about him.

They sat down, cross-legged on the ground, and Ian didn't miss the irony of the situation as he loosened his tie. Jemma passed around wooden bowls for the soup, then a quart-sized mug, which smelled of wine and honey, into which he looked suspiciously before he passed it on. Owain and Evan each took a sip from it, as did Jemma when it came back to her. Owain called Rolf, who joined them for the drink but didn't eat, and the three natives began to talk quietly among themselves.

Ian asked Jemma, "How is it you know Gaelic?"

"I studied it while awaiting trial. It was obviously a bad gamble. Welsh seems to be closer."

To Celtic, if you believed her. He didn't bother to consider the possibility. "How did you manage to get out of your country?"

"Careful planning." She gave him a placating smile, no doubt in deference to his profession. "I gradually converted all my assets to cash—ostensibly to pay my lawyers—and transferred the funds to my father. He used the money to get what I needed and set things up for my getaway."

That part was undoubtedly true. Matthew Henderson had admitted as much.

"...All I had to do was get to Britain. And when you have money..." She helped herself to some rabbit and offered it to Owain.

Owain reacted to the rabbit more negatively than Ian had to the wine—he wouldn't even touch it, neither would Evan or Rolf. Jemma shrugged and told Ian, "More for us."

The meat was perfectly done. He asked where it came from, thinking perhaps she'd brought it with the rest of the supplies, but she pointed to the woods. "I caught it with a snare."

"Why do you suppose they won't eat it?"

"Not kosher, maybe?"

The food improved his disposition, and he felt more inclined to be civil. The soup was delicious, flavored with bacon. He thought the bread tasted like sourdough—Jemma confirmed that it was— and he tried some of the wine when the mug came round again. It was mead—fermented honey—and was excellent. After a second sip, and a third—as the wine dulled his anger—he relaxed. He began to see his situation as a case to be solved. To prove or disprove a theory, one had to have data. He decided he would have to gather more. He would have to catch Jemma contradicting herself and face her with the contradiction. Which meant he'd have to talk to her.

There were dozens of things he'd like to ask her—where, for instance, did a surgeon learn to snare and cook rabbits?—but even in his head, they sounded officious. Matthew Henderson had been right—wherever they were, it was outside his jurisdiction, and without the authority, he couldn't compel her to answer.

Jemma resolved his dilemma. "You're dying to ask me something," she said. "Go ahead. If I think it's impertinent, I'll say so."

"How is it that your father's a British subject but you're an American?" It wasn't what he'd meant to ask.

"My mother married Matthew Henderson because he was rich and handsome and famous—not necessarily in that order. She left him because he was totally dedicated to his work. It was an amicable settlement. Both of them had money, so there was very little maneuvering; and I've never wanted for anything. She got custody, of course, because that's how it was done, and since she was an American, we went back there to live. But I spent my summers in England—it's always been a refuge from the insanity of the States— so it was natural for me to come back."

"What made you think you wouldn't be extradited?"

She smiled—genuinely amused, he thought, and charming. "But I haven't been."

He wondered why she hadn't used that charm to woo the jury.

"I didn't plan to stay," she continued. "I wanted to say good-bye to my father and, of course, to use his machine."

"I suppose you'll claim you were unjustly convicted?"

"Not at all."

He thought he detected amusement, as if she thought him terribly naive, but then she seemed to sober and she asked, "Are you married?"

"Widowed."

She nodded, once. "Children?"

"Two." He began to feel resentment for the reversal of their roles.

"Still at home?"

"No."

She seemed relieved. "Did you have a partner?"

"Did have?"

"When you blundered into the time machine, were you alone?"

"I *entered* a small building. Before someone struck me."

Jemma made a wry face. "It was a tree that you hit."

"Right!"

"You were alone when you entered the shed?" She sounded anxious. Why?

"Yes."

This seemed to please her. "Then thank God! No one was killed." He raised an eyebrow, and she added, "There was enough explosive in that shed to blow up a city block."

He remembered the letter her father had given him. *When you read this, I will be long dead.* She'd planned to make it look as if she'd died.

Jemma was saying, "...you were very lucky."

Lucky! "My children must be nearly mad with worry. What've you told them?"

"I? Nothing." More gently, she added, "They almost certainly believe you're dead."

If that were the case it would be a mercy, he thought. Eventually one dealt with death. It was uncertainty that drove one 'round the bend. And the worry, when you didn't know, was a great deal more painful than the certain loss.

But, in any case, CID wouldn't be fooled. Even in the most thorough bombings, they'd find the grisly bits. He hoped that when they didn't, in this case, Andrew would have sense enough to let Peter and Margaret think he *was* dead.

Who are these people? he wondered. *How can they do this to other human beings?!*

Rolf tapped Jemma's arm with the mug and up-ended it to show that it was empty. She got up and refilled it from a large wineskin she brought out of the tent.

Her questions had started Ian thinking about his family, wondering how long this exercise in lunacy would last. He might never see Peter, Margaret or Susannah again.

Don't think like that! he told himself.

He suddenly didn't want to talk to Jemma any more. He loosened his tie further. The planet was only eight thousand miles in diameter. Wherever they were, if he traveled far enough in one direction, he would eventually come to a seacoast. And if he followed the seacoast he'd find a port, with sailors and someone who spoke English. When the wine came around again, he took a hefty swig. Though he could feel it going to his head, he didn't care. He caught Jemma watching him. She quickly shifted her attention to Rolf.

"*The Celts take small sips but they do it rather often,*" she said, quoting one of the ancient historians. Ian was too affected by the wine to remember which.

Owain and Evan, who'd been talking quietly in their strange tongue, suddenly raised their voices to demand something of Rolf. He stood up unsteadily and began to rant, swearing—Ian was fairly certain—and shaking his fists toward the northwest. The others weren't managing to calm him. Ian stood up. Rolf became more agitated, grabbing his sword and swaying precariously.

Jemma leaned over the tablecloth and tugged on Ian's trouser-leg. "You can't reason with him. Sit down and let me try."

He'd seen women police constables succeed with drunks where burly men had failed. He shrugged and sat. Jemma tapped Rolf on the leg and said, "Rolf," in a loud voice. When Rolf looked down at her, she lowered her voice and raised her hand in a gesture indicating a cup. "Would you like more wine?" She pantomimed drinking.

Rolf nodded.

Jemma motioned for him to sit, and he did so. "Inspector Carreg," she said, without looking at Ian, "would you please get Rolf some wine?" She smiled at Rolf and added, "Put lots of water in it."

When Ian half-filled the mug with water from the kettle, he noticed that Owain watched thoughtfully, though Rolf seemed not to notice.

Jemma, meanwhile, was trying to distract Rolf with gestures and Gaelic phrases, but he was too drunk to make any sense of it. He was about to get up again when she started to sing "Frère Jacques." She had a clear alto voice and she immediately had everyone's attention.

"*Frère Jacques, frère Jacques, dormez vous? Dormez vous? Sonne les matines. Sonne les matines...*"

Ian forgot the mug in his hand until she substituted for the last verse, "Give him wine. Give him wine."

Ian obeyed. Rolf took the mug and settled down to enjoy the recital. Owain smiled. Jemma sang another round of "Frère Jacques," then began a medley of Christmas tunes with "What Child Is This?" All three of the natives were mesmerized. Owain and Evan swayed slightly in time with the music; Rolf began to nod. The wine mug he'd neglected to pass sagged, and Owain quietly put a hand under it, easing it from his grasp. As Owain sipped from the mug, Rolf stirred briefly, then closed his eyes.

Owain passed the mug to Ian, who gave it to Jemma. When she paused to drink, Rolf stirred, so she quickly handed it to Evan and began to softly sing the "Riddle Song." "*I gave my love a cherry...*"

Rolf quieted.

Ian found himself relaxing. When Owain passed the mug again, he sipped without thinking, then held it out to Jemma, who shook her head, and pointed to Rolf. She kept singing. Owain took the mug, sipped, then passed it back.

Drugging me, Ian thought, *that's what they're doing*. Somehow it didn't matter. *They'll do what they want with me anyway.*

As Jemma ended the song, Rolf's heavy breathing became a snore.

Ian stretched his eyes wide in an effort to keep them open, but he felt himself slipping. He pulled off his tie and pocketed it as he tried to concentrate on the others.

Jemma went into the tent and came out with blankets; she spread one over Rolf. "Inspector Carreg," she said, "would you like to sleep in the tent?"

His own, "No, thank you," sounded slurred and distant. *Too much wine. Too much too much.*

She handed him something, but he couldn't think what to do with it. Couldn't think what it was. She was incredibly beautiful but there was something—he couldn't remember what—that made her dangerous…

Darkness seemed to have arrived. The stars were a spill of stolen diamonds on black velvet. He noticed the air was frosty, though he didn't feel cold. Owain appeared from nowhere and threw more wood on the fire, and asked Jemma for another song. Ian felt he was possessed of tongues, for he understood the request. Or had Owain been speaking English? It was too much of a puzzle.

Jemma sang, "*Now I lay me down to sleep. I pray the Lord my soul to keep…*"

Yea, though I walk in the Valley of the Shadow of Death, I will fear no evil, Ian thought, *not even Jemma. Into the valley of Death rode the…*How many was it? Five. No, six with the boy…

It seemed to him that, just before he lost track of things, she weighted him to the earth with a shroud of wool.

Later, his head cleared as the cold seeped in. They were obviously in the northern hemisphere. The two Ursas ambled across the heavens with frigid indifference, and later still—or earlier, depending on your view—Orion stalked the sky. Only *they* called him Cernunnos.

As he lay there, with a murderess and among men who might be lunatics or felons, he recalled that he had never feared dying, though in years past he'd feared leaving Marjory to raise their children alone. Now, he feared death even less. Dead was beyond caring, beyond pain and fear and rage. Corrosive rage. Distracting rage. Thought-stopping rage…

Cold woke him again, and his bladder drove him to the clearing's edge. From that vantage point, he could hear Owain and Evan muttering to each other in their strange language. He stumbled back to his blanket, not caring if they cut his throat in his sleep.

24 mawrth

Ian's third awakening was for breakfast. He had been dreaming he was lunching at Rule's. Though the restaurant vanished when he opened his eyes, the luscious aromas remained. He looked around and began to believe he was back in Britain—the sky was overcast and threatening. But the agony that racked him when he tried to move brought his actual situation stabbing back. Every stick and pebble on the ground beneath him was a log or boulder. The muscles of his back, and all the muscles he'd discovered riding, were locked in position. He couldn't sit. With a great deal of effort, he rolled over and pushed himself to his knees, arching his back to unlock his spine and neck. He got up one leg at a time.

A sensation of being watched spun him around to face Rolf, who bleared greenly up from where he'd passed out the night before. He looked even more depressed than yesterday and was, undoubtedly, hung over to boot. Ian felt foul enough, himself, to manage a wickedly cheerful good morning. If Rolf didn't understand the words, he got the meaning, for he scowled back.

Ian found it more comfortable to turn his whole body around to look for the others. Jemma was sitting beneath the raised flap of the tent, pouring soup into her patient. The cooking fire danced under a large pot, from which emanated the tantalizing aroma. Evan and Owain were nowhere in sight, but by the time Ian had relieved himself and limbered up, they returned from the direction of the stream. And by that time, Jemma had served the morning meal.

The food was simple—some kind of grain porridge with honey, reheated rabbit which the other men continued to eschew, and water.

Rolf sulked in front of the fire and ignored the food, staring at a point halfway to the henge. He was oblivious to the urgings of Owain and Evan to eat. Ian didn't blame him. His own head was none too steady. It ached and his nerves felt stretched beyond hope. He was acutely aware of how provoking Jemma smelled as she moved around the fire. He noticed Owain was affected, too, for *he* made the sign against the evil eye when she came near. As well you might, Ian thought.

She wore no make-up. Her brows and lashes were a darker gold than her hair—wheat-straw gold. Her eyes were cornflower blue and deep as…Drowning pools! Ian thought savagely.

Ian had noticed that Owain's chin was clean-shaven, and after they'd eaten, he tackled the job of requesting a razor. It turned out to be a flat, kidney-shaped piece of bronze with a whetted edge. Owain laughed uproariously when Ian didn't know what to do with the thing, but patiently demonstrated its use, substituting oil for shaving cream, and using a tiny bronze mirror he took from his kit and hung on a tree.

Ian's first attempt with it was nearly suicidal and amusing even to the grieving Rolf. As Ian tried to staunch the blood, Owain took pity and finished the job as deftly as any barber Ian had patronized. While Owain scraped the last of the stubble from Ian's neck, Ian consoled himself with the knowledge that if they were going to cut his throat, they'd have done so while he slept.

Jemma watched the lesson without comment or hint of amusement. "We need meat," she announced when they'd finished. "Would one of you gents volunteer to go hunting?"

The three natives stared at her as if waiting for a translation, then looked at Ian. He shrugged.

She tried again. Taking a stick, she sketched the outline of a deer with quick, deft strokes. The three nodded as if all of their heads were animated by a single mind and common thought. But they kept waiting. She fetched Rolf's spear, which had been leaning against a tree. She startled, perhaps frightened them, but made her point when she plunged the spear point into the stick figure. Rolf took the spear and went to get the horses. Owain and Evan got their weapons, and the three were quickly mounted.

"I don't suppose you brought any fishing gear," Ian asked when they'd gone.

"I did, as a matter of fact. I'd forgotten." She took a small leather pouch from a bag packed with commendable efficiency and withdrew a packet of assorted fish hooks. He selected one. She gave him a six-inch stick, with black line wrapped around it, and a cork. "If you catch 'em, you clean 'em," she said.

"Only if you'll cook them."

"Fair enough."

He turned over several logs on his way to the stream, and collected an assortment of grubs and spindly worms. These he put on a slab of bark and protected with a handful of humus.

The fish liked them. The first pale worm floated and writhed below the surface, racing the cork downstream, until something large and silver arced out of the water—as slick as an ad in a fishing brochure—and swallowed it. Without a reel or net, he was forced to drag the pretty fish up on the bank. As he was not inclined to torture the creature by stringing a line through its gills, he left it on the bank to die as quickly as possible, and covered it with leaves to keep it while he caught another.

He hadn't fished with a hand line since his boyhood—the summers he'd spent with his paternal grandparents in Wales, running wild and exploring, and occasionally justifying his long absences with enough fish for supper. He'd taken Peter fly fishing since then, but of course, this wasn't the same.

He'd dropped the line in again when he wondered, *what if she uses my absence to escape?* He rolled a large rock onto the end of the fishing line and half ran back to the clearing.

She—as he'd come to think of her—had rolled up the sides of the tent and was changing the boy's bandages. All else was quiet. Feeling foolish, he hurried back to his fishing.

After luncheon, when the food had been put away and the injured boy had nodded off, Jemma scraped the cookery pots clean and enlisted Ian's aid in hauling the lot down to the river. The place to which she led him was a point where the stream curved broadly southward, and the banks stood three feet above water level. On the inside of the curve, the water slowed enough to drop its sediment, building a little flat bench on which grass had taken root. Jemma scrambled down the bank and carried her pots to the upstream side of the bench, where new sand was being deposited. Ian followed.

As he watched, she scrubbed the pots out with sand and a flat stone. He didn't comment on the bizarre lengths to which she was carrying this back to nature romp. At her request, he returned to camp to check the boy. That done, he hurried back to see she hadn't hooked it.

She met him halfway to the stream.

"Where're your pots?" he asked.

"I left them to soak. I think they're safe."

Ian shrugged and allowed her to precede him back to camp.

Late afternoon shadows barred the clearing, and sunlight lay on the campsite like honey, thick and golden. It warmed Jemma where she sat on a pile of rugs, turning her skin to gold and her hair to brass. Ian's suit was a loss, so he gave up trying to spare it and sat cross-legged in the sun, on the blanket he'd used for a saddle, and he wrapped the other around him like a shawl. He listened to Jemma amusing herself by memorizing bits of the natives' strange language, pronouncing the words aloud. The effort seemed as futile to him as learning Esperanto—as if another language was needed in this Babel world.

It had never occurred to him, before, to wonder how prisoners passed their captive hours. That he was a prisoner was beyond question. Although there were no walls or chains holding him, he was as surely contained by the impenetrable forest and his own dearth of woodsman's skills as if he'd been chained to one of the trees.

The thing was, he decided, to be patient, to see if one could tell what language they spoke when they slipped out of character. Thinking this, he dozed.

He had the gift of dozing, while on surveillance, so fitfully that any movement by the subject would arouse him.

Jemma's departure woke him. The glimpse he caught of her back, gold hair trailing, brought him wide awake and to his feet. He followed her by sound.

After she was well away from camp, she made it easier by humming. He noted—with admirable detachment, he thought—she had a first-rate voice. But this he knew already from the previous night.

Soon the rush of water drowned the murmur of her humming. Sweat soaked him. What if he lost her? Yet there was no hurrying without giving himself away. He stopped when he judged she'd reached the stream and he peered through the brush.

She stood on the grassy bench, among the pots she'd left there earlier, and was twisting her hair up on her head, skewering it in place with what looked like an ivory pin. Sensible course. Less likely to catch it on snags or brambles. Then she slipped out of her sandals.

Ian's policeman's sixth sense made him ease backwards, into hiding, as she looked around for watchers. Seemingly satisfied, she picked up her footwear and strode over to the river bank and began undoing her belt. As she slipped it off and laid it on the bank with her sandals, he realized that her rendezvous was with water and soap, not a co-conspirator. Even murderesses bathed occasionally. He felt his face go crimson as she pulled her tunic off.

But perhaps she was meeting someone after her bath. He would wait to see what she did when she finished, though he wouldn't watch her bathe. He started to withdraw to a modest distance when he realized here was an opportunity to search her clothing for a transmitter or a clue to where they were. If he could get to her wardrobe unseen.

He glanced at her again—just a peek to locate her. She'd stepped out of her skirt and smalls and was completely naked. Her white form was arresting.

She walked over to the pots and began pouring water on herself as Japanese people do in public baths, using the smallest pot for a dipper. Sun-warmed water. No Spartan she. A small breeze stirred, and the cold made her nipples as erect as if she'd just been made love to. He found himself becoming aroused. Confound the woman!

For a fraction of a second, he flushed with an emotion he recognized with shock.

Lust!

Then a wave of shame replaced it, and a blush burned his face and neck. It was impossible not to look, but extraordinarily embarrassing. What if she should turn and catch him? What did one say to a naked woman upon whom one has been spying? A lovely naked woman, he admitted grudgingly. Her skin was unblemished and white as raw milk. She had voluptuous breasts—Good Lord, what breasts!—and full hips, though by no means too broad hips, a mature woman's figure that reminded him of Marjory's.

Bloody hell! What an obscenity to think of this woman in the same thought as Marjory!

And she was bathing with the cookery pots!

His annoyance strengthened his determination to continue. He was behind her as she poured the sun-warmed water over her, two paces from the garments she'd laid out on the bank. When she began to soap her face, he stepped out of hiding. A quick feel of the skirt revealed that nothing was hidden in hem, waistband, or seams, and that the garment had two pockets. The right one held a sewing kit with thread and needles, a small sharp scissors in a leather case, and a clean but rumpled handkerchief. The left contained a small leather pouch of silver and gold coins, a piece of chalk, a small spool of cotton twine and a primitive-looking safety pin. Nothing high tech. Nothing electronic. He returned the skirt to the bank and went over the tunic. It, too, was without secrets.

He glanced at Jemma. She'd lathered herself to her waist and was passing the soap over her hips and buttocks. Ian felt a shiver pass through him and looked away quickly. Her sandals seemed to have no hidden pockets or compartments; her belt held only her hunting knife. That left her undergarments.

Ian's experience of women's undergarments was limited to the things Marjory'd worn, the frillies Margaret had occasionally left in the bath, and to the sometimes surprising items worn by crime victims—little frothy tidbits whose sole function seemed to be the arousal of any man who clapped eyes on them. Jemma's serviceable but ugly undergarments were not what he'd expected of her. He was reluctant to touch them, but if he wanted to search thoroughly, he must. He did. Again, he found nothing.

So. She had taken a chance and left the radio—if she had one—with her other things. He quickly placed everything as nearly as he could to as he'd found it and stepped back out of sight.

He couldn't resist one final backward look.

Jemma was emptying the last of the warm water over herself. The late sun caught her in a net of glittering rivulets and glowed back from her creamy skin. *Piel du lait.* She seemed to have a sort of gravity that held the water to her curves and contours as it trickled earthward. And held his eyes. And raised the tide of his lust like the moon. And speeded his departure.

He was methodically searching her luggage, when a blow between his shoulder blades nearly brought him to his knees. He regained his balance as he whirled about, ready to defend himself. From Jemma!

She stood with her hands fisted and her face flushed. "You

crazy old man! What the hell are you doing?"

Ian paused. That's how she thought of him. Old man! The insult stung, and his own sudden anger left him shaking. "I want out of this charade. I want to go back to England. *Now!*"

"I can't send you back."

"Very well, I accept that. Let me speak with someone who can."

"I don't seem to be getting through, Inspector Carreg. Let me state it as clearly as I can." He nodded. "We came here through a sort of time-tunnel, created by a time machine, which *stayed* in the twenty-first century. There is no time machine in this century. Therefore you *can't* go back."

"That's nonsense!"

"Seeing is believing—look around you!"

"I see a very intricate hoax, though I don't see the point."

"Okay, I was wrong. Apparently, believing is seeing in your case."

She paused, and he was aware of his own rapid breathing.

Why is it she can make me so angry?!

Then Jemma said, "I'm sorry," and started to turn away. "I can't send you back…"

Whatever else she'd been going to say was forgotten as the rumble of horses hooves drowned out her words. The Celts were returning. The hunt had put them in great good spirits and they raced their horses across the meadow.

March 27

Rain sheeted over the blue-slate roof-tiles and rivered down Christ Church's limestone gutter, spitting from the mouths of gargoyles to pool on the flagstone walk and float a vehicular armada in the new-formed car park sea.

Professor Henderson shook it from the lapels of his black suit coat as he paced the front portal of the church. His umbrella dripped against the wall by the great, paired doors.

When the doors opened, half the village filed out in somber dress, in groups of two or three. Among them, Mrs. West leaned heavily on the arm of the pub's landlord, and uniformed police constables mingled with Scotland Yard officials in funereal suits. They paused in the portal to open their umbrellas or put on raincoats. Some waited for the next of kin or for the vicar. A few stepped aside in ones or twos to gossip or reminisce.

Andrew Blemming wiped his broad face and sparsely red-furred temples with a large white handkerchief as he waited next to Henderson. The vicar appeared, accompanying Susannah and Peter, who carried a folded umbrella. Margaret joined them, holding tight to Michael Gwaed.

Blemming offered Peter his hand. "I can't tell you how sorry I am."

Peter shook and nodded, but he had heard it too often.

Blemming shook hands with the vicar, towering over him. "First rate eulogy, sir." He turned to Peter. "You'll let me know if there's anything I can do?"

Peter nodded wearily as Blemming turned to leave, then he

spoke to the vicar. "Thank you, Father."

The vicar nodded and shook his hand, then watched with Henderson as Peter and Michael opened their umbrellas and held them up to shelter the women from the rain. The foursome stepped off the porch.

Henderson started after them, but stopped to open his umbrella. He gave it up when the catch wouldn't take hold, and hurried after them, umbrella trailing.

"Mr. Carreg?"

Peter stopped and turned.

"I'm most sincerely sorry about your father."

Peter nodded, trying to be polite, but he was tired of dealing with strangers and anxious to be away. Henderson seemed unsure how to proceed; Peter waited.

Finally, Henderson said, "The papers reported that the police didn't find..." There was no way to phrase it delicately. "...er... any remains."

Peter, Susannah and Margaret reacted with the beginnings of outrage to this breach of decency. Michael was alert and quietly interested.

Henderson didn't notice. "...There's a very good chance that your father wasn't killed in the explosion."

"What?!"

The old man talked fast, wanting to get it all out before he was interrupted or overheard. "You see, my daughter didn't die in that explosion, and there's every chance that your father is with her. She's going to send me a sign that she's safe. Perhaps she'll also send word of your father."

Peter, Susannah and Margaret scarcely dared to breathe. Michael's interest intensified until he was like a cat sitting over a mouse-hole.

"Where is she?" Peter demanded.

"Somewhere in the third century, I believe."

"What?"

"You see, I built a time machine and, after she left, I blew it up…"

Margaret and Susannah relaxed. Peter surged toward Henderson. "You crazy old man!"

Susannah grabbed Peter's arm but didn't speak.

Margaret stepped between the two men. "Peter, forget it!" She turned her back on Peter and said to Henderson, "I'm sorry, Professor Henderson. You'd better go. My brother's not ready to hear what you have to say."

Henderson was astonished. With his umbrella half open, upside-down and catching rain, he stood and watched them as they walked away.

29 mawrth

When Jemma pronounced the boy well enough to travel, they managed to sling a litter for him between Rolf's horse and Evan's, using Rolf's saddle and Jemma's pack saddle to suspend it. Most of their gear went on the pack saddle, so Evan had to double up with Jemma. He didn't seem too keen on the idea; but the gray horse didn't mind, and Jemma was indifferent as far as Ian could tell. Gestures and stick-figure drawings had given Ian to understand that their destination lay three days' journey to the southeast—three days, he discovered, on unburdened horses.

They followed the river south and east, traveling in the shallows in places where the forest crowded the water's edge. Nowhere did he see a modern artifact—none of the careless discards or lost articles that usually pollute the most secluded wastelands. Ian hadn't seen a plane since his arrival, and wherever they were, it was well away from any highway.

Eventually they came upon a track that had been well if not recently traveled. It ran along grassy ridge-tops, showing signs in spots of having been mowed by grazing animals. In other places, the horses trampled fetlock deep in mud. Birds marking their territories with song fell silent as the party passed.

The going was extremely slow. Paces quicker than a walk were agony for the injured boy and tended to exhaust the encumbered animals, even where rocks underlay the track and abated the ubiquitous mud. Sitting a horse all day—when one is used to it and provided with a saddle—is rigorous enough, but riding bareback was impossibly difficult.

Once, when they stopped at a clear spring to water the horses, Ian slid off to stretch his cramped legs and nearly fell. His clumsiness occasioned much discussion among the men. Farther on, as the mare he'd come to think of as his own plodded through the lace-work of shadows, Ian's throat burned. His face felt as if some giant burning glass had concentrated the thin, spring sunlight on his skin. He could feel the dry irritation in his lungs that often signaled the onset of a cold. His head began to ache. The world narrowed. He felt light-headed and sleepy. The three men, chattering in their unfamiliar tongue, were as inconsequential as birds twittering in the surrounding wood. His face blazed like a furnace, and he became uncomfortably aware that the mare between his legs seemed on fire. His mind turned and returned to Jemma.

Her insistence that they were in Roman Britain made him doubt, at first, the veracity of every statement that she made, so that if she said something as simple as "lunch is ready," he found himself looking for the food. But as the days passed he found it easier to imagine he had been transported back in time. And Jemma was as lovely a creature as he thought he'd ever seen. For riding, she wore a divided skirt that rode up her legs and showed her shapely calves and knees. A man would have to hate her dearly not to be attracted.

Ian didn't hate her. Not yet. He didn't know her well enough for that. And there was no harm in looking.

My Lord, Carreg, he thought, *she's a bloody killer!*

He caught all three of the other men looking at her from time to time, but as frequently making the sign against the evil eye.

What would you do if she got drunk or crazy enough to invite you into her bed?

Ian's inward grin was more a grimace as he contemplated the possibility. Rather a sad joke. Probably go quite limp. Hadn't tried it in so long he'd probably forgotten how, though he'd never had any trouble satisfying Marjory. God, but that was one of the least things he missed. You'd think, at this age, the desire would pack it in, but it seemed one just developed better self-control.

When *did* it diminish, anyway? Seventy? Ninety? Opportunity dwindled, he was sure, long before desire.

1 ebrill

By the third day, Ian ceased to question Jemma's assertion about their place in time. He'd seen no evidence to contradict it and could think of no way to gather any. Late in the afternoon, they came to an enormous grove of oaks, each several feet in diameter and dozens of feet in height. The largest of them had a monstrous human face carved into its side, as high above the ground as a man could reach from horseback. The wound in the living bark had begun to close over the face, giving it a cowled, mysterious look. Mistletoe festooned others of the oaks. The grove had a feeling of great age and mystery, but none of the malevolence with which movies tend to endow such places.

"Nemeton," Owain said, encompassing the grove with a gesture. He sounded awed. And the place *was* like a cathedral—high-vaulted and quiet, with foliage so dense that very little would grow under the canopy after the leaves were out. Now, the grove was laced with shadows and carpeted with blue flowers.

Rolf urged his horse up next to Jemma's and tentatively touched one of the dead rabbits tied behind her saddle. Her frown made it clear that she didn't understand even the gist of the speech that accompanied the gesture, but she didn't protest when he dismounted and carried the dead animal into the grove. Without dismounting, Ian started to follow him, but Rolf's horrified reaction made it clear the horse wasn't welcome.

Ian dismounted and watched with the others as Rolf buried the rabbit in the clearing along with the game bag containing his brother's remains and heat-killed sword.

• • •

The forest gradually subsided, giving way to open grasslands and small farm fields bordered by stone fences and hedges. This open land resembled northern Scotland—beautiful and nearly empty, with distant hills shrouded by mist. Eventually, the gray walls of a citadel painted themselves on high ground, languishing in the distance like a romantic watercolor. The fortress was the object of their journey, it seemed, for sight of it occasioned much discussion on the part of Rolf, Owain and Evan, much laughing and pointing.

They rested the horses below the fort, which was situated atop the tallest hill in the area. Ian could see that the structure's irregular perimeter was bounded by a high, grassy bank crowned by a weathered wooden palisade of twelve-foot poles sharpened at the top. It was an *oppidium*, the fortified village of a Celtic clan. Outside the protective bank, there was a ditch, nine feet deep. Beyond the ditch, a patchwork of small farm fields surrounded the hill. Deer-colored sheep, shaggy, long-horned cattle and small, woolly horses could be seen grazing on the new grass showing in a few of the fields, while in others, grass poked through stubble from last year's harvest and the manure spread out over it for fertilizer. The hills beyond the fields were blackened to the horizon by mantles of dark woods.

They arrived at the entrance of the oppidium, where the approach road disappeared between walls that overlapped to form a corridor—twisting clockwise around the fortress—that was easily defended from above. Ian had the impression it had been there forever. The few new, yellow poles in the weathered gray of the walls were an unexpected detail that lent authenticity to the scene.

Stuck on poles six feet above the ground, five human heads, in various stages of decay, guarded the entrance. One was skeletal. The freshest was clean-shaven and short-haired, its skin dry and translucent. A crow perching on it flew off as they approached.

Though devoid of the gore that is modern horror's stock in trade, the skulls, especially the newest, were more shocking than the bodies Ian had seen cremated days before. He felt nauseated. He had to look away and swallow hard to avoid losing his dinner. Owain pointed after the bird, then at the head on which it had been perched.

Ian caught one word of his pronouncement and asked Jemma, "Did he say Roman?"

"He may have, though I'd think it would be dangerous to kill a Roman."

"Oh, for God's sake!"

"You'd forgotten the Celts are headhunters?"

Before he could respond, people began spilling out of the oppidium, crowding and elbowing and asking questions. Most were dressed in bright clothing—checks, plaids and bright solid colors with embroidery on the sleeves and yokes. The clothes seemed to be mostly of wool, though a few of the shirts appeared to be linen. Some of the men wore knee-length tunics, without trousers, over knee-high boots, but most wore clothing styled like Rolf's.

Ian noted a discrepancy in the tableau. They seemed excessively clean for ancient people—odorless and clean-cut—like weekend farmers from London in their expensive tweeds. They seemed awed by Ian's clothes and Jemma's horses, a nice touch. Even the sentries, armed with spears and swords, observed from the ramparts with patent interest.

Rolf, Evan and Owain dismounted. People lifted Alf's litter down. A woman with pale gold brows and lashes and a wide mouth looked the new arrivals over carefully, asked anxious questions, which Owain answered quietly. She began to wail, hanging her arms at her sides and clutching her skirts. Apparently, she was the wife or sister of one of the murder victims. A word from Rolf, and two of the older women took hold of her and hustled her back into the fort. The rest of the people milled around, jabbering and plying Rolf and Owain with questions Ian didn't understand.

Everyone stopped talking when a man appeared, whom Ian judged to be in his sixties, though his hair was completely white. He was of medium height and slender build—on the declining side of his physical powers—but with the eyes of a chief superintendent or a fencing master. He wore an ankle-length tunic of natural-colored wool, which was finely woven and embroidered around the yoke and sleeves with the stylized floral patterns favored by the Celts. He wore his hair and mustache long, in the Celtic style; below the mustache, his face was clean-shaven. His gold torc and finger rings, belt buckle and dagger hilt were patterned with a dragon motif. Faded, blue dragon tattoos curled around his wrists and forearms.

The old man's costume brought to mind the neo-pagans who congregated at Stonehenge on the solstices, but he had the bearing of a magistrate. The crowd parted respectfully to let him through. He asked a question that was unintelligible to Ian, and one of the sentries pointed back toward the entrance of the oppidium.

"Stay on your horse," Jemma told Ian.

"Why?"

"It gives you a psychological advantage."

"How long are you going to continue this charade?"

Before she could answer, Owain pushed forward and made some explanation to the old man, whose face gave no clue to his feelings or beliefs. His nods and comments were receipts, not opinions. Then Owain made introductions all around. The old man's name or job description—Ian wasn't sure which—was Drullwyn.

Drullwyn addressed Ian and Jemma in his own tongue, and when he got only blank looks, he tried again, in another.

Latin! Someone, Ian thought, during the gestation of this scheme, must have looked up his early school records and discovered that he'd studied Latin. Too remotely long ago for any to remain, but he could, of course, still recognize it. They'd know he would. It was part of the rehearsal. If they could drive a hard-headed police inspector mad, what chance had a clerk or a diplomat?

He said, "Latin!"

"Yes, Latin," Jemma said. "Shut up!"

"*Nobody* speaks Latin!"

"*Oh, butt out!*" She turned to the old man and answered him in Latin.

Ian caught only *Cymry*, a Welsh word meaning compatriots, and *Brythons*, which he recalled was a name some of the Celtic tribes gave themselves.

Drullwyn nodded and gestured an invitation to dismount. Ignoring Jemma's scowl, Ian accepted.

A murmur from the crowd signaled the arrival of another official, in his mid-thirties, Ian judged, at least six feet tall, 180 pounds, and muscular, with light brown hair and blue eyes. He was dressed like the common folk except for his gold torc and arm bands, and a gilt scabbard. He nodded noncommittally, when Owain introduced him as Houel, and waited.

Drullwyn demanded something of Owain, who plunged into a long, incomprehensible tale—what had befallen them since leaving home, presumably. Ian looked around as nearly all the people listened with apparent awe. Only Houel, Drullwyn and Jemma seemed unimpressed.

When Owain finished, Drullwyn questioned Jemma in Latin, and she translated for Ian: "What brings you here?" Her own Latin wasn't fluent. She had to assemble the sentences slowly as she answered, reiterating frequently so that she didn't lose sense of the beginning before she got to the end. But she was clearly speaking Latin.

The old man's awkward responses made it evident he was only slightly more conversant, but with frequent pauses and much gesturing, they eventually came to an agreement. Drullwyn conferred with Houel, then asked Jemma something, to which she shook her head and said, "*Non.*"

It was obvious Houel didn't need a translation. He nodded and said something in his own tongue. When he finished, the old man translated for Jemma, and she for Ian: "He says that the families of Alf and Owain are in our debt, and we're welcome to stay as their guests as long as we abide by their laws."

"Ah," Ian said, "but will they take American Express?"

April 1

What furniture remained was shrouded by dust covers. Ian's books had been placed in cartons on the floor, and Peter was sitting at the desk sorting through his father's papers when Margaret entered, followed by Charles. She'd been crying. She put down the box she was carrying and picked up the cat, holding him against her face. With a little-girl voice, she said, "I never thought of his job as dangerous. He'd always go off to work like a solicitor or stockbroker. He didn't carry a gun. And he always let the constables arrest the rowdy ones." She paused. "I just wasn't prepared for this."

She looked around, trying not to cry again. She spotted the portrait of her mother on the desk and smiled ruefully. "He said I look more like her every day."

Peter picked up the picture and something dropped from behind it onto the floor with a loud clunk. Margaret retrieved the object and held it out.

"Peter, look." It was Ian's gold, Celtic ring. "Here. I'm sure Da would have wanted you to have it."

He hesitated, then put the ring on his finger.

7 ebrill

I

Sparrows, nesting under the eaves, kept up a constant chirping as Ian lay staring at the smoke-blackened ceiling. The house had no chimney—smoke from the open hearth wafted upward and hung below the roof in ghostly layers, probing thatch and rafters for an exit. Only the ceiling's height saved them all from suffocation. He supposed that vermin would quickly be exterminated, and his supposition was borne out by the haunches of smoked meat that hung there untroubled by flies.

His room was a little cubicle in the house Rolf shared with his gray-eyed wife and their daughter. The cubicle had a plastered wattle outside wall, cut by a small, high window. The inside walls were wicker. Ian's bed was a pile of clean straw covered with a sheet of hessian, which Jemma called burlap, and several woolen blankets. He'd stuck his reading glasses on a little shelf wedged into the corner above the bed and hung his suit coat on a stick protruding from the wicker.

He shifted his position and noticed a suspicious bulge beneath the blankets near his feet. Rolf's mongrel wolfhound. The dog's large feet and exuberant, uncoordinated movements labeled it a pup, though it had needed only two days to mark Ian as easy meat. Ian called it *Clyfar*, Welsh for clever.

He thought back to the day of his arrival. With Rolf as their guide, and with what must have been half the population in tow, Jemma and Ian were officially welcomed with a tour of the village. To his surprise, the entourage included children—several infants and toddlers, a handful of mid-school aged children and half a dozen teens in addition to the adult actors. Nondescript dogs, built like small wolfhounds, followed them like rats after the Pied Piper.

The oppidium covered several acres and consisted of twenty-odd houses, sheds for animals, and a small shrine—judging by the offerings of flowers, heads carved of stone and wood, and human skulls. Next to the shrine was a well. Cattle pens containing only two small, shaggy, brown milk cows lay beneath the western wall of the fort, and pigpens nestled against the rampart on the village's lee side. Nondescript chickens wandered at will among the buildings. Here and there a small, hairy, half-wild pig rooted around a foundation or dozed in a shady spot.

The people's houses clustered in the center of the hill fort, on the crown of the hill. Except for minor details, they were similar to those Ian had seen in the farmstead at the Butser Ancient Farm Research Project in Hampshire. With a single exception, they were circular, seven to fifteen meters in diameter, and constructed of timbers set in the ground and connected with wattle and daub—a basket-weave of hickory withes plastered over with clay. The conical roofs were thatched with straw. The village's single rectangular house was sided and thatched with weathered wood shakes.

"What do you think of it?" Jemma had asked, indicating the oppidium with a broad sweep of her hand.

"Very impressive," he said, dryly.

"Did you think they'd be living in caves? This is the *Iron Age*, Inspector Carreg."

The Iron Age! The period in history when iron replaced bronze in the production of tools and weapons. It was a subject he'd studied as a boy but hadn't thought about since he'd left school. He hadn't even heard the term in years. He wished he'd paid closer attention when he'd studied Celtic art. Whoever these people were, they seemed determined to pattern their community after the Celts, and he wished he knew the ground rules. Before Jemma could feel too smug, he'd said, "I'd give a week's pay to know why."

"Why what?"

"Why go to all this trouble? It can't be for my benefit. I haven't any special skills or talents, nor any government secrets."

She shook her head and shrugged. "I can see there's no point in discussing it."

Four days later, the question remained—*Where on earth am I?*

The answer was *on earth*. But where?

He'd read novels, the plots of which revolved around enemy organizations setting up model villages—schools for spies—where agents could immerse themselves in the culture of the spied upon. It would make sense, here, if the village were contemporary—a school for modern spies set up to study British or American ways. But no one was going to infiltrate an extinct culture.

He'd spent hours poking about the village, studying the construction of the buildings and the way the people went about their daily chores. He'd found no zippers or safety pins, concealed radio parts or anything made of plastic. The villagers said nothing. They treated him with the sort of strained tolerance accorded an eccentric. He'd grown tired of asking: "Does anyone here speak English? *Sprechen sie deutsch? Parlez vous français?*" People just looked at him oddly, or made the sign against the evil eye, or walked away shaking their heads.

He'd seen the television series, "The Prisoner". Probably this village was similarly designed to make its victims crack. Such a conspiracy was the most plausible alternative to the theory that the village was a hippie commune. Conspirators, on the whole, were more disciplined and ruthless than hippies, and these people were disciplined enough to always stay in character. Always. The problem with the conspiracy idea was motive—why go to all the trouble? That left anthropologists living the lesson, trying to recreate the life.

Jemma's response to the question was impossible. The idea of time travel was preposterous—not that they hadn't prepared carefully for the illusion, gleaning every product of modern manufacture from the environs and replicating Celtic artifacts and clothing, even creating a facsimile language. They'd got the latitude right, too—selecting a location where the position of the sun on the horizon was as northerly as in Britain at the equinox. It was almost too good to be a set up. It had to be...

No! That's what they intend me to believe!

Make it easier for a man to believe what *you* want and he'll succumb. Make him doubt his own logic and his knowledge; he'll follow yours. These were *not* Celts! These were kidnappers. They had a *reason* for convincing him that he'd been transported to the past. He might never discover that reason, but he was confident it existed.

There was a faint creaking of the wicker partition, and a tiny voice said, "Ian?" Rowena, Rolf's daughter. "Are you awake?"

Ian smiled as he rolled over on his side. How many times had Margaret waked him with that question? And Rowena was too young to be party to the conspiracy. He said, "Yes, Rowena."

The girl scooted around the partition that formed the wall of his room and knelt at the edge of his bed. She sat back on her heels, smoothing the yellow wool of her dress over her knees. "Papa says we will *aradig* today."

Rowena had Rolf's fair skin and her mother's dark hair—nearly black, with red highlights when the sun hit it just right. Her cornflower-blue eyes were darker than Rolf's. She'd got her permanent front teeth, upper and lower, but there were gaps at the sides where adult pre-molars were still sprouting. That put her between eight and ten years of age if his forensics still served.

She spoke Celtic. Ian thought of it as that for want of another name, though he didn't for a moment suppose it was the Celtic of Roman Britain. "What is *aradig?*" he asked—also in Celtic.

They were conditioning him just like Pavlov's dogs. They would only respond if he spoke to them in Celtic. The language was akin to Welsh as Old English is akin to modern English. He'd learned Welsh as a child to communicate with his paternal grandmother, a strong-willed woman who, in her dotage, had refused to speak anything else. He'd taken a refresher course the previous fall and, now, he found that gradually, almost imperceptibly, he'd come to understand these pseudo-Celts as he'd come to understand Chaucer at university, by the slow process of persistent exposure. There was no time he could point to, that he'd been able to say, "Aha, now I see," but gradually he'd become aware that what he understood to be the gist of conversations was what was actually being said.

Rowena didn't answer at once. She was watching Ian's blanket come alive as Rolf's dog roused himself beneath it.

The gray canine had adopted Ian. At his insistence, the animal would lie down outside the room at night and, as long as Ian watched him, would stay outside. But as soon as Ian closed his eyes, the animal would start to inch his way closer to the bed until, around midnight, he'd be curled up on the foot of it. Ian was used to Charles sleeping on his feet and never noticed until morning. Sometimes, as now, he would find the creature under the blankets by daybreak. Ian gave the dog a nudge with his foot and the beast scrambled out of the bed and back across the imaginary line that marked the doorway. The room was so small that when the animal lay down across the line, his nose almost reached the bed.

"*Aradig?*" Ian asked again.

Rowena thought further, then scrambled around on her knees to roll back the reed mat—the only flooring—from the earth floor. She pulled the bone pin from the brooch holding her hair back from her face, letting the hair fall loose. In an older female, the action would have seemed provocative, but it only added to Rowena's charming animation.

She scratched a square on the floor and said, "*Cae.*"

Cae. Field. The word was the same in Welsh.

She scored parallel lines across the square and said, "*Aradig.*" Ian nodded. *Plow.* It was thus that they'd learned to bridge gaps in his understanding of their tongue.

The girl let the mat fall back in place and pinned her hair back up. She began to tease the dog, pretending to hold a tidbit just beyond its reach, switching the imaginary treat from hand to hand as the dog got near it. The dog's feet scrabbled loudly on the reed mat.

Ian said, "Be still or you'll wake your parents."

"Oh, they're not asleep." She let the dog see that her hands were empty and the game ended.

Ian said, "They're being very quiet."

"That's so I won't ask about what they're doing."

"What *are* they doing?"

"A grown-up thing."

Ian nearly choked.

Rowena added, "Mother says I'll know when I'm a woman and that's soon enough."

"I dare say she's right. Why don't you go along, now, and let me get started with my day?"

"Mens sano in corpore sanem?"

He had determined to remain fit so that if the chance to escape presented itself, he would be able, literally, to grasp it. To that end, he had been exercising every morning, before the diversions of the village stole the day away. When Rowena first noticed him doing calisthenics, she'd asked why, and he'd answered her with the Latin phrase.

She added, "Drullwyn says that's a good motto."

"But did he tell you what it means?"

"A sound mind in a sound body."

"That's right. Off with you, now. And take the dog."

She grabbed the dog by the fur behind its ears and backed out of the room.

As he began his exercises, Ian tried not to think about what Rolf and his wife were doing that was not sleeping.

The latrine was a midden hole, an abandoned grain pit used for refuse disposal, and Ian inspected the oppidium as he made his way toward it for his morning visit. The irregular arrangement of the houses around the village center and the constant activity of the colorfully clad villagers, their children and livestock gave the impression that the life concentrated within the hill fort overflowed its protective palisades into the surrounding farms and valley. It was like a movie set done right. There were no false fronts. And no tracks set out for camera dollies. For that matter, there were no cameras. Ian had looked carefully.

Returning from his morning inspection, he spotted Jemma feeding the small fire in front of the carpenter's rectangular house. He nodded to acknowledge her presence without returning her "Good morning"—something Rowena, waiting in front of Rolf's house, didn't miss.

As Ian gathered up kindling from the pile near the doorway, she asked, "Don't you *like* Jemma?"

It was a hard question.

He found he couldn't honestly say he disliked her. If she were a harridan, if she were hard or sarcastic, it would be easier to keep in mind what sort of woman she was, but since their arrival, she had been courteous and cheerful. And it seemed that, since they arrived, she'd been called upon to treat nearly everyone in the village for one malady or another, from ingrown toenails to serious heart disease. She had even stitched a bite wound on Houel's favorite horse.

He decided to equivocate. "Let's say I don't approve of her."

"Why?"

"Because she's not what she seems."

Rowena laughed. "Of course not. She's a goddess."

"That's another thing she's not."

"Father says she is, and so she must be. He says you're a god, too."

"Humph."

"But Drullwyn says you're crazy." She looked at Ian, assessing his reaction to this verdict.

Ian gave her an "is that so" look and said, "You spend a lot of time talking to Drullwyn."

"He's a great teacher and a poet." She smiled. "He says I haven't the Sight, but I have good insight for a child. And if you haven't true Sight but you are clever, insight and learning will suffice."

"That sounds like the voice of experience."

"You and Drullwyn are a lot alike. Sometimes he talks in riddles, too." She twisted a strand of her hair around a finger until the end of the finger turned red. "Do you think Jemma would teach me to be a healer?"

"She might."

"Perhaps I could foster with her."

Fosterage, far from being an institution for unwanted children, was an educational system analogous to arranged marriages. For a fee, parents fostered their children—girls and boys—with a family of equal or higher social standing. Foster families treated their wards as their own, teaching them necessary skills and social behavior in preparation for adulthood. Fosterlings were often, simultaneously, hostages exchanged between clans to guarantee the loyalty of the clan's allies. Alf, who'd been fostered with Rolf's dead brother, was said to be the youngest son of a neighboring clan's chief. Rolf claimed that Jemma had averted war by saving him. Ian didn't believe any of it but that Jemma had saved the boy's life. However, it made a good story.

Rowena loosened the hair around her finger, letting the blood flow resume. "I'm surely old enough."

By two or three years, Ian thought, but he only said, "Bring the fire, please."

He began to lay the kindling in the hearth just outside the door. He'd begun making up the fire for breakfast the first morning of their stay. He'd considered that it might constitute collaboration but rejected the idea. He had always earned his keep and he wasn't about to try changing a lifetime habit.

The villagers kept their fires going continuously, banking them when they weren't cooking. At night, they carried them into hearths in the houses. It was a wasteful method that devoured wood. Ian had accompanied Rolf to the forest twice, in the week past, to replenish their fuel supply.

It reminded him that all Europe had been forested once, as this place was. The entire Mediterranean basin had been covered with timber until Iron Age peoples, with their high-tech-for-the-times—iron tools—felled the trees to smelt the iron and to make room for crops. Once, there had been cedars in Lebanon. How many people ever thought of that? How many would give a damn?

. . .

By the time the fire was well established, Rolf's wife, Gwen, was ladling water into the wrought iron kettle of meal that she'd brought from the house. The water was kept in an oak bucket on a stump near the door. It was Rowena's job to keep it filled from the well—another task Ian had been helping with.

Gwen smiled at Ian as she lifted her kettle onto the firestones. She had gray eyes in an oval face. Her figure was stunning, and her smile dazzling. Lucky man, Rolf.

She made no effort to avoid bumping her husband as she reentered the house. Meeting her in the doorway, Rolf yawned and stretched, and they danced the little waltz of lovers, pressing from shoulder to knee as they half-turned around each other.

Ian stanched the up-welling of pain and rage that flooded him. Had his captors known? Was it part of the great game that these two should so resemble Peter and Susannah?

"Ian!" Rowena's voice broke through his preoccupation. "Ian, you aren't listening!"

"Yes…er…What is it, Rowena?"

"Maura's here." Maura was the carpenter's wife, the woman in whose house Jemma was staying.

"What is it, Maura?"

She was a brown woman, brown hair, brown eyes, skin browned by the sun. She trembled and hid her hands in the folds of her skirts, making the sign against evil, no doubt.

"Speak up, woman. I won't bite you!"

"Epona…" Maura began. "Epona commands…" She hesitated. She swallowed. "Epona requests…your presence…She requires a translation." She blinked and edged away.

Rowena had told him Maura thought he was a god and, it seemed to Ian, Maura truly believed it. Either that or she was the best actress he'd encountered yet. Or she was simple. Obviously she was simple.

Since the entire village seemed to claim that Jemma was a

divinity, Ian wondered how Maura could stand living in the same house with her.

The woman's timidity brought out the bully in him. He fought the urge to shake her and instead said, "Is it urgent?"

She seemed to be trying to guess what he'd like to hear as she swallowed again. "Y-yes."

"All right. Tell her I'll be along."

Maura scrambled away.

"Ian," Rowena said. "Can I go with you?"

"That's up to your mother."

II

The carpenter's house was the only house in the village not conforming to type, being rectangular and constructed of carefully mortised and dressed timbers. It was sided and shingled with wood shakes. The carpenter's occupation, like that of many other villagers, could be inferred from the tools hung on the outside of its walls. Draw knives and saws, chisels and axes and froes were sharpened and oiled against rust and arrayed neatly beneath the eaves.

As they approached, Ian noticed a crow perched on the ridge-pole like a great, black chicken. It flexed its wings and settled itself with a caw that sounded like a chuckle. The bird reminded him of the one that had perched on the totem heads at the hill fort entrance when they'd arrived. He felt an echo of the disgust he'd felt then. He scowled and looked around for a rock or stick. He spied a dog gnawing a bone in front of the neighbors' house and two women watching the crow.

Ian rushed the dog and seized the bone as the dog shied away. He put all his weight behind the bone as he aimed for the bird. His curse caught the creature solidly, but the bone merely brushed its feathers. It skittered over the ridge-pole as the bird escaped.

The two watchers signed against the evil eye, and one covered her face and ducked back into her house. Ian looked down at Rowena, who seemed amazed. She reached up and grabbed his hand with both of hers and squeezed it.

"Now what have I done?"

"Papa's right. You must be a god, attacking Morrigan's bird. Or maybe it was Morrigan herself, come to steal Jemma's patient away."

"Nonsense! It was just a bird."

The eaves hung below the windows, blocking most of the light from entering the house. Inside, it was dark and dusty, so Jemma usually conducted her surgery in the sunny garden behind the house, or under the little wild-grape arbor beside it. Ian wondered what she'd do in the winter. *Winter!* He'd be away long before then. Or he'd die trying!

"What kept you?" Jemma spoke English, and he could tell by her color she was furious.

"If it's urgent," he said, "we'd better not waste time quarreling."

She gripped her lower lip between her teeth and almost bit through it, but swallowed her retort.

He said, "What's the matter?"

Jemma stepped back and gestured toward a distraught young woman seated under the arbor, holding an infant that, to Ian's unpracticed eye, looked only a few hours old. The child was an unhealthy yellow.

"A form of anemia caused by incompatibility between the mother's blood and the infant's," Jemma said. "I'll have to get a history to be sure. And you'll have to explain the treatment to his mother and get her permission."

"What treatment?"

Jemma laughed without humor. "Ordinarily, a complete exchange of blood. But we'll have to settle for a partial replacement. And pray he's strong enough to take it."

For a moment, Ian felt almost faint with rage. He was being

forced to play the game again. For higher stakes this time. A child's life.

She waited for him to replay the argument in his head that they'd so often had before: *The child belongs in a hospital. Have you seen a hospital hereabouts? No. Then we will have to treat him.* She seemed to take it for granted he would decide rightly.

In the end, he knew that he would help her. She spoke with the authority of her profession and with total conviction. If *she* didn't treat the child, no one would. And if he didn't help her, she would not succeed.

He glared at her. "What did you want me to ask?"

She seemed grateful. Perhaps she hadn't a choice in the matter either, was also forced to play the game. Even more than he hoped that was the case, he wished he knew for certain.

"I need to know who the baby's father is."

Ian translated, and translated the reply.

The woman dropped her eyes. "My husband is Dyfyd."

Ian had always trusted his intuition, feeling it was a gift—like perfect pitch—that was not susceptible to analysis. For fear of being ridiculed, he had never spoken of it to anyone but Marjory, to whom it had seemed natural. Now, as he watched the woman speak, he could see that his gift was nothing more mysterious than a knack for interpreting body language. She was lying.

"Rowena," he said. "We will need to talk to Dyfyd. Would you please ask him to come?"

Jemma looked at him curiously but withheld the obvious question.

"Your husband is not the baby's father," he said when Rowena was well away. "Who is?" She hesitated. "What you tell us will not go beyond these walls."

The outpouring that followed made Ian acutely uneasy. She had a confession. As a policeman, he was used to hearing confessions. But she wanted absolution, and he was not a priest.

Five years of childless marriage had left the couple frustrated and angry, desperate and blaming. The husband had taken a mistress but hadn't had children from her. The wife had prayed, finally, to the god of the season, and Lugh had taken pity on them. On Lughnasad, she'd taken a lover, and Lugh had given her a child.

"Whose child? The truth. The child's life depends on it." The woman moaned. Ian waited.

"Rolf's brother."

"The one who died?"

"Yes."

"Dammit!" Jemma said. "That ends that line of enquiry."

"He *must* live!" the mother said, rocking the infant for emphasis. "If anything happens to Mathe's baby, this will be her husband's only child."

Jemma was ignoring what the woman said. "This is not her first child," she insisted.

"She says it is."

"Then she's had a miscarriage."

Ian fumbled for the right word. It had not been a topic of polite conversation in his grandmother's house, in his grandparents' time. And he couldn't remember what his grandfather called it when the cattle aborted. He finally settled on "child born dead."

The woman shook her head. No children. None born dead.

"Ask her if she had an especially bloody menses after her first time with a man. Or bleeding at the wrong time of the month."

The woman was amazed. "How did you know?"

"She's a *healer*," Ian said, using the local word.

"Who was the first man?" Jemma asked. "The one before the bleeding?"

"I was not yet betrothed. It was Samhain," the woman said. Ian knew she thought she had done something wrong—she probably wasn't sure what—and she surely had incurred the wrath of some god.

"His name," Jemma demanded. She spoke in Celtic. She'd learned enough to ask that.

The woman looked away and said, softly, "Houel."

"Excellent," Jemma said, "now we're getting somewhere."

"Shall I send Rowena for Houel when she returns?"

"Not necessary. I know his blood type. I made him pay for the horse's care with blood."

"Jemma," Rowena called out. "Dyfyd is here."

Dyfyd preceded Rowena into the room.

"I'll need a few drops of his blood," Jemma told Ian, and when he'd translated, and Dyfyd had asked why, she said, "For the ritual."

The "ritual" turned out to be a standard test for blood type, done on a glass slide with chemicals Jemma kept in small glass vials. Ian had seen it done before, in the forensics lab, but to primitives—if one believed they were not merely fine actors—it must have seemed as eerie as a black mass. The test confirmed that Dyfyd was not the infant's father, and gave Jemma the confidence to proceed.

"The baby's Rh positive; his mother's negative. I typed them after the delivery."

The transfusion was almost an anticlimax. Jemma sent the parents away, saying "He'll probably survive the procedure, but I'm not sure his mother would." She let Rowena assist.

She tied a thong around her own left arm and pulled it tight, using her free hand and her teeth. Then she threaded a needle into her vein like a practiced addict. She bled the infant through a vein in his leg, catching the blood in a bowl, and resanguinated it through a vein in its umbilicus. When she'd finished, she tied off the cord and dealt with her own vein while Rowena applied pressure to the infant's. Having seen horses gelded and cattle butchered, the girl was unperturbed by the procedure. Ian translated, and acted as a second pair of hands where they were needed. He was amazed at how thoroughly he'd become accustomed to the letting of human blood.

When they were finished, and Rowena dispatched to return the child, Jemma asked him, "What's your blood type?"

"None of your affair."

III

Ian had been riding every day, so it seemed natural to catch and bridle a horse to go any place—however close—outside the oppidium. The horse paddock was an acre of overgrazed grass enclosed by a fence of split poles slipped through mortices in the fence posts, fixed by wedged pegs. The gate was a section of fence where the pegs were unwedged so the rails could be easily removed. Ian leaned on the fence and called the horse he'd come to think of as his own by rolling grain between his palms. The subtle sound it made was irresistible to the mare. When she reached for the grain, Ian put a hand behind her ears, to keep her from backing away, and eased the bridle bit between her teeth. Rowena walked up as he slipped the headstall over the mare's head. Rowena was wearing a broad-brimmed hat of woven grass and her oldest dress.

"Ready?" he asked.

"Can I lead her out?"

"Why not?" He finished buckling the cheek strap and handed her the reins.

He slid the rails back, and she led the horse through, holding it while Ian replaced the gate. When he lifted her onto the horse, her skirt flew up, revealing skinny white legs, causing her to blush and giggle. She clamped her legs around the mare and tucked the skirt beneath her legs and bum. "You'll have to get a riding skirt like Jemma's," Ian told her.

He shoved the mare around, against the fence, and used it to mount behind Rowena. Then they were away.

• • •

Rolf's fields, held by right of family membership, were about half a mile east of the hill fort, across the river—now swollen with melted snow and relatively deep—that curled around the oppidium before bisecting the surrounding valley down its long axis. The valley extended to the southeast horizon, its walls gradually diminishing in height. The land on either side was a patch-quilt of small fields— brown from freshly turned earth, bright green with winter oats, or gray with last year's stubble. Rising from the cropland to the valley walls, greening pastures reached for the forested hills above the valley. Across the river, to the northwest, the brooding dark giants of the sacred grove crowned a hill that was twin to that occupied by the oppidium. Grazing sheep and cattle looked, in the distance, like miniatures and, on the farthest slopes, like moving dots. Paralleling the river, a road surfaced with river gravel disappeared in the distance, with unpaved tracks branching off to the small stockades and circular houses of the freeholders and cattlemen who lived outside the hill fort.

As they rode out, Ian thought about ritual. Everything the villagers did seemed to be accompanied by a ritual or a song, though some of the latter seemed optional. Drullwyn, who was the village equivalent of both priest and magistrate, greeted every sunrise with a chant that was usually taken up by anyone out and about that early. Fictional characters accepted ritual, magic, time travel, and the appearance of aliens or dinosaurs without question. If one wished to retain a naive faith in the goodness of humanity, or to deny one's own hostile or xenophobic impulses, such acceptance made cock-eyed sense. But Ian had long since come to terms with his own prejudices and hostilities, and his job had left him willing to believe anyone capable of unspeakable acts. He could, and simultaneously did, hold the belief that these people were loving, admirable and ordinary, and that they were kidnappers.

If there was a ritual for plowing, they'd missed it. By the time he and Rowena arrived, Rolf and the two sun-brown men helping him had tilled a quarter of the field. There *was* a song. The three men were taking turns singing a verse about plowing that had a randy double meaning.

They broke off singing, and Rolf introduced his helpers. Bran and Cae were bondsmen, Rolf explained, who sold themselves into a slavery of limited duration to pay off their debts. Ian thought they were particularly unservile for slaves—more like union workers who know they can't be sacked. They were dressed in the same coarse wool tunics and trousers Rolf wore, the same leather boots and, in the Celtic fashion, they had long hair and voluminous mustaches. Neither wore a torc, but like Rolf, they wore leather gloves. Rowena pulled on a pair, from a pile next to the spare tools, as soon as she'd tethered the gray mare in the next field with Rolf's shaggy dun.

Rolf drove the oxen that pulled the plow to cut the soil in parallel, east-west rows. The bondsmen followed with a deliberation that seemed sloth-like as they turned the sod over and beat the soil loose from the roots with flat-edged shovels, pausing occasionally to let Rowena pull out the more obdurate weeds. These she beat against the ground to loosen the soil from their roots, then threw on a pile at the edge of the field.

At first, Ian only watched.

The work was hard and dusty, but Rolf made it look easy. He had an understanding with the oxen, though he showed them none of the affection he lavished on his horse. He was patient with them, and they worked for him. The animals were trained to obey simple *gee* and *whoa* commands but they were slow to respond, as if it took time for sound to penetrate their bony skulls. They were the height and color of Jerseys but boxy, like beef cattle, and shaggy. Rolf called them Shirker and Complainer, which seemed to fairly summarize their characters. Complainer might also have been called Kicker, Ian learned, when the beast planted a huge foot on his thigh. If the ox had been two inches closer, it would have broken Ian's femur.

One could imagine the plow having been beaten into being from a sword. There was not much to it—an iron-clad blade and a beam to which the team was hitched. It had no mold-board to turn the furrow over. Ian had seen plows like it, called *ards*, at Butser.

"Ian," Rolf said, after what seemed like an hour, "would you like to try?" There was no hint of reproach in his question about Ian's failure, thus far, to lend a hand. That was Rolf.

Ian had found it impossible to dislike him. He was generous and gregarious, with the cheerful bravado of a child. His affection was more difficult to resist than the material deprivation, the isolation or the maddening circumstances. It was a trap, Ian knew, but oh, what a soft, enticing one, a deliberate, canny employment of the phenomenon whereby the captive becomes emotionally bonded to his captor. If they'd used a woman—Jemma, for instance—to cozy up to him, it would have been too blatant to be borne. But Rolf was a seductive acolyte. Like a brother. Or a son. Ian felt himself responding in spite of himself.

While Rolf waited for an answer, Bran complained under his breath. "His majesty wouldn't soil his hands with common work."

"Rather let a child labor," Cae agreed, nodding at Rowena.

Rolf heard and glared at the men, and they quickly made themselves busy. Rolf said, "I apologize for my servants, Ian. They must have been sleeping it off somewhere when the gods handed out brains and good manners."

Ian wasn't sure whether to resent their attempt to shame him into helping or to agree with them. Exile to this village was, if he was to follow his custom of earning his keep, a life sentence to hard labor. Or, at least, an indeterminate sentence. But as inactivity would surely drive him mad, hard labor was preferable. He shrugged. "They may have a point," he said. "If Rowena can do this, I suppose I can manage." He got himself a pair of gloves and a spade, and joined the laborers.

The work was harder than it looked—clods loosened by the *ard* were anchored in place by roots—so the almost retarded movements of the laborers made sense. They wouldn't burn themselves out. Ian felt the strain in his back and arms and the backs of his legs almost immediately. Tomorrow, he would be a virtual cripple. But today— now—the rhythm of the activity was mesmerizing.

After a while, the spring sunlight that had seemed a blessing when Ian was merely watching, became unbearable. He tied his handkerchief over his head, pirate fashion, and took off his shirt. But his vest offered his arms no protection from the sun, and dust stuck to his sweaty skin, desiccating it. He soon removed the vest and put the shirt back on.

When they finished scouring the field with east-west furrows, Rolf watered the oxen and began driving them in north-south lines.

By noontime, a gnawing pain had lodged in Ian's middle. Never in his life could he remember having been so hungry. The pain stayed an hour before subsiding, leaving him light-headed. But he persisted, following the rhythm—now autonomic—that he'd set up. He found himself looking for Jemma when Gwen brought them food mid-afternoon. Ian was only a little uncomfortable leaving Jemma behind. It was probably foolish to depend on anything in this looking-glass world, but he had begun to trust that she would still be there when he returned, sitting with the women who were spinning or grinding cereal crop, or in her dispensary, dealing with patients. There would probably even be a list of prescriptions for him to dispense or translate when returned. The very routine of it had become comforting. He was annoyed with himself when he felt disappointment at not seeing her.

Jemma turned up an hour later looking cool and lovely, wearing a hat fashioned from a reed basket. She asked Rolf—a trifle too sweetly, Ian thought—"Could I have a small corner of the field to plant some herbs?"

Ian didn't see how any man could have refused her. Not Rolf, certainly. "The whole field, if you like, Lady," he told her.

"A corner will be enough," Jemma said.

Rowena gave up the weeding to help her plant and mark the rows of seeds she'd brought with her from her former life. When they finished, Rowena returned with Jemma to the oppidium.

The men kept working. By teatime, the tepid water and bland, unsalted food Gwen brought them seemed like a banquet, and by dusk, even half-spoiled meat, unrefrigerated for days, would have been appealing. Ian wondered if his moral standards were slipping as badly.

8 ebrill

I

The Celtic day ended when the western horizon bisected the sun's red disk. By that time, the four men had finished cross plowing the field and Rolf was satisfied that they'd done enough for the day. They left the plow in the adjacent field, which they would work tomorrow. Bran took up the tools, and Cae led the oxen off to groom and feed them. Rolf and Ian rode back to the village in silence.

There was no bridge over the river. The track between Rolf's fields and the hill fort crossed it at a place it broadened and grew shallow flowing over a gravel bar. The ford, Ian would've bet, was man-made. When they came to it, he stopped the mare.

"I want a wash," he told Rolf.

No one else was around, nor likely to be at this time of day, so Ian tied the mare's reins to a bush and slipped out of his clothing. He didn't expect to get clean in cold water, without soap, but he splashed into the cramping-cold water and managed to remove the dust from his hair and skin. By the time he'd beaten the dirt from his clothing and shivered back into it, he was shaking uncontrollably but he felt better.

Rolf, meanwhile, dismounted and splashed water over his head and neck, and rinsed the dust from his arms. He didn't miss Ian's stiff movements as they remounted. "I'll have Gwen make you some willow bark tea."

• • •

Ian was uncomfortably aware of their vulnerability as they passed into the fort. The left-handed turn where the walls overlapped at the entryway forced them to present their right sides to the scrutiny of the sentries. He remembered reading that in the ancient world, the shield was held in the left hand so that the right would be free to wield sword or spear. The clockwise twist of the entrance forced invaders to present their unshielded side to the defenders.

Their entrance was accompanied by a clanging of iron on iron. Rolf would've ignored the sound, but Ian detoured to discover its source.

The younger man followed. "Gof's back," he said.

"Gof?"

"The smith. He went north to buy iron." Rolf urged his horse ahead of Ian's and reined it toward one of the houses. "C'mon, I'll introduce you." He led the way around the house and dismounted. Ian followed more slowly to give himself time to study the scene.

Tacked onto the side of the smith's house, the smithy consisted of a thatched lean-to under which the smith kept work-in-progress and his stock of iron bars, tools and firewood. His anvil was mounted on a large tree stump near the fire pit, far enough from the buildings to reduce the chance of igniting them. A small boy sat next to the fire pit working a bellows that was just a leather bladder pressed between two slats of wood, with a clay nozzle affixed to the end that pointed into the fire. At first, the smith paid Ian and Rolf no notice, but beat on the horseshoe he was fashioning as if it were an enemy he could pound to dust.

Rolf said, "Ian, may I introduce Gof?"

Gof didn't even look up. He was a head shorter than Ian and had pale blue eyes bracketed by networks of crows' feet. His voluminous mustache and braided sideburns were roaned with gray. Too many teeth in his mouth overlapped to fit in. He had the arms and shoulders of a bodybuilder, and the joints of his huge hands were enlarged by decades of gripping and hammering.

When he finally deigned to acknowledge them, the smith looked Ian over contemptuously, then asked Rolf, "Who's the foreigner?"

"Epona's kinsman."

"Her bond-slave, more like, from the look of him. Where's his torc? What are his clan and family?"

"Some of my ancestors were Stewarts," Ian said defensively.

"Is that a clan?"

Ian nodded. "Scots."

"Your tribe? Never heard of it."

Ian just shook his head and shrugged. The smith pantomimed dismissal.

"Come on, Ian," Rolf said. "Gof's in a bad mood. Let's not disturb him further."

Rowena saved him from nodding off into the beef stew at supper. "Ian, wake up!" she said. She was giggling.

He sat straighter, reluctantly. He'd begun to stiffen as soon as he stopped moving. The muscles of his legs and back and shoulders were knotted, but he forced his attention on the food.

To go with the stew, Gwen had baked bread in a sort of Dutch oven, and she served barley beer—*corma*—to wash it down with. Though the *corma* tasted terrible, it had as high an alcohol content as wine. Ian was getting used to it, but he would've given plenty for a pint of almost any modern brew. The bright spot in the meal was that Gwen hadn't been stingy with the salt, which always seemed to be in short supply.

An eternity later, he lay on his straw bed, waiting for the moon to rise. He studied his position again.

He had lost his home, his work and all the people and material comforts that had made life bearable without Marjory. Worse yet, he would never again see his children. They were as dead to him as Marjory. No. If Jemma's fable were right, it was *he* who had died—

seventeen centuries before his birth. But such an absurdity could not be! Jemma was lying.

She claimed they were in England. Well enough. When one traveled south and east from nearly anywhere in England, one came to the Channel or the sea. If, as he supposed, they were actually somewhere else, traveling south and east would disprove the time travel nonsense and put him in contact with someone who could help him get home. Or if it were true, he would come to know it with certainty once and for all.

It was time to escape the village and end the charade. If he took both Jemma's horses, left undetected, and put a night's ride between himself and the village, he could probably pull it off. There wasn't a horse in the village that could hope to catch the grays. They would have to come after him in modern transport, and perhaps he could put his hands on whatever they came in, and get clear away. Tired and stiff as he was, he thought it was worth a try.

He listened for the sounds of the others' breathing and heard only Rolf's near-snoring. There was none of the rustling of bedding that would signal anyone having a bout of insomnia. He would get up and gather his things together. He would lift Rolf's hunting bag, which, he knew, contained enough salt and dried meat and fruit for a week, from where it hung on the wall. He'd wrap his cloak around him and slip out when the village was asleep. That was the plan.

But in fact, any thought he had of stealing away that night was bludgeoned to death by the rigors of the day. Even had he been able to slip away unnoticed, or had a clue as to where to go, by the time the village had settled itself for the night, he was dead to the world.

II

When Ian peered out the east-facing window of his room, clouds above the horizon were glowing red as the coals in the blacksmith's hearth. Light splashed over everything, transforming bands of northern mares' tails into a spectacular daylight simulation of the aurora borealis.

Time to go. Time to find his way out of this wonderland and get back to his own life.

With the sun rising, the dogs ignored him. He carried Rolf's game bag and his own belongings quietly to the paddock, where he caught and bridled his gray, saddled her with his cloak and tethered her to the fence. Then he caught Jemma's horse. No need to take it along if he could just remove one of its shoes. He could be well away by the time the smith could reset it. He lifted each of the mare's feet, testing for any give, and got lucky. The shoe on the off-side front hoof was missing two nails. He had nothing to use as a pry-tool but his knife, but the knife sufficed. The back of the blade straightened the nails and a few taps of the hilt knocked them free. Ian pocketed the nails and dropped the shoe into the paddock near one of the fence posts—a new shoe, for an animal with feet as large as Jemma's mare, might be hard to come by. He released Jemma's horse and mounted his own.

No one was about yet. He held the mare to a walk as they approached the hill fort entrance, though he would have liked to have given her her head.

He hadn't counted on the sentries. Two of them stood on the rampart, over the gate, still wrapped against the night air in the near-black cloaks that were the uniform of the village constables. Ian recognized them. Joess and Pyrs. Joess was the largest man in the village, dark and tall, heavy-set and curly-haired; Pyrs, his constant companion, was as tall but pale and thin, with straight, ash-blond hair. At sixteen and seventeen they were considered adults, but as the youngest of the village PCs, they drew the least desirable duty—and frequent graveyard shifts. They were fighting sleep as Ian guided the mare at the narrow passage below their position. Before he could enter, Joess said, "I'm sorry, sir, but you may not pass."

Ian decided to ignore him, to see what he would do. He nudged the mare forward.

"Hey!" Pyrs said, trotting along the catwalk to keep even with him. "Stop!"

Out of the corner of his eye, Ian could see Joess race around Pyrs to vault the wall and drop into the passageway ahead. When Ian tried to goad the horse around him, he grabbed the reins and stopped the animal as firmly as if he'd snubbed her to a post. His attitude was fearful but defiant—as if he were afraid of Ian, or his reported powers, but determined to avoid the dishonor of showing it.

Ian let all the rage he felt sound in his voice. "Let me go!"

Joess said, deferentially, "I'm sorry, but you may not leave without an escort. I have my orders." He gave the impression one would have to strike him dead to move him, and Ian remembered that he was Houel's son. Although physically unlike Houel, he seemed to have the same imperturbable self-possession that marked his father as a leader.

Then Pyrs dropped into the passage beside him.

"This is absurd!" Ian told them. "You didn't stop me yesterday."

"You were with Rowena, yesterday," Joess said. He turned the mare around—a tight squeeze in the narrow passage—and let her go. Pyrs slapped her rump.

Ian gave it up and let the mare make her way back to the paddock.

By the time he had put the horse up, the village was well into its morning routine. Jemma was sitting on a stool in front of the carpenter's house, humming while she combed her hair. It seemed to have grown paler as her skin darkened in the sun.

He stopped to watch. He couldn't help himself.

He was not sure of when, precisely, he had become obsessed with Jemma, but she invaded his thoughts, waking and sleeping. He found himself constantly trying to reconcile this woman, the healer, with the murderess he'd been sent to take in charge. He was overwhelmed, as well, with the thought that his situation was impossible. Such a thing could not be happening! But of course, that was the same feeling hostages and innocent prisoners the world over felt when wrongfully detained. It was just that the particulars of this situation lent it a Kafka-esque poignancy. The feeling was an echo of the emotion he'd experienced after Marjory's death—a familiar sensation, comforting only by its familiarity.

But on a planet with eight billion inhabitants, circled by communications satellites, infested with off-road vehicles, it wasn't possible that any temperate zone location would be unvisited for weeks by tourists. Not even the Antarctic was immune.

To quote Sherlock Holmes: *When you have eliminated the impossible, whatever remains, however improbable, must be the truth.* This, of course, was precisely the logic "they" wanted him to accept, but how could one not?

He began to doubt his own doubt. Was his refusal to accept this world merely denial? Could going through a time warp change a person?

I haven't changed!

But Jemma might have. He longed to ask her about the circumstances of her conviction.

His common sense told him that this woman wasn't a felon. Perhaps this wasn't Jemma Henderson. Perhaps there had been a switch, with this woman substituted for *the* Jemma Henderson.

Jemma noticed him staring and stopped humming. "Good morning, Inspector Carreg. Have you been out riding already?"

She was mocking him. Ian felt himself flush. "Er…the early bird…"

For a moment, as she finished combing and began to plait her hair into a French braid, she seemed to stop listening. Once she had a good start, she was able to resume sparring. "So, you're going fishing later?"

"I beg your pardon?"

"With the worm?"

That didn't merit an answer. He changed the subject abruptly. "Your horse has lost a shoe."

"What?"

"Your horse—"

"I heard you. What has that to do with…? What were we talking about?"

Good. She was off balance. To keep the advantage, he changed the subject again. "What was that you were singing just now?"

"Just a tune…Who's Rhiannon?'"

It was Ian's turn to say, "What?"

"Yesterday I was singing that song and Houel called me Rhiannon's bird. What did he mean?"

"Rhiannon was a goddess whose birds sang so sweetly that men who heard them forgot time, and their homes and duties, and lost years of their lives listening."

Canny metaphor, Ian thought. Canny fellow, Houel.

"Oh, a siren," Jemma said. "The flatterer. Tell me about my horse. The smith's back. Can he reset the shoe? Would you be good enough to arrange it for me?"

It was blasphemy, but the way she took charge reminded him of Marjory.

"I'll ask him."

"Thank you."

She gave him a smile that would have made most men's hearts stop, and Ian felt a little thrill of—

Good Lord! *She's a murderess!*

He kept forgetting! She was a woman toward whom—out of habit, it sometimes seemed—he had become antagonistic. But he had to keep reinforcing the habit to maintain it. If he wasn't careful, he'd come to regard her as ordinary and benign.

No. Never ordinary.

He was nearly finished with his breakfast, watching Gwen start her morning chores and reflecting how he missed his morning caffeine, when Rowena planted herself in front of him.

"Ian, aren't you happy here with us?"

She seemed distressed and he wanted to reassure her, but he wouldn't lie.

"I miss my family. I have a son your father's age and a grandchild coming." He reached up and stroked her hair.

She touched his face, wrinkling her nose when her fingers encountered the rough stubble on his unshaven jaw. "You'll just have to go back to them. Jemma will understand."

"I can't." He tried to find the words to explain a time machine to someone who'd never seen the telly. Impossible. "I'm banished," he said, finally.

She looked as if she'd cry. She stepped closer and put her head against his chest and patted his shoulder. She didn't speak.

When Ian arrived with the mare and her shoe, Gof was sitting in front of his house, shoveling porridge into his mouth. The linen tunic he was wearing hung between his legs to cover his privates, but left a great deal of hairy knee and leg showing. His legs were as scarred as his forearms—white marks against his sun-darkened skin testified to the burns and kicks and gouges that were the hazards of his occupation. He finished his porridge before getting to his feet.

When he got up, he ignored Ian, but walked around the horse like a curator appraising a work of art, running his hands over her cheek and down her neck, peering into her mouth, even pulling her eyelids down to look at the membranes. The mare demonstrated her good manners by standing perfectly still, then by shifting her weight off each leg as the smith lifted the foot. He started with the near front and finished with the off front. His gentleness was a mirror image of the hostility he'd displayed toward Ian.

"She didn't lose the shoe," he said when he was finished with the inspection. "It's been removed."

"So?"

"A trick."

Ian sighed. "You'll be paid to reset it. What's your price?"

Gof looked at him speculatively, pursed his lips then, finally, said, "Your belt."

Ian wondered if his astonishment was obvious. The belt was leather, with a buckle of some indeterminate metal. It cost, at most, five pounds new. As with the rest of his wardrobe, he considered it a loss, but it *was* holding up his trousers. He said, "Er…are you sure you wouldn't prefer silver?" He was sure he had seen silver coins in Jemma's pocket.

"Your belt," Gof said, again. He seemed immovable.

Ian shrugged. A rope would hold his trousers up. He slipped the belt off and handed it to Gof.

The smith examined the buckle as if he had never seen such a thing before, taking his knife from his belt to scratch off the finish on the back, frowning without comment. Finally, he hung the belt on a peg on the wall of the house and took the horse's lead from Ian's hand. "Do you have the shoe?"

Ian held it up; Gof nodded and started around to the smithy. Ian followed. When they got near the fire, which the same boy was diligently feeding, Gof thrust the lead back into Ian's hand. "Hold her."

He left him holding the mare while he put on his leather apron and checked the blade of his hoof-knife. Then he took the horseshoe, examined it briefly, and dropped it in the fire. The boy doubled his efforts with the bellows; the coals reddened.

"You'll have to pay for nails," Gof said.

Ian dug the nails out of his pocket and handed them over, and the smith dropped them into the fire as well.

"People say you're a god, but I don't believe it," he told Ian. "I think you're a clever charlatan."

11 ebrill

I

The night of the quarter moon, Ian slept fitfully, feeling something was afoot. There had been such a strong undercurrent of excitement and secrecy at dinner that the meal had been almost unpleasant. Rolf refused to explain, growling it was women's business. Ian hoped to ask Jemma, later, but he couldn't find her. He had just gotten to sleep when a dog barked. Another answered it. Clyfar whined, and Ian told him to be still. A muffled, familiar voice told the dogs without to be quiet. Ian sprang awake. The moon was just rising and, though most of the cooking fires had been extinguished, he could easily make out through his window hole the figure he'd come to love and hate. Jemma was camouflaged by a dark cloak but unmistakable as she hurried through the dim light between the houses, burdened by her medical satchel. Someone was ill. *Or wounded!* Ian snatched up his own cloak and followed, closing the door on Clyfar. He kicked the first barking sentry that appeared into silence; the others slunk away.

He paused under the eaves to look at the rising moon. It appeared as it always had, though he realized he had never studied it before. It might be a different, very similar moon. He couldn't tell. He decided that when he was well away, he would memorize it—every nuance and crater—so that if—

No! When he got home, he could recognize the subtle differences between this alien satellite and his own familiar one.

He stayed out of sight. Jemma was silently admitted to the house of Absinthe, one of Houel's cousins. Ian slipped into the black shadow under the eaves and followed the curve of the wall until he found a window from which light escaped. And laughter.

He peered cautiously around the window frame.

The interior was illuminated by a fire in the central hearth and oil lamps suspended from the roof. Light like liquid amber bathed the participants—all women—glinting off their hair and from the fresh straw covering the floor.

The room was filled with women, seated around the fire, golden and animated in their conversation. It was a party to which they'd worn no jewelry, a working party judging by their dress. He watched Jemma take off her wrap, and she too, was dressed for work—in the white tunic she'd worn to stitch Alf's leg, on which yellow traces of blood could still be seen. Jemma's hair was braided and pinned out of the way. She sat down and Ian could see Gwen there, too, and Maura and Houel's wife—all of them dressed in clothing that was old but clean, all of them with their hair tied back and their sleeves rolled up. Maura shifted, and Ian could see the fifth woman next to the fire. Absinthe sat naked and sweat-covered, the muscles of her neck and arms and swollen abdomen knotted.

Ian blushed to the soles of his feet as he realized he was spying on a birthing. He started to turn away, but Absinthe let out a little cry—an almost disappointed sound, and the conversation around her ceased. When the contraction was over, she lay back on Gwen's lap and spread her legs, and Jemma got down on all fours to check the infant's progress.

What a contrast from the procedures Marjory'd described to him that were designed for the doctor's convenience. He didn't know from experience. He hadn't been allowed to participate in— or even observe—the births of his own children. If he waited just a few more minutes, he'd witness the miracle here. Now. What harm would it do to watch?

He hesitated. Jemma said something, and the other women helped Absinthe to her knees. They held her arms, supporting her weight as she bore down. Sweat condensed all over her as her body contracted, and they chorused their support.

A shiny, dark-blue bulge appeared between her legs. Gravity maintained her gain while she rested between contractions. The next gargantuan convulsion brought encouragement from the team and transformed the pendulous bulge into a pointed head and a squeezed-together face wrapped in slippery cellophane.

Absinthe screamed, "Cernunnos!" and stared straight at Ian. He was transfixed. The other women stared at Absinthe, who convulsed again—not in pain, but in absolute effort—and the child dropped, steaming and squirming into Jemma's waiting hands. The mother sobbed. Her tears were indistinguishable from the sweat that drenched her, from the birth water on the child Jemma clutched. The mother chanted, "Cernunnos, Cernunnos," and they all took up the chant as they stared at the marvelous child.

Except Jemma.

Jemma looked at Ian through the window and gave him a sort of a knowing, mischievous smile. She deliberately closed her eyes as he disappeared into the night.

Cernunnos!

II

That afternoon, he came upon Jemma napping in the dappled shade of a flowering apple tree. White, spent petals settled on her like large snowflakes, and the sun dropped coins of gold light in her lap.

Ian was overcome by an awful sense of *déjà vu* as her sleeping form revived a memory.

It was late July or August. They had been punting on the river, a perfect idyll. Marjory was stretched out, golden and languorous in the bow, he lounged at the oars. The water seemed as viscous as oil, tea-colored and amber, and pale blue and gold-green where it reflected sky and grassy bank and overhanging trees. New-cut grass perfumed air neither too hot nor cold. It was one of those moments that by its near perfection impresses itself in memory with absolute clarity.

She'd smiled and yawned and said, "Promise me that you'll

remarry if I should predecease you."

"Good Lord! What a thing to say."

"You're so impractical, Luv."

"All right. To be practical, women outlive men by a good number of years. So I don't think you have to worry about me on that score."

She smiled again. "Don't just fall for a pretty face. Find someone smart. Someone who'll take care of you. Promise?"

"If I lose you, I shan't want another wife."

"But children need a mother."

"We haven't any children."

"Mmm," she'd said. "Not yet. Not for eight months."

The beloved apparition faded. Jemma glowed in the pied shade like a specter mocking Marjory's words. Pretty was an understatement. And she was smart. But a murderess! A kidnapper! A woman young enough to be his daughter!

13 ebrill

Two days after Absinthe delivered her baby, everyone participated in the planting as they would in the harvest. Even Absinthe helped, keeping the toddlers out of harm's way. And Mathe, Rolf's brother's very pregnant widow, tended the soup the women had prepared.

There was a ritual for planting, and a chant that was a blessed relief, stopping his obsessive thoughts of Jemma and of the impossibility of his situation.

Great Modron, Good Modron, Merciful Mother, hear our prayers. Spread Your legs. Accept our seed. Bear us Your fruit. Give us Your Life. Merciful Modron.

The villagers' frank acceptance of their sexuality had shocked Ian at first, but after a while it had begun to seem so natural that he accepted it. The women were not intentionally provocative, but neither did they hide their virtues or their appreciation of things sexual. In this, Jemma seemed to fit perfectly.

The planters went from field to field as Drullwyn blessed each one. They opened the earth with sticks—some simple, some ornately carved with the heads of serpents or other fabulous beasts—before dropping in the seed, planting broad beans, oats and barley, and a community field of leeks and garlic. While they worked, the women swapped recipes and gossip; the men made jokes under their breaths: "I'd like to plant *that* field."

Jemma started to sing along with the others. "It's a pretty chant," she told Ian, when their respective tasks brought them near. Her proximity made him uncomfortably aware of his own sweaty stench, though she didn't seem offended. He translated for her, and

117

she blushed, but later, he noticed, she was still chanting.

When they finished, one of the children presented her with a necklace of violets. It began to rain. Drullwyn waved at the sky, and told Jemma, "You held the rain off until the planting was finished. Our harvest is assured."

14 ebrill

The day after planting, Ian watched with Jemma as Gwen took several handfuls of the carded wool, which was stored in nets hung under the eaves, gathered it loosely in a mass she hung from a hook suspended from the rafters, and began to twist it into a thread that she attached to the end of a hand spindle. "This work we usually do in winter," she told Ian. "But Epona has asked to see how it's done." She dropped the spindle, twisting out half a yard or so of yarn, which she wound around the spindle shaft. When she'd got the rhythm of the procedure down to her satisfaction, she sat down to work, feeding more wool into the growing thread so deftly and quickly that Ian had to watch for several minutes to understand the process.

Jemma seemed to catch on immediately and repeat the procedure without the least fumbling. She had a surgeon's hands, dexterous and graceful and strong. And extremely beautiful. From time to time—as he watched them—Ian's thoughts stumbled on the things those hands could do to a man. For a man. Such thoughts embarrassed and angered him, and left him irritable. He wished to heaven he had never seen her naked.

It was a common misconception that she belonged to him, perhaps because they'd come together, and nothing he said seemed to change people's minds. Her grasp of Celtic had advanced to the point where she was able to hold simple conversations without him. He asked her what she'd told the villagers about them.

"I said that you're my kinsman. That seems to cover any number of possibilities."

"But it's not true!"

"Perhaps you'd like to explain it to them?"

He thought about it. What could he say? That she'd abducted him? That she was mad and claimed to have a time machine? *Nonsense!*

On the other hand, all the villagers were relatives by blood or marriage, or by fosterage or clientship. To them he and Jemma must seem related.

The village was like any other farming community save that the farmers took frequent holidays from their work to practice swordplay and javelin throwing and vaulting onto their horses with full battle regalia. Ian declined to participate in their mock battles—some of which were sufficiently competitive to result in real injuries—but he watched them closely.

The women worked constantly. When they were not grinding oats—which Jemma persisted in calling wheat—or cooking, or caring for children, they were spinning yarn. They didn't seem to notice, much less resent, the fact that the men never helped with any of this work.

Ian found life in the village not particularly unpleasant. There *were* advantages—fresh air, healthy food, and no want of useful exercise. Though there were things that drove him mad as well— moldy meat and awful beer, and fleas and flies, and other vermin. Hot baths were unheard of and the simple act of brushing one's teeth became a chore. Nevertheless, it was only the involuntary nature of his stay that prevented his enjoying it. He awoke every morning with a new plan for escape, but every day some new amusement presented itself for his edification and held him for the day—the assembly of a new loom by the carpenter; the manufacture of a *fro* by the smith; the breaking-in of a half-wild yearling by one of the warrior farmers or his son or—to Ian's surprise, for it seemed out of character—by the farmer's daughter.

Rolf dug him up a rusty, pitted and corroded spear point, which he presented apologetically.

"Maybe you could fix this up."

The villagers didn't own a decent whetstone, and it occupied the better part of the afternoon to scrub the rust off with sand and put new edges on the blade. The point was of poor quality iron, but Ian managed to temper it without benefit of the smith's help. Gof guarded his prerogatives zealously, and clearly disapproved of Ian.

Village life had a definite rhythm, which after the first week was predictable and comforting. Ian marked the passage of time by the gradual lengthening of his hair and mustache, and the deterioration of his clothes. The days flashed by like strobe light as he learned how the villagers managed their everyday business without running water, refrigeration, indoor plumbing or electricity.

One of the principal reasons he couldn't fathom living in this time, though, was that there was no work for him. In his former life he'd had a purpose. Here, there wasn't much crime—only occasional fights, petty larceny and the sort of mindless vandalism unsupervised children engage in. Houel commanded the group of young men who acted as constables and sentries. They broke up fights and returned lost children or property. Ian could see no work for a detective, and he had no aptitude for farming, nor anything beyond an academic interest. No one but Jemma seemed to expect much of him. Often people seemed to be waiting as if watching to see what he would do. Jemma seemed only to require translations, but she was fast learning the language and soon would translate for herself. The skills that he could have taught were largely irrelevant to these people. And the village had a blacksmith.

The smith's antipathy had became a challenge. Every time Ian came near the smithy, Gof told him to go away. At first, he complied, but the smith's unwillingness to have him around made him wonder what the fellow was up to. He would wait until the ringing of iron on anvil signaled that Gof was preoccupied, then he would quietly approach. Gof put all of himself into his work, so that Ian was often able to watch him for long periods of time before being noticed. Gof's reaction was always the same: "Go away, old man!"

Rolf told Ian that the smith never let anyone watch; he was afraid people would steal his secrets. So after the first time, Ian didn't take it personally.

He was poking about under the eaves, one day, when Jemma came along and asked, "Lose something?"

"An operation of this complexity has to be coordinated by radio. Sooner or later I'll find one."

"You still don't believe me."

"That we've traveled into the past, I'm forced by the evidence of my eyes to accept. But I want to go home. You can tell that to whoever's orchestrating this charade."

"What possible purpose…?"

"I confess, I can't imagine. I have to give you credit. Three weeks, here at Berlitz camp, and not one of you has slipped out of character. But someone will. Sooner or later. And I seem to have nothing to do but wait." He started to walk away and stopped. "The worst is all the men you've killed for this horrific little god-game! There can't be anything to justify that."

She seemed truly horrified. "Can you really think I'm such a monster?"

He truly didn't know what to think. "You have the brass to ask? You've taken my life. My children think I'm dead or worse!—Do you know how hard it is on the families of people who just disappear?"

"Yes, and I *am* sorry. But since you're here, and the machine was set to blow up right after I left, I think it's safe to assume they think you're dead."

"Is that supposed to set things right?"

"Most people outlive their parents, Inspector. They survived the death of your wife. They'll get over yours."

It was no more than he'd expected from a woman who'd shot her lover, who'd committed premeditated murder.

• • •

That afternoon he asked her, "What's *gwraig gwneuthuriad?*"

"Curious, aren't you?" She seemed to have forgotten their hard words earlier. "Where did you hear of that?"

"Some of the women were talking. No one seems to want to explain it to me." He waited.

She shrugged. "When a girl reaches marriageable age, her women friends hold a sort of coming-of-age ceremony for her, and one of them surgically severs her hymen. Under anesthetic. So when she takes a husband, or participates in the festivities at Samhain or Cetsamhain, she won't experience pain with intercourse. It's quite a useful custom."

Ian felt himself reddening. Jemma only half tried to hide her amusement. "Inspector Carreg, you're blushing. Have you hang-ups about sex?"

"My *hang-ups* are none of your affair."

"I hope that doesn't mean you'll wait to call, when you need a physician, until you're on your deathbed."

"What makes you think I'd call you?"

"You don't seem suicidal." After he blinked, she added, "And I'm the only show in town."

15 ebrill

Jemma had been taking skeins of yarn as payment for her services since they arrived in the village, and one morning, when her own business was slow, she asked Gwen to show her how to dye it. They started early, dropping the dampened yarn into a large pot of plant leaves simmering over the fire. Gwen called the dye "woad."

"It came from the leaves of *Isatis tinctoria*," Jemma told Ian. "Only they won't call it that for hundreds of years."

That made him realize, with a jolt, that he'd been accepting the scenario as perfectly natural. As if modern chemical dyes had never been invented.

The ivory-colored wool turned pale blue almost immediately. As they stirred the steaming mixture, the wool grew deeper and darker blue, and the pot liquor gradually lost its color.

"What's on your agenda for the day?" Jemma asked affably. Her eyes were the same blue violet as shadows on wet pavement on a sunny day.

Ian dragged his attention back to her question. "I thought I'd give Ty a hand." Ty was Maura's husband.

In furtherance of his plan to placate Gof, he'd been forced to prevail upon the carpenter for the loan of an ax.

Ty had the most impressive tools in the village, including at least three or four axes. He'd offered Ian a deal. If he would help fell and split a large tree—how large was not specified—he could have the unlimited use of Ty's axes, and the use of a wagon to boot. It seemed a fair bargain.

• • •

Ty was both woodwright and wheelwright. A flamboyant character—as flashy as Maura was plain—he was much given to bragging and brawling, and quite fond of drink. Yet no one accused him of false boasting, nor was there ever any talk of his having been bested in a fight.

"Of course, it's the wrong time of year to be doing this," he told Ian, apologetically, "but this tree was recently killed by lightning. If I leave it until next winter, the wood may be ruined."

Ian had to think for several minutes before he figured out why. Wood has to be cut while green to minimize the splitting that accompanies shrinking as it dries. He had always purchased seasoned wood for his projects and had never given a thought to how it was produced. For that matter, he had taken nearly everything for granted before.

The work took an hour. Ty brought a great two-man saw, with which they cut a large wedge from the trunk, on the side toward which the tree would fall. Before they finished, sweat soaked their clothing. The muscles of Ian's back and shoulders and his triceps were in agony; he knew that within hours his hands would stiffen like an arthritic's. A chainsaw would have had the tree down in minutes with less effort than changing a tyre.

But the ease of doing it with a chainsaw would've taken the impact from the task. With every painful drawing-back of the blade, he was aware of the time taken by nature to produce the tree, thirty or fifty or 100 years—he'd know when they finished and could count the rings. It seemed fitting that it needed effort to undo all that time of quiet growing.

Labor-saving devices were all well enough, but they let one evade the question of whether the task was worth doing. Something he'd never before considered.

As the blade closed in on the wedge cut, the faintest creaking began to warn that something was happening. The sound wouldn't have been heard over a chainsaw. They stopped to listen. Ty pulled the blade from the kerf and pushed against the trunk, and the two of them stepped back to watch the huge tree topple.

The smith was unimpressed by the wagon load of firewood. "A bribe," he said, but he didn't object when Ian stacked it under the lean-to, nor did he tell Ian to go away when he went back to his task. He was fashioning a sword, incising the hilt and the upper part of the blade to take an intricate bronze inlay.

He was soon interrupted by one of the farmers, who sidled up with a broken ard blade and stood waiting for Gof to pause in his work.

"What?" Gof finally demanded. The farmer looked at his plow. Gof scowled. "You can see I'm occupied."

Plainly unwilling to enrage the town's only smith, the farmer said nothing. But he didn't go away. It probably was his only plow, and until Gof fixed it, he had nothing better to do than wait.

But having someone watch him work did not improve the smith's disposition. "Come back tomorrow," he curtly told the man.

The farmer hesitated. Clearly he was as unwilling to lose a day of planting as he was to incur the smith's wrath.

Time to intervene, Ian thought. He said, "Master, why not let *me* fix this man's plow?" He watched as amazement, rage, and then curiosity played across the blacksmith's face.

"What?" Gof said. "You?"

"It would leave you to do the skilled work without interruption."

"What do you know about working iron?"

"Enough to fix the ard."

"Show me," Gof demanded.

And Ian did.

16 ebrill

I

Rolf woke him before sunrise, announcing that the village needed fresh meat, insisting that Ian accompany him hunting. A more logical course, in Ian's opinion, would simply be to slaughter one of the cattle. Rolf was disappointed when Ian said so and refused to bound joyfully up to follow him. Rolf capitulated only to the extent of postponing for an hour. After breakfast, he went to get the horses while Ian went into the house to collect Rolf's spears for the expedition.

Ian was in his own "room" when Gwen brought Jemma into the large common area of the house to show her how to set up the loom that stood below the single tiny window beneath the eaves. As they came through the door, Jemma said something Ian didn't catch, to which Gwen replied, "Why don't you tell him how you feel?"

They didn't know he was there; it was impossible not to eavesdrop. "He hates me," Jemma said.

In the dim light, Ian couldn't judge her expression. He wondered who she meant.

"Surely he can't?" Gwen said. "Why would he?"

"Because I killed a man." Gwen must've seemed incredulous, because Jemma elaborated. "The bastard raped me."

The man she'd murdered! It wasn't what the papers had reported.

"…So, I killed him."

Ian hadn't considered the possibility that she was innocent. But even in America, juries based their verdicts on the facts.

"And he hates you for that?" Gwen persisted. "What sort of monster is he?"

"He doesn't know the whole story. He never asked."

Surely they were referring to him. He *hadn't* asked.

"And why did he never ask?"

Why, indeed?

Jemma didn't answer. Ian peered through the cracks in the wicker wall. He couldn't see their faces. He noticed that Gwen had slipped the knotted ends of skeins of yarn into notches in the top of her loom frame and hung every other skein on the opposite side of a horizontal pole below. The order of the yarns' colors gave a hint of the future pattern—blue and green plaid or perhaps checks. The last three notches were empty.

"This isn't going to be enough," Gwen said. "We'll have to get the rest before we start."

After they'd gone, Ian was careful not to be seen leaving the house.

II

The hunting party included Owain, and they brought Rolf's affable dog, Clyfar. The number of the complement seemed to be important—one, three, and three, with the horses—for a total of seven beings. Seven. As they passed beneath the watchful eyes of the sentries, Rolf asked, "Ian, do you feel lucky?"

"Not particularly."

"Then perhaps I should choose our direction."

"Not on your life. We'll go east." East was the direction that held the most promise of returning to his own world, should he manage escape. This would be a chance to reconnoiter.

It took an hour, walking and cantering, to get beyond the cultivated lands east of the hill fort. On the edge of the wilderness, the fields gave way to partially cleared lands where oak and hazel coppices predominated. The track climbed gradually into the sky, for it seemed as if the upper branches of the forest had reached up to trap a cloud. Distance was impossible to judge in the mist—objects farther away than a hundred meters simply dematerialized.

As they penetrated the forest, Ian saw evidence of game, but no animals. The horses' hooves cut decaying leaf mold underfoot and stirred up the earthy odor of mushrooms and compost. The forest was wondrous in its variety of colors and patterns, odors and textures, and alive with the fluttering of unseen creatures curiously muffled and disembodied by the fog. It was easy to believe in spirits and apparitions. Ian was struck by an eerie sense of déjà vu. He remembered, with surprise, how as a child he'd felt the magic of the wasteland.

Though intellectually he'd known even then that the wood was bounded by highways and seacoasts, it had the power in his imagination to go on forever, like the enchanted forests in fairy tales. In his mind, what lay beyond the wasteland was the misty expanse marked on old maps: "Here be Dragons."

They let the horses choose the path; they chose the easiest. Game trails opened up before them and branched and intertwined and vanished. Clyfar raced ahead and circled back, materializing and dematerializing. He'd snuffle frantically near the feet of the horses, then hang back, then dash off on little side excursions—always silently.

They crested a slight ridge, and Ian found they were on a track that perfectly fit C. S. Lewis's description of the road to hell: *The gentle slope*...It was a good metaphor for this whole bloody world, and for his sojourn in it, though Lewis had neglected to mention company—congenial companions and beautiful adversaries.

Rolf stopped his horse where the path widened out on either side of a ford across a small stream, which meandered between the fog and mist. Ian's two companions began to go through their belongings. Owain produced a boar's tooth, and Rolf brought out a fawn Ty had carved for him the previous day from willow wood. Each tossed his offering downstream with a brief prayer to the god of the place for good luck in the hunt. Then they looked at Ian.

Clearly, he was expected to make an offering as well. But what?

He was dashed if he would give up his watch or pen or keys, or even a page of his jotter. And he carried no coins. What did that leave that would satisfy a pagan god? What would one of his companions find entertaining? He did a brief inventory of his clothes and pockets and settled on a button. His shirt was, after all, already a loss and, in any case, the lowest button never showed beneath his belt line. He pulled out the shirt tail and yanked off the button, skipping it into the stream.

"Here's to good luck!"

Suddenly Clyfar started baying, startling Ian, who hadn't heard the sound before.

Rolf and Owain shouted, "Deer!"

The dog began to circle in a clockwise direction—sunwise, Rolf called it. The men followed him by sound as he drove their quarry north, then gradually eastward. When it became apparent that dog and prey were circling, Rolf signaled for the party to move south to intercept. The track widened and petered out in a small meadow. The three horsemen positioned themselves at the points of an equilateral triangle just within the event horizon of the mist-bounded space. Clyfar's disembodied voice circled south, then west and north. Ian glanced at Rolf and Owain, and gathered from their amazement that the chase was not going as expected. Clyfar's voice continued to spiral toward the meadow. When it had finished two complete circuits, a deer broke toward Rolf from the mist. Rolf was ready, aiming the spear just far enough ahead of it to anticipate the animal's forward motion. But just as the weapon left his hand, the animal veered toward Owain. Rolf's horse plunged in a half-rear and Rolf's spear sailed over the deer's back.

Owain was also ready. Before Rolf's curse reached him, he reined in his horse and launched *his* spear, also aiming ahead to allow for the deer's forward movement. But just before the spear left his hand, Clyfar broke from the mist with another of his hair-raising yowls. Owain's horse bucked in protest, and the deer veered toward Ian.

Ian's mind raced. The deer seemed to move more slowly with

each change of direction, but it would soon change course again and disappear in the mist. Ian could see that he was all that prevented its escape. He *must* act! *He* must act. He had the time, time enough to notice how graceful the animal was, dark-eyed, tawny-coated. He had more than enough time to note his horse standing quietly, to experience his own reluctance to take the deer's life.

The hunt wasn't frivolous, he reflected, not a mindless idyll, but an ancient ritual. The creature would be eaten—not hung on a wall to prove some macho point, but shared with the neighbors. Its death would serve a purpose, and no part would be wasted. He was expected to do his bit.

And so he flung his spear with the same exasperated resignation with which he'd thrown his button in the stream, without a thought for aim or trajectory, but with a prayer for the life he was taking: *Forgive me.*

Even as the spear left his hand, he knew it had to miss. He had time to notice Rolf grab for his lost weapon, to observe as Owain hauled his horse up on its haunches, to see Clyfar bound toward the deer—all huge feet and uncontrolled momentum. Clyfar bayed again. The deer jerked as if shot and leaped, almost sideways, to meet the point of Ian's spear with the base of its throat. Ian felt the point strike with a wave of shock that was not pain but adrenaline. The deer arced forward from the point of impact and crumpled, landing in a tangled heap. Clyfar skidded and slid, almost overrunning the remains. He sniffed the corpse, then sat down next to it and raised his muzzle to howl like some feral dog.

"We must have had just the right numbers," Rolf said. "One, three, three, seven."

Respective numbers of dogs, men, horses and living participants.

"No," Owain said, quietly. "It was Ian's offering, his words. Or else he drew the deer to him with his magic."

He looked at Ian, waiting for confirmation, Ian supposed.

"It was just bloody, stupid luck," Ian said.

Rolf nodded. "The god…" He indicated, by gesturing at their surroundings, the god of the place to whom their offerings had been directed. "…must have approved."

With that, he handed his spear to Owain. For the moment of the exchange, Ian was reminded of an oil he'd seen in the British Museum, of an exchange of gifts between two American Indians. The resonance that the image set up in his mind was like an electric shock, a déjà vu. The humanity of the gesture spanned cultures, continents, and time with the speed of thought, and with the strength of the human species.

III

When the hunters returned to the hill fort, they stopped their horses below the gate, by the five skulls mounted on their poles, to let the sentries appreciate their kill. Ian had been passing the heads for days without noticing them particularly, but the mood of the day seemed to bring them out of the background. He couldn't repress an involuntary shudder.

Rolf noticed. "Can it be you're afraid of our guardians?" he demanded, only half joking.

"Trophies, don't you mean?" Ian said to Rolf's puzzlement. "… Badges. Decorations."

Rolf was horrified. "Oh, no! No! You have it wrong." He looked at Ian and seemed distressed to see he was serious. "The head is the dwelling place of the spirit," he said, "and where the head is, the soul must remain. It's thus…" He nodded toward the disembodied guardians. "…we compel these warriors to guard us from bad luck and evil spirits. Only the bravest may be so honored."

"My family's most prized possession," Owain added, "is the head of a Catuvellauni; they say he slew fifty men in his lifetime. My grandfather turned down three gold torcs for it."

A long silence ensued while Ian absorbed this new perspective.

"Ian," Rolf said, "in your land, who protects you from demons and evil spirits?"

"Where I come from, we're not troubled by evil spirits, only by evil men."

"Who protects you from evil men?"

"The police." His own irony mocked him as he hauled his horse around with far more force than necessary and spurred her into the oppidium.

Jemma was leaning over the fence of the horse paddock when they arrived, stroking the neck of her own gray. Ian felt a little surge of pleasure at the sight of her, then shame. Where she was concerned, he knew he was not quite rational. His mind played little tricks—he would say to himself: *If only she were not a murderess...*

But, of course, she was. Her own words condemned her. She may have told Gwen it was self-defense, but the first day they'd met she'd admitted that she hadn't been wrongly accused.

Why, of all the women he'd encountered since Marjory's death, had he become infatuated with this one? There *had* been other women, though they'd wanted him far more than he had wanted them. Claire would've married him if he'd asked her. And Brigit, the redhead from the BBC, had been so hot to get him in her bed that her determination quenched his own desire. Perhaps he just knew less of women than he'd thought. He hadn't been a virgin when he married, but neither had his bachelor days been a chase. Marjory had been his first love. His only love. The only woman who had stirred his lust. Until now...

"Ian," Rolf said. "I'll put up your horse. You can go with Owain and collect our share of the meat."

Ian would've preferred to groom the horses. Watching a butcher work was not his idea of entertainment, but to remain meant being alone with Jemma and the discomfort of making unstrained conversation. He told Rolf, "You've a deal." He nodded at Jemma and said good afternoon as if he hadn't seen her yet today.

In the end, he found himself alone with her. Owain asked him to bring her some of the meat, and there was no gracious way to refuse. Ty and Maura were away. Ian found Jemma in her dispensary, the little arbor in Ty's garden.

Though she tried to hide it from him, her brimming eyes and reddened nose gave her away. She'd been crying. He had never, before, seen her show any sign of weakness and it was unnerving. He felt an alarm he tried to keep from sounding in his voice. "What's wrong?"

"Nothing."

"You're crying!"

She squeezed her lower lip between her teeth. He waited. Finally, she said, "So?"

He kept waiting.

"These people are so amazing," she told him, finally. "They say prayers for the animals they kill. So their spirits will be reborn."

It was not what he expected.

17 ebrill

Having been convinced that his new apprentice could handle horse-shoeing, Gof took the day off. Ian had the smithy to himself and he kept it to himself using Gof's tactic of scowling at would-be watchers. Two farmers left horses to be shod, and Ty requested some simple hinges for the door of a shed he was building, so Ian had work enough. But as he waited for the iron to heat, he had time to ponder his predicament.

His life in the village could have been quite pleasant, but there was always a tension between come or go, fight or passively resist, believe or disbelieve. Most days his conflicting emotions fought themselves to a standstill, and he was immobilized. And he often felt an urge to put hands on Jemma, to throttle or savagely kiss her, to pummel her or drag her off to his bed. The latter was the most debilitating impulse of all. A woman he loathed.

At such times he found himself missing Marjory. He could have talked things out with her. She would have been delighted with the novelty of the village. She would have found some sensible way to settle the dilemma.

His children he missed slightly less. It came to him, at odd times, that the uncertainty of his fate must be driving them mad. He hoped, for their peace of mind, that they'd assumed him dead. They'd deal with the pleasant shock if he reappeared.

If! Was he beginning to believe Jemma? Was he truly caught forever in another time? Everything confirmed it, and logic could provide no other explanation for the perfection of the illusion. *Illusion?*

He took a horseshoe from the heat and rested it on his anvil. The iron was glowing red and yielded like plasticene when he struck it. That was how they were shaping him, heating him with rage and beating him, with gentle blows, to the form they wanted. When he started to resist, they would thrust him back into the furnace.

"Ian, Jemma wants you." Rowena stood back and called. She was afraid to come near the smithy, afraid both of the smith's curse and the tongue-lashing he gave anyone who displeased him. Gof had banished all children save his own from a ten-meter radius around the premises. While she waited for Ian to answer, Rowena peered around as if expecting a troll.

Ian paused and dropped the shoe he was pounding in the fire, and wiped the sweat from his face. "Is someone dying?"

"That's a silly question. Of course not!"

"Then tell her I'm busy."

Rowena's eyes widened.

The pigpens lay against the oppidium's outer wall, on the lee side of the hill fort. The morning breeze had died of heat prostration, and *muget du cochon* hung on the air like an olfactory boundary warning.

As with any work Jemma did outside the privacy of Ty's garden, this project had attracted an audience, including Gwen and Rowena. The group parted to let Ian through, and he could see that the pens contained two sows, bedded on straw, imminently ready to farrow. They were not the placid darlings of parish fairs, but beasts only a generation or so removed from dangerous wild animals. One of them was squeezed into a narrow chute that looked like two board and batten doors placed parallel to each other. A yoke-like affair, at one end, kept the sow from moving forward or turning her head more than a few centimeters. She was prevented from backing out by stout poles fixed behind her rump and hocks. Her captivity was mitigated by pannage and water within reach, and she seemed only mildly alarmed by what was going on around her.

The pig's owner was leaning down to drape a sopping blanket over her—a good idea in the heat. The man's name was Moch. He was large, and as solid as lean pork. His fat face and small, close-set eyes made him look as much like a pig as a human could. His slovenly personal hygiene made a splendid argument for the contention that people take on the characteristics of those they live with.

Jemma sat on a stump near the captive pig, looking like a dignitary who's been kept waiting, and she seemed to be trying to get herself in hand. Her instruments were laid out nearby. Before Ian could say anything, she said, "I can't operate without at least six buttons, and you have the only ones in the village."

She spoke English, so he answered her in English. "Surely, you're jesting." Jemma shook her head. "You're going to perform surgery on a pig?"

"You haven't met a veterinary surgeon hereabouts, have you?"

"With shirt buttons?"

"Please! You can have them back as soon as the pig heals."

The situation suddenly seemed so absurd that Ian had to laugh. He couldn't even muster a shard of anger over Jemma's assumption that he'd volunteer his property for the well-being of a pig.

"You're going to sew buttons on a pig?! Haha. Hahaha."

"Ian," Rowena demanded. "What's so funny?"

Ian laughed again and translated; "The doctor wants to sew my buttons on that pig."

"What's buttons?"

"This…" Ian plucked at the one in the center of his shirt front.

"What's funny about that?"

Ian laughed again, this time at himself. They thought Jemma was a goddess, and so, of course, nothing she did would seem absurd to them.

Jemma said, "Well, Inspector?"

Ian gave up. He shrugged, then unbuttoned his shirt and

tossed it to her.

She thanked him. She removed the buttons, dropping them into a cup near her instruments, and returned the shirt. "You can go back to what you were doing, Inspector. Rowena will assist with this."

He nodded, but remained, curious to see what she would do with the buttons.

She took a tiny amount of white powder from a polyethylene package and mixed it with a clear fluid in a small glass vial. The white powder and its packaging looked familiar. Ian said, "What is it?"

Jemma seemed annoyed, then resigned. Without any obvious sarcasm, she said, "A local anesthetic."

Ian moistened the tip of his finger and touched it to the powder. The taste, when he touched the finger with his tongue, was familiar. "Cocaine!"

"That's right, Inspector." As she spoke, she drew the solution from the vial into a syringe. "A perfectly acceptable local anesthetic, which has the advantage of an indefinite shelf life."

Ian could feel the muscles of his jaws tensing.

Jemma nodded at Moch, who moved around to the sow's head and took hold of her snout and left ear. Jemma walked around to the right side of the pig, saying, in English, "They don't know the potential for abuse, here…" She took hold of the animal's ear and began to inject it with the cocaine. "…And *I'm* not going to mention it."

Looking at the sow's ear, which seemed to have been inflated with a tyre pump, Ian forgot to reply. The sow kept trying to shake her head while Jemma worked, and did shake it when Jemma'd finished and Moch let go of her head.

"What's wrong with it?" Ian asked.

"A haematoma," Jemma said. "That's self-perpetuating. Every time she shakes her head, she starts internal bleeding in the ear, and the resulting blood clot pushes the skin out and prevents it from adhering to the underlying structures. Rowena, scalpel and sponges, please."

"So why not sew it together?"

"That's what I'm doing." Jemma made an incision in the skin on the top of the pig's ear and pressed on the ear. A large clot of dark blood squeezed out. "The buttons will prevent the sutures from tearing through the skin when she shakes her head." She made a small hole three centimeters from the incision and said, "Drain." Rowena handed Jemma a dripping piece of string that she fished from the cup Jemma had dropped Ian's buttons into. Jemma squeezed out the excess liquid and threaded the string in through the hole and out through the incision, which she sutured all but closed around the string. She tied the two ends of the string together, saying, "So much for the drain." Then she proceeded to "quilt" the ear together by sewing the buttons on it in pairs, one on top, the second underneath, connected through the ear by a suture.

Ian walked away thinking the performance well worth the six-button price of admission. Now he *had* seen it all!

18 ebrill

Since his arrival in the village, Ian had been watching Houel take on all comers at *fidchel*, a game similar to chess in its employment of strategy, but played with pegs instead of chessmen. It was Ian's understanding that only Drullwyn had ever beaten him. Ian watched Owain's mistakes and Rolf's debacles until he thought he had the gist and, one noonday, he got Houel to agree to a match.

They set the board on a low table in front of Houel's house and took their places on stools opposite each other. The game took all afternoon. People drifted by, stopped to watch, wandered away, returned. The shadows beneath them slipped eastward. Each player had the other in check half a dozen times, but neither would concede.

As they played, Gwen and Jemma sat nearby watching. Jemma was embroidering a shirt, Gwen grinding oats. Rowena came along with a comb and watched the game for a while, then said, "Mama, will you help me?"

"With which hand?" Gwen said. "Ask Jemma."

"Jemma?" Rowena said, shyly.

Jemma put down her sewing. "I'd be delighted."

As Jemma combed her hair, Rowena fingered the shirt she'd been stitching. "What words do you say to make such a pretty design?"

"I pray that the wearer will prosper and be content with his life."

"And be fearless in battle?"

Out of the corner of his eye, Ian could see Jemma nod.

"You ought to make one of these for Ian," Rowena said. She spoke louder than she needed to. Ian caught Houel sneaking a glance at the girl, but he didn't comment.

Jemma seemed to be trying to not smirk. "You think he needs one?"

"I'll say. It's almost indecent how he dresses."

Ian felt himself blush.

Houel quickly dropped his eyes to hide his laughter, but he couldn't control the shaking of his shoulders. Ian took the opportunity afforded by the interruption to checkmate.

"A good tactic," Houel said, when he'd had time to study his defeat. "Having your womenfolk create a diversion."

"Oh, they don't create diversions," Ian told him. "But, I'll grant you, they are diverting."

19 ebrill

After fitful sleep punctuated by the sporadic barking of dogs, Ian awoke unrested. When he came to breakfast, he thought Rolf and Gwen must've had a fight, for he was gone and she was out of sorts. Rowena had the edgy look of a child in the middle of the wrong things, but neither she nor her mother would say what was happening. Ian ate quickly and went to search out Rolf.

Rolf's horse was gone and Jemma's was as well. Ian wondered if their going together was the cause of the tension he'd sensed in Gwen and Rowena. He caught and bridled his mare and asked one of the sentries which way they'd gone. He tried to tell by the signs how long ago they'd passed, going how fast, though the sentry had told him some time ago and at a walk. Jemma was leading. The larger prints of her horse's feet were overstepped by the smaller hoof prints of Rolf's pony. Ian kicked his mare into a canter and made up some of their lead as the trail passed from the farm fields into pasture.

Overhead, the inverted bowl of sky was bright blue, fading to nearly white at the horizons. The greening of the land was a commonplace miracle he hadn't taken notice of in years—not since Marjory's death. He hadn't let himself feel the wonder and rebirth spring engendered. The early sun transformed the meadows he passed through into fields of blue diamonds. And one could hyperventilate trying to breathe in enough of the morning air to memorize the aroma.

The track crossed a small stream and forked into the forest to the north and west. A scratch on a half-buried stone in the trail and a silver thread from the tail of Jemma's mare pointed to the north fork. The hoof prints confirmed it as the track crossed a small clearing and the grass bent northward, pointing their direction. Beyond the clearing, in the cool wood, dew still dampened the undergrowth and underfooting. Sunlight showed through incomplete canopies of emerging leaves and glinted off new foliage. The horse's hoof beats were soft thuds, and thought was unimpeded by extraneous noise.

Ian considered the problem at hand. Rolf wasn't the sort he'd imagined Jemma would fancy. Houel was more her type.

Lord, Carreg, he thought. *A woman goes riding with a man and you've got her sleeping with him. It's unfair, at the very least. You wouldn't touch her if she'd have you, but let another man show interest…*

God help me, I'm besotted. Thank God they can't read minds. But what else would they be doing out together? Learning to hunt? Hunting for medicinals? Consulting their writers?

He had to know. He urged the horse faster.

He thought they both looked guilty, when he found them, or unhappy, which is nearly the same—but Rolf could not resist a glance backward, toward where they'd come from. Ian couldn't stop the "What've you been up to?" and he didn't need to hear Rolf's unconvincing, "Nothing." He kicked his mare, pushing between Rolf and Jemma, forcing Rolf's smaller horse off the track.

"Wait!" Jemma insisted. "Where are you going?"

He ignored her.

The trail widened into another tiny meadow whose grass was bent, coming and going, almost to the far side. A small white bundle under a little tree seemed to mark the turning point of their journey. Ian raced Jemma for it, and his mare almost trampled it as he pulled her up. He backed the horse up so fast he almost brought her to the ground, swarming off of her, then shooing her away. She skittered off, reins trailing. Jemma reined in and dismounted, letting her horse follow Ian's.

Ian ignored her. As he turned his attention to the prize, he felt the sort of sickening shock he imagined a man might feel who's discovered his best friend is a murderer.

A naked, newborn infant lay on a square of linen beneath the tree, wedged between something under the cloth that prevented any movement to his sides. His tiny face scrunched tight as a fist—all wailing mouth and wrinkles—and his tiny arms flailed uselessly. Flies had gathered on the child's umbilicus.

The dreadful ratchet of his cry struck at Ian's innards. He whirled on Jemma and demanded, "What deviltry is this? Who's caring for this child?" He spoke English. He was too disturbed to play the game.

Rolf pulled his horse up behind Jemma, who translated Ian's question.

"He's in the hands of the gods," Rolf said.

Ian waited for Jemma's answer.

She seemed nonplussed for the first time since he'd met her. She answered, finally, in English. "Turn him over."

Ian wasn't sure how to handle the child. He hadn't held an infant since his daughter was small. He knelt down and reached under the cloth and removed the rags that formed the wedges holding the child. Holding the small body through the cloth, he rolled it over on its face.

The infant convulsed with spasms of pain. Its anguished cries set Ian's every nerve on edge, and his brain refused to interpret what his eyes beheld. A knot of grayish tissue, the size of a walnut, bulged from the child's spine. And Ian noticed for the first time that his legs weren't moving.

Jemma said softly, "Spina bifida. There's a very high incidence among the Celts. Nothing can be done for it."

"But…"

"It's customary, here, to take the victim somewhere the dogs won't find him and let him die quickly of exposure."

"My God! You're a doctor!" He wasn't sure why it surprised him. A woman who'd kill her lover in cold blood wouldn't hesitate to commit infanticide, especially if it involved no more action than neglect.

"In a modern hospital, with the best pediatric surgeons, he'd have a chance to live. Not here. I *can't* help him."

Ian was speechless.

"This is the best way. The kindest, short of slitting his throat."

"Why *don't* you just slit his throat?"

"I can't!" She seemed distressed. "This is their way!"

"It's barbaric!"

"Is it any more barbaric than subjecting him to numerous painful operations that would—at best—leave him crippled, and at worst a human vegetable?"

"You can't know that."

"I know that in this place—whatever you believe it to be—there is no remedy for spina bifida, no medication, no surgical procedure that can do anything but prolong his suffering."

"You're a surgeon!"

"Not a miracle worker." She seemed to grasp his great frustration, for she said, more gently, "Under conditions here, it's impossible."

He turned to Rolf and switched to Celtic. "She could fix it!"

Rolf looked sharply at Jemma.

"Perhaps I could save his life," Jemma told him, "but he would be a monster, not a whole, sound person. I couldn't enable him to grow normally, to bear arms, to win a wife or father children. He might survive. He might even make a bard or teacher, but he would never walk or ride or have control of his bowels or bladder." Jemma was on the verge of tears and seemed almost ashamed. Ian found he was convinced of her sincerity and could see that Rolf was also.

Rolf turned to him. "Put him back where he was." He saw that this wasn't acceptable. He said, gently, "Does he not have an immortal spirit?"

"Yes, but…"

"Then why do you grudge it the chance to be reborn in an undamaged body? If he cannot do any of the things we live for, why should he live? Wouldn't it be better for him to start over, better, even, to live as a whole dog or rabbit than a damaged man?"

"No!"

Rolf shrugged.

"What about the child's mother? Surely she didn't abandon him willingly?"

"It's our way to accept what we cannot change."

"She'll take him back." He picked up the child and wrapped him quickly in the cloth, then he started to go around Rolf, toward the horses.

Rolf quickly stepped in front of him. "No!" He seemed to realize the rage his defiance kindled in Ian, for he added, quickly, "You'll have to kill me before I let you take him back. Mathe has suffered enough."

Shock brought Ian up. Mathe was his dead brother's wife, this child his nephew! And Rolf hadn't stood up to him since the first time they met, so his determination was more daunting than armed resistance would have been. Ian didn't understand it. He looked at Jemma and found no help. She'd crossed her arms and was hugging herself, but she, too, stood between him and the horses.

He felt suddenly hopeless. "I can't just leave him…"

"Stay with him if it comforts you," Jemma said. "This once. You'll see the wisdom of the custom."

The baby whimpered with pain as the linen rubbed tissues meant to be enclosed in tubes of bone.

Jemma rummaged around in her shoulder bag and brought out a small flask, which she handed to Ian. "You might need this."

"What is it?"

"A few drops will act as a sedative, a little more a general anesthetic. An overdose depresses the central nervous system and causes death."

He discovered, after they left, that it was mead. He swallowed quite a bit of it before he could bring himself to give any to the child—only enough to still its cries—and he was painfully aware it was his own discomfort he was easing.

When dusk came, he sat at the base of the small tree and wrapped them both tightly in his cloak.

20 ebrill

I

He woke with a start to the familiar agony of muscles locked by cold. He moved tentatively and winced. The small body on his lap, at first, brought Charles to mind. But Charles was always warm. The infant was cold and still. He'd relaxed his vigilance and Death had stolen in.

He felt profoundly sad, and discouraged. He felt as abandoned as the child. *Who will mourn my passing?* He wasn't unaware that it was his own losses he mourned most. Power. Family. Home. Work. Purpose.

Still, the child is, was, would be—if Rolf was right—a human being and deserved a human burial. Its face, relaxed by the cessation of pain, looked like an old man's who'd died in his sleep. As if he'd lived a full lifetime.

Ian looked around. The sky was a flat, uniform gray. Swollen clouds to the southwest hinted at great quantities of water. There was no sun. Mist had settled on the shoulders of the forest and drifted down between the trees. The woods were empty save for himself and the gray horse. There was nothing to suggest that men had ever been there. It needs a churchyard, he thought, and some small monument—even a faceless stone—to mark the grave. He knew the nearest he would come, here, to a churchyard was Nemeton.

He put the tiny corpse down while he relieved himself and caught the mare. He had to mount from a fallen tree trunk, with care for the tiny body and for his own too mortal bones.

The mist, condensing on the upper branches of the trees, dripped down and stained the gray trunks black, painted the lichens jade and turquoise. Lilies of the valley rang where bluebells had carpeted the forest floor a month earlier and tiny fringes of bronze-green flowers replaced the bare crowns on the oaks, but Nemeton was otherwise as he remembered it. Solemn and awfully quiet. He threw a leg over the horse's neck and slid off, leaving her, with reins trailing, to graze near the track while he entered the sacred grove on foot.

He laid the tiny corpse on the grass and used his knife to scoop a hollow among the roots of a giant oak. He hacked off the end of his cloak, and used it to line the grave. Then he curled the child into the fetal position in the hollow and covered the body with the free end of the cloth. As he pushed the earth back in the hole, he found himself reciting the chant from his childhood with which his Welsh Gran had consigned beloved pets to earth: "Ashes to ashes, dust to dust, flesh to earth, and iron to rust."

After he'd rolled the largest stone he could find over the grave to mark it and protect it from animals, he poured out a libation from Jemma's flask for the spirits of the place. He wasn't sure why. He didn't believe in spirits. He had not been a believer since his youth, but he was an observer of convention. Ritual gave the mind direction when it was too numb with joy or grief to function. And the ritual was a comfort.

II

Drullwyn was sitting cross-legged on the grass by Ian's mare when he returned to her. "What have you done with the child?"

"I buried him," Ian said, nodding toward the grove.

Drullwyn nodded. He didn't fit the part. He looked more like Sir Alec Guinness as Obi-Wan Kenobi than the villains of Roman report. "That is not our custom," he said, "but I doubt the gods will be offended." He was wearing trousers. The effect was as if the local vicar had traded his Roman collar for a set of hunting pinks. He noticed Ian staring and said, "The robes of my office are not suited to riding." That made Ian look for his horse. The gray mare grazing near Ian's own was the best horse he'd seen in the village barring Houel's stallion.

Drullwyn held out a hand; Ian automatically helped him to his feet. The druid caught his horse and waited next to it. Ian found himself lacing his fingers together to give the older man an assist. It brought back the day he'd met Rolf, nearly a month ago.

A month already!

He wondered how his children were doing. It had taken a year for Margaret to speak of her mother without tears. Peter never spoke of her, though Susannah, who hadn't known Marjory long enough to know her well, had said Peter was only just getting over it. He tried to remember how he'd felt a month after his father died, but that had been too long ago.

Drullwyn swung stiffly onto the horse and gathered up her reins. Ian was surprised. The older man had never shown signs of disability before. He patted Ian's shoulder. "Come break your fast with me, and you can tell me what's troubling you."

"I've already told everyone in this bloody place what's troubling me—I want to go home!"

Drullwyn shook his head. "That is between you and Epona." He glanced at the sky. "It will rain soon. We'd better get going."

Ian caught his mare. There was nothing close at hand to mount her from, so he used the child's trick of jumping up two-handed to heave himself, face down, across her back and balance in that undignified position while he dragged a leg over her rump. The mare stood patiently until he'd collected himself. "Untrue," he said, finally, as if there had not just been a long pause in the conversation and a change of subject. "I've been told several times that I can't leave without an escort."

Drullwyn pantomimed looking for Ian's escort. When Ian refused to respond, he sighed and said, "Epona told me that among your people, you have a weapon that throws thunderbolts. But since you did not bring this weapon to our land, you are helpless here.

She asked that we detain you until you have learned our ways and made alliances that will protect you. If you demand a judgment, I will require her to show on what authority." With another glance at the sky, Drullwyn kicked his horse into a canter. Ian's mare followed. The easy gait swallowed up the distance. The still, saturated air condensed in the distance to a soft haze that eased the contours of the valley and mitigated the stark blackness of the tree-clad hills above. To the southeast, the hill fort rose out of its surrounding farmlands, no longer the fairy-castle of a month earlier. It should have conveyed romantic images of love and valor, but Ian felt only an anticipation of comfort—both its physical amenities and the emotional insulation of friendship. And there was Jemma…

Recognition was as shocking as the great drops of rain that fell faster and closer together until a curtain of water closed between Ian and the view. Long before they reached the gates of Drullwyn's farmstead, they were soaked.

Servants and acolytes opened the gates as they approached. Without a word from Drullwyn, his people led the steaming horses to shelter.

Drullwyn walked slowly through the falling water, his earlier stiffness gone or, Ian suspected, hidden from his inferiors. Ian curbed his own urge to hurry. He could not get any wetter. The house they approached was as large as a barn, circular with eight gables—facing the four directions and the four points in between. It was sided with vertical planks that had weathered silver-gray and were stained charcoal gray where the rain hit. Each gable had a small, shuttered opening, just under the ridge that was blackened by smoke and all but the east facing gable wall had a shuttered window. The east wall of the house was dominated by a double-door entrance beneath a massive lintel. Doors and lintel were ornamented with bas-relief carvings of boars, horses, dragons and several varieties of birds. The doors opened noiselessly as they approached, and were closed behind them.

Compared to the houses of the villagers, the interior of the spacious house was brightly lit. Windows in the gable ends of the leeward side were all open, admitting rain-gray daylight, and oil lamps burned in the recesses of the windward side. Flagstones covered the floor and were, in turn, covered by wool rugs and wild animal skins. The interior walls were plastered with white lime, and the hearth was ringed with square-cut stones and roofed over with a funnel-shaped sheet of bronze that formed a primitive chimney below the roof. Smoke ultimately escaped through the shuttered openings, below the gable ridges, which could be closed during inclement weather. Drullwyn motioned Ian to stand near the coal fire glowing in the hearth, and servants moved quickly to remove their wet clothing and provide dry robes. They sat on a rug near the fire and a man set a low table before them. A young woman Ian had never seen before brought them bowls of hot mutton soup. Drullwyn introduced her as his wife, Llynda. She was young enough to be his daughter, but her eyes followed the old man with unconcealed idolatry. She spoke quietly to the servants, and they brought bread and butter and cheese, dried fruit and fresh greens. The best restaurants in London had never served anything so good! Ian remembered Jemma's flask and sent a servant to fetch it from among his things. Without being asked, Llynda set two cups on the table, then vanished. Ian poured mead in the cups.

"To creature comforts," he said, and drank.

Drullwyn nodded and tasted the wine.

"This is very good."

They ate and drank the rest in silence. The servants cleared the table and brought fresh water and bread soaked in honey. Over the dessert, Drullwyn said, "Alf told me that he was being slain by outcasts when Epona appeared and frightened them away with thunder and lightning. He knew her for what she was by her horses. Then you appeared, in your strange clothes. But he couldn't guess your identity. Nor can I. People tell me you ask questions, in all seriousness, that would embarrass a child and you speak with Rowena as an equal. Yet you assist Epona with her magic. What am I to make of you?" Ian said nothing. "There is some talk that you're Gofannon, the god of smiths, but I think you're a teacher like myself."

"And they say *you* know about things before they happen."

"The birds and animals, and people's actions tell me something has died," Drullwyn said. "I leave it to my eyes and ears to tell me what, and to my wits and experience to tell me why."

"That's not what I've heard."

"In the absence of facts, people become quite inventive."

"Hmpf. What do your wits and experience tell you about my chances of ever seeing my family again?"

The old man raised his eyebrows. "A wife? Young children?"

"Dead. Grown."

Drullwyn nodded as if he understood. "Ah, grandchildren." He sounded sad.

I will never see my grandchild! Ian felt tears welling and remembered Marjory telling him, once, that women cry for rage as well as grief. Now he knew why.

Drullwyn was saying, "It's in the hands of the gods."

How comforting the gods were. Anything beyond one's control, any failure or anything neglected or overlooked could be laid at their feet—even neglect or oversight must be their work.

He must have been shaking; Drullwyn said, "What is it you fear?"

"What makes you ask that? As a matter of fact, I was more angry than anything, just now."

"Can you deny that fear and anger are twins joined at the heart?"

Ian felt he'd been invited to draw an obvious conclusion, but to draw it of his own free will. He said, "No."

"Ah, then you can discover where your rage gives way to fear?"

"Fear has nothing to do with it. Wouldn't anyone be angry who was forcibly taken from his home...*And kin,* and made to accompany a stranger to an alien place, forced to accept *barbarous* customs?"

The druid shrugged. "Say you are slave to your destiny. Accept what you cannot change."

It was there again—the fatalism that, to his modern sensibilities, seemed so absurd.

• • •

The rain ceased, and by the time they finished their discussion, Drullwyn's people had dried Ian's clothes and replaced his wet saddle blanket with a dry one. Changed and mounted, he thanked Llynda, who'd come out to see him off. She invited him to return. Drullwyn mounted his mare and personally escorted Ian to the boundary of his lands where a herd of rain-wet horses grazed. Most of the animals were sleek and fat, and they sat for a time discussing the virtues of this animal and that.

"But there's one that does you no credit." Ian pointed to a bay mare that was little more than a skeleton. The way the animal stood—head down, heaving for air—made him think it afflicted with the equine equivalent of emphysema. The horse was standing as if she'd been running hard. "It'd be kinder to put her down."

Drullwyn nodded. "I would, but I took her in payment for a judgment from a man for whom she was too dear a price. To destroy her would be to devalue his payment and my counsel. Besides, she'll foal in a month, if she lives, and the foal might survive. It's in the hands of the gods."

21 ebrill

Rumor—in the person of one of Drullwyn's bondsmen—
interrupted breakfast to report that he and his fellows had had to
drive a herd of wild pigs from the sacred grove. Rolf, of course,
immediately changed the program for the day, and he and Ian
were soon mounted and armed, and off in search of Owain.
Moch, the pig keeper, insisted on joining them, but as four was
an "inauspicious number" they invited Pyrs and Joess, and Pyrs's
younger brother along to bring the group to seven. The hunters
brought along nets to catch the little pigs and spears to get the big
ones, and left Clyfar home because the game was too dangerous to
risk an inexperienced dog. The three canines they did bring were
scarred veterans, but by the time they'd located the swine, one of the
dogs had disappeared. Rolf and Owain were uneasy. "Not a good
omen," they kept repeating.

The remaining canines, a dog and bitch, cut the boar out of the
herd, and Moch drove the sows and piglets off in the direction the
missing dog had taken. Dogs and hunters cornered the boar against
a little dirt embankment in a small clearing. The beast was half-again
as big as the next largest of its tribe and made itself seem larger by
lifting its back hairs as it filled the air with its appalling squeals.

The dogs attacked. The men dismounted and sent the horses
off a safe distance with the boy. Then they advanced on foot,
spears ready.

The fearsome snarling of the dogs joined the pigs' squeals; the
smell of blood mingled with the odors of pig and dog, and with the
smell of fear. The grass was quickly churned to bloody mud.

The boar tossed the bitch aside. She rolled—a ball of wiry fur—until she thumped against the base of a tree and lay still. Instantly, the boar had the dog by the skin of its throat and was shaking it, tearing the throat. Joess cursed the pig and charged it, but his spear glanced off its leathery flank. It caused no more damage than a shallow, bloody furrow, burying itself in the blood-soaked ground. Before Joess could free it, the boar dropped the dog and turned its fury on him. Joess jumped backward but failed to notice the recovered bitch crossing behind him. He tripped. The boar caught his leg and tore into the flesh of his calf. Skin and underlying tissue ripped as Joess kicked the beast away. He scrabbled backward on his rump, with the boar pacing his retreat, climbing in his lap to savage his inner thigh. Joess doubled up and pressed his hands defensively over his privates.

In what seemed like slow motion, Rolf jammed his spear into the animal's ribcage. With like deliberation, Owain circled and rammed his spear at its heart.

The beast writhed and coughed, showering the hunters with a froth of bloody saliva. Its feet thrashed the body of its victim. It bathed him in blood as it whirled from side to side, trying to dislodge the spears, clacking tusks against the hardwood shafts.

With horrifying slowness, Ian rammed his own spear in where he judged the boar's kidneys to be and pumped on the shaft. The rage he felt had overcome his earlier reluctance to take life. The beast tried to turn on him, but was constrained by the spears protruding from its sides, by the men thrusting them deeper. Then Pyrs, who was trying to skewer the pig without striking a fellow, managed to find its haunch with his point. The pig screeched more furiously as it was again prevented from turning on its tormentor.

The four men, of one accord, began to draw the pig backward off its victim. The bitch sank her teeth into the haunch opposite Pyrs and tugged as well. The boar's movements slowed, and it lost ground as its life-blood showered out over Joess from wounds and mouth and nostrils. The hunters cursed it in unison. They called on Cernunnos to take its life—even Ian prayed.

The shaft of Pyrs's spear snapped off with a crack like a shot. The beast gave a small leap forward and collapsed—a quivering heap of pork—across Joess. Rolf and Owain quickly put feet against the body and withdrew their spears, Rolf barking at Ian to do the same. Then they scrambled to roll the carcass off the boy. The pig's body was greasy with blood and filth, and they wasted precious seconds trying to get a hold.

Joess lay very still. The weight that had knocked the breath out of him seemed to have crushed his very will to breathe, but a crimson fountain springing from his inner thigh spurted and ebbed with the pulsing of his heart. The Celts were immobilized by the damage.

"Rolf!" Ian said, "Put something on that wound. Quickly!"

"He's dead," Rolf said, surprised.

"He bloody well will be! Wipe your hand clean and press down on that wound. Now!"

That got to him. He wiped his right palm on his trousers and placed it gingerly over the gusher.

"Harder," Ian snapped.

Rolf pressed harder.

Ian, meanwhile, wiped the blood and mire from the youth's face and, pinching his nostrils shut, began to blow air into his mouth. Joess's chest rose and fell. Ian began to feel giddy. As he wondered how long he could keep it up, Joess coughed and began breathing on his own. The awed Celts mumbled to one another.

Ian felt profound relief. "Pyrs," he said, "go tell Jemma what happened so she can get ready."

Pyrs nodded, grimly, and charged at the boy who had crept as close as he dared with the six plunging, skittish horses. "I'll get Drullwyn, too," Pyrs shouted as he sped off at horse-killing speed.

Ian raised Joess's eyelids and noted, with satisfaction, that the pupils contracted. If they could keep the bleeding checked, Jemma might be able to save his life.

Suddenly, the clearing was pandemonium. Moch reappeared with the missing dog and the balance of the pig tribe in a frenzy of noise and a roiling mass of smooth pork and wiry dog meat. Rolf,

Owain and Ian roared their disapproval in unison. Rolf crouched over the injured man and did his best to protect himself and Joess from flying feet and flailing tusks. Ian grabbed the shaft of Pyrs's broken spear and swung it like a cricket bat, scattering bodies in every direction. Then the herd coalesced on the far side of the clearing, and the turbulence subsided as they leaked away among the trees, washing Moch and the bloody dogs away with them.

The sudden quiet mocked the still form at the center of concern, the cold, white body.

"Owain!" Ian demanded. "A stretcher! Boy," he told the horse handler, "get those horses upwind of the blood!"

Owain nodded and hurried to comply as the boy struggled with their mounts. Ian began to strip his shirt and vest off to make bandages…

Everyone in the village who owned a riding horse seemed to have come out to meet them. Houel led the rescue party himself. He quietly assessed the situation, then sent men to retrieve the dead boar and help Moch round up the surviving pigs. The stretcher Rolf and Owain had rigged was transferred to fresh horses, and blankets were piled on the bloody shirts Ian had put over Joess to keep him warm.

The procession that continued grimly toward the hill fort had a funereal air that didn't diminish when Drullwyn met it, near the display of severed heads, and pronounced Joess, "In the hands of the gods."

Ian, quite naturally, demanded a second opinion. Jemma would have the last word. For all the animosity he bore her, Ian would still trust his life to her skill as a surgeon. Even here.

The funereal procession followed the stretcher to Ty's garden, where a door had been fetched and set up as a table. Jemma's instruments, alcohol, plastic tubing, glucose solution and needles were laid out on a linen-covered bench. A dozen kettles of water stood at hand, cooling. The villagers found the preparations fascinating, but Houel quickly ordered all bystanders away. He took up a position at the head of the operating table and demanded to know what he should do to help. "Pray," Jemma told him.

She started an IV before beginning the difficult repairs, and spent most of the next hours cleaning dirt from the wounds before suturing them. Ian assisted.

Jemma wiped her gloved hands on her apron and sent Houel to ask his wife for more linen to use for bandages. Ian's feeling that the boy was doomed was subsiding, and he complimented the doctor on her workman-like job.

She looked grim. "He'll probably die anyway. He needs blood, and no one else here has his type. You don't happen to have O-negative, do you?"

"I do, as a matter of fact." Obviously, she knew it—as she knew so much else about him, but it was apparent she'd be willing to let the boy die if he didn't volunteer. It grated to be forced to capitulate again. He looked at her. "Well?"

She frowned as she thought about it, then brightened. "If we dope you up with anticoagulant and transfuse directly, he may have a chance."

Maura was sent to make willow bark tea while Rolf and Ty fetched another door. Ian stretched himself out on it with a familiar apprehension. Jemma tied a tourniquet around his biceps and scrubbed the inside of his elbow joint before threading a needle into the vein there.

He had donated blood before. At this point, in that past experience, the sister taped the needle to his arm and allowed the blood to flow down the tube into the collection vessel. Jemma had no tape. She took a length of homemade bandage and wrapped the tube and needle against his arm, tucking the loose ends under the wrap to hold them. Instead of a collecting vessel, she attached the other end of the tube to a needle in Joess's arm. When Jemma was satisfied that things were proceeding on schedule, she spoke in English.

"The trick is knowing when to stop it. We've no way of measuring the flow." She smiled wryly. "And we don't want to exsanguinate our donor."

"Why not collect it in that empty glucose packet?"

"I've run out of anti-coagulant. There's a huge chance of clots with this method, but less than if it's allowed to pool."

They watched together in silence as his blood flowed into Joess. He began to feel light-headed, then to feel nothing…

22 ebrill

For a moment, when he awoke, he was home. Saturday morning. Sleeping in, with Charles curled against his feet.

But then the smoky odor of Rolf's house brought him back, and the warm body at his feet grew to Clyfar's proportions. A small, cool hand settled on his face.

"Ian?" Rowena whispered.

When he opened his eyes, he thought she seemed relieved. "You're not going to die?"

"Just sleep," he told her. And he did.

The second cool hand that awoke him belonged to Jemma. He felt it on his face, then on his wrist before he opened his eyes.

She smiled.

When he tried to sit, she stopped him with a firm hand on his chest. "You've given more than the usual pint, Inspector. Please take it easy."

He knew that his surprise showed.

"A waste," she added. She looked exhausted.

"He died?"

"No. But the prognosis is very poor. He still hasn't enough hemoglobin by half and there'll almost certainly be complications." She sounded so discouraged that he stared at her.

"In other words, it's in God's hands?" It must be hard for her, he thought, to relinquish control. Even to God.

"So it would seem. Although Drullwyn's decided he might have a chance after all, and he's leading the cheering section. If Joess dies, it won't be for lack of prayer."

"Then I suggest, Doctor, that you take your own advice and get some rest."

She gave him a fleeting, dazzling smile and was gone before he could think of what to make of it.

Later, when the need to visit the latrine drove Ian from his bed, he stopped at the carpenter's house to look in on the boy. He was pale but still breathing steadily.

Ian thought about Jemma's confession. She'd taken more than a pint of his blood—a curious malpractice, yet apart from a slight headache and the odd giddy fit, he hadn't suffered any harm.

24 ebrill

For two days, Jemma responded to questions about Joess's prognosis with, "We'll see."

On the third day, she ventured that he'd live.

25 ebrill

Traders came the day Ian slept in. The aromas of wood smoke and porridge woke him, and the need to void drove him from his bed. The morning was foggy and damp. Ian cursed his unknown captors as he made his way toward the midden hole. Surely inadequate plumbing could be seen as a form of torture and was prohibited by Geneva Convention rules. He limbered up as he walked back to the house, swinging his arms vigorously and pausing to stretch his hamstrings.

Rowena was waiting impatiently with his breakfast. She couldn't sit still as he poured milk and honey over his porridge.

"What's going on?" he asked. She hadn't shown so much enthusiasm last night, when they'd discussed today's program. "Has the circus arrived?"

She jumped up and down as she answered. "Traders have come."

"Oh? I didn't see any traders."

"Papa says Houel won't let them within the walls until everyone's here. In case they're treacherous."

"Sounds a sensible course."

"Papa asked me to ask you to wear your god-coat."

His suit coat that people still insisted on calling a god-coat, as if it was something of divine manufacture. They still, occasionally, made the sign against the evil eye when he wore it.

Ian shrugged. "Why not? Go get it for me?"

• • •

He missed his *Times*. He thought about it as he followed Rowena. He found himself crowding around any visitor—shepherd or trader—to hear the news. The latest had been that Prasutagus of the Iceni was gravely ill, not expected to live. The names meant nothing, but were vaguely familiar, like a forgotten history lesson. The fact was, he remembered little of ancient British history, so their efforts to flamboozle him were largely wasted. He remembered Boudicca, of course, and Cartimandua and Caratacus, and that the Catuvellauni, the Belgae and the Atrebates were tribes. But there'd been no Caesar to enliven the conquest of Britain for future students of Latin, and so his recollection of it was dim at best.

The villagers, he admitted to himself, were not the actors he'd first assumed. They were too good, too constant in their roles.

Most of them were waiting in the commons, the large clearing in the center of the village, and all the men who owned swords were wearing them—twenty, at least. Jemma, Gof and Drullwyn were the only adult residents Ian didn't see among the crowd. Obviously, visitors were an event. The weather wasn't dampening anyone's spirits.

The traders were a rag-tag lot. Ian stood between Rolf and Houel to watch them parade in. Six armed men and four armed women, two infants, and five persons—three women, a teenaged boy and an old man—who looked like poor relations. The latter were ragged and unwashed and walked between the company's two wagons. The armed members of the group were better dressed, in Celtic style—gaudy checks and tartans, swords and spears and jewelry—brooches, torcs, rings and bracelets. The women wore gold or copper earrings. A two-penny colored lot, Ian thought.

"A pity they don't have a singer," Rolf said. "We could do with some entertainment."

"No self-respecting bard would travel with this vermin," Houel told him. "Look at their horses."

The horses were bony, and shaggy with winter hair that should have been combed out. The dampness in the air had condensed on them, turning the dust of travel to thin mud. The tack looked as if it hadn't been cleaned in months.

While the others supervised the unloading of the wagons by the ragged women, the head trader extolled the virtues of his wares like a carnival barker. He had a face scarred by acne, a thin mustache, thinning brown hair and shifty eyes.

"Ian," Houel said, "you should have a new sword." He pointed to a pile of iron trading blanks—pieces of iron roughly the size and shape of a sword—spread out on hides on the ground.

Ian inspected several of the blanks and shook his head. It was not a particularly good quality iron. "If I were to spend time and energy forging a blade, I'd prefer to use material worth the effort."

Houel shrugged. He and Ian separated, as if by mutual agreement, to look at the other offerings—salt, wine in sealed amphorae, jet and glass and amber beads, needles made of iron and bronze, cloth, furs, pottery and bronze drinking vessels, as well as other articles of bronze—jewelry, brooches and horse hardware.

Then, in the bed of one of the wagons, Ian noticed a nearly naked man. Most of his body was covered with blue tattoos—stags and fabulous plants, boars, and dragons of the sort that adorned Drullwyn's wrists. The man had been beaten—yellow bruises blotched his face. His limbs were bound with heavy rope, and a metal collar around his neck was attached to the cart by a formidable chain. His body was scraped and pocked with festering sores, especially on shoulders, elbows, back, knees and heels. His hair and beard were matted and filthy. He stared defiantly at Ian but said nothing.

Ian summoned the head trader, who was followed by one of his fellows, a red-haired, red-skinned man. "What's *he* done?" Ian said.

"Stubborn bastard wouldn't walk," the head trader said. "Would've let us drag him to death." Ian noticed him eyeing his suit coat, but he didn't comment.

"But what's he done? Why is he in chains?"

Houel walked over to see what was going on, and the trader said, "You've acquired a comic since our last visit, Houel." He sobered somewhat. "Has he money, or is he just wasting our time?"

Houel seemed amused. "Why don't you ask him?"

The trader turned back to Ian. "What's your interest in this fellow, Grampa? You looking to buy? What would you *do* with him—set dogs against him?" He said to his companion, "There's something I hadn't thought of. We could charge admission."

"Not here," Houel said, sternly.

"Just a thought." The head trader turned to Ian again. "Well, Gramps?"

Ian ignored the insult. "*What has this man done?*"

"He's one of the painted people."

"That's a crime?"

"Oh, you *are* funny."

"He's serious," the second trader said. He rubbed the peeling skin on his red nose and asked Ian, "What one-eyed village are you from that you never heard of the painted people?"

"He's committed no crime?"

"He's a captive, a slave."

"A prisoner of war?"

"Exactly."

"Then he'll be treated like one!" Ian pulled his knife—a gesture both outsiders found threatening, for they stepped back and reached for their swords. Ian pointed the knife at them. "I wouldn't, if I were you."

As they looked around to see if he had any backing, Ian cut the ropes binding the painted man. The man tensed his muscles, causing the rope to fall away, but otherwise remained motionless.

"Houel," the first trader roared, "call off your man, here. That slave cost me a mare in foal!"

Ian ignored the trader and told Rowena, "Go get Jemma."

"She's coming," Rowena said. "She's sent for."

Ian pointed to the lock fastening the chain to the man's neck. "Where's the key?"

"Oh, no," the trader said, "not 'til we've agreed on a price. Then, if you lose him, it'll be your pocket that's empty."

They expect me to buy the man's freedom! It was a test. If they could get him to accept slavery, they could get him to acquiesce in any atrocity.

The man was very angry as a real slave merchant might be under the circumstances. And Houel appeared amused. Nice touch. He wasn't taking sides. No one was taking sides—not a good sign for the trader if the transaction were as represented. But neither was anyone offering to back Ian.

They want to see how I'll react. So be it.

"Rowena," Ian said, "go ask Gof if I may borrow a cold chisel and hammer."

"Houel," the trader said, not looking at Houel but watching Ian closely. "I won't be deprived of my property by this...who do you think you are?" he asked Ian.

Ian didn't answer.

Houel said, "Most think that he's Gofannon."

A god could take whatever form he pleased, even the identity of a crazy foreigner like Ian. Houel wasn't, himself, convinced—Ian knew—or that was the way he played it, but he also wasn't above using the other villagers' belief to take advantage of the outsiders. With part of his mind, Ian admired this game within a game.

The trader said, "Bullshit!"

As the stand-off continued, Ian could feel his heart hammering and was aware of his own rapid breaths. The trader's anger—red and white, sweaty, veins out—must be a mirror of his own rage.

Across the common, Jemma came out of her house and made her way toward the action.

Then Rowena returned, not only with the requested tools, but with the smith as porter. The sight of the tools and apparent reinforcements unbalanced the moment. The trader shouted, "I demand a judgment!"

And Drullwyn appeared like the granting of a wish.

The traders all made the sign against the evil eye.

"What is it you want judged?" Drullwyn asked, quietly.

Everyone had to strain to hear him. Consequently, he had their complete collective attention. The head trader seemed taken aback.

Then he realized he was getting his hearing. He said, defensively, "This man…" He pointed at Ian, and Ian didn't miss the fact that he'd dropped the "old" in the presence of one even older. "…is trying to steal my property."

"What property?"

"My painted man." Getting hot again, the trader pointed at the wagon. "I paid a mare in foal for that slave. I won't take less for him."

Drullwyn walked to the wagon and looked in. "It must have been a poor mare."

"You can insult me all you like. I won't lower my price."

Drullwyn turned to Ian. "You *were* planning to compensate this man?"

"You can't *own* a human being. Apparently the only crime he's committed is being foreign."

"We will have to discuss philosophy another time. The man came here in the possession of these traders, and you will have to give them their price if you wish to have him." Before Ian could object, he added, "That is our law and my decision."

This was intolerable! "*Slavery is wrong!*"

It was Jemma who answered in English. She stepped between him and Drullwyn, facing Ian, and said, "But it's legal and customary here."

He felt an overpowering rage. She, of all of them, should agree with him. "That doesn't make it right!"

She seemed simultaneously fearful and angry. She grabbed his lapels. "It's their way!"

A thrill like an electric current stabbed him. He felt her tremble.

"You can't interfere!" she said. "You'll be thrown out!"

She'd apparently said all she had to say. She closed her mouth and stood breathing as hard as if she'd just run uphill. Then she seemed to realize she was still holding his coat. She let go—vehemently—and backed up. She glanced at the Celts, causing him to wonder what they thought of her tirade. They looked like children whose parents have been battling. Jemma, too, seemed genuinely dismayed. She added, "There's nowhere else to go."

Something made him hold back the "Oh, right!" that was about to burst forth. He was, suddenly, too aware of her tantalizing proximity, too conscious of his own urge to put hands on her and shake sense into her. Or was that it? Was it the urge to drag her into Rolf's house and his own bed? The brutal self-honesty startled him and he took a step back as if she, not his own lust, had made the obscene suggestion.

He tried to keep anger between them like a shield. "You asked them to keep me here! How dare you?"

"Inspector Carreg, you were in an unfamiliar place, unarmed and unfamiliar with the customs. You were not fluent in the language, nor had you learned what constitutes proper etiquette in this part of the world. Of course I asked them to detain you."

He recognized that there was no point in arguing. Jemma was like Marjory in one respect. Marjory had stood against him only a half a dozen times during their life together, but once she'd taken her stand, she had never budged. Neither would Jemma.

She seemed to notice that her proximity was an affront, because she took another step back and dropped her eyes. "I'm sorry."

He felt incredible relief. What could she do with it if she suspected the intensity of his feelings? What advantage could she take if he weakened even momentarily? He looked at the others. Which of them knew the plot? Was his seduction—either by Jemma or one of the others—part of it? She hadn't made any overtures. But she must have done her homework, must know that any blatant pass would repulse him. It was enough that she was blond like Marjory, and sensible and direct like Marjory. It was enough that she was exquisitely beautiful.

Ah, Marjory. There's no fool like an old fool. Why couldn't I fall for someone like you?

Stupid question. Marjory was one of a kind.

Very well. They might have figured out what sort of woman he favored, but he needn't let them know how he'd come to feel about *her*. He turned his back on her and told Drullwyn, "I haven't got a mare in foal."

Drullwyn raised one eyebrow. "But you could trade for one. One for which you wouldn't have to pay too dearly."

The wording of the suggestion and the phrase *too dearly*, brought to mind the bargain he was sure Drullwyn had in mind, a mare in foal he needn't hesitate to offer a slave trader. "You have such a mare. What would you be willing to accept in trade?"

Drullwyn merely raised his eyebrows. Ian mentally inventoried his remaining possessions. He could not do without his reading glasses and he was not going to offer his Rolex for the screw. Nor did he wish to part with pen or jotter. That left his keys, ID and remaining clothes. His suit coat was the least essential item of clothing. In parts of the world, a man might be knifed for things in worse shape. Ian grasped the lapels. "Would you take this for the mare?"

Drullwyn seemed surprised. "Surely that's worth more than *one* horse?"

Ian took off the jacket and held it out. "A mare in foal is two horses." Even to himself, arguing for a lower price sounded strange. To the onlookers, it must seem mad.

Drullwyn took the jacket with a shrug. A murmur passed through the crowd.

The head trader told Ian, "I'll give you the slave for that."

Ian held his hands up in an exaggerated what-can-I-do? gesture. "It's no longer mine to trade. Besides, you said you wouldn't take anything but a pregnant horse for him."

"Nothing less," the trader said. He turned to Drullwyn. "Well, sir?"

"I haven't any need for a worthless slave." He turned to one of his bondsmen, watching the drama from the edge of the crowd, and handed him Ian's jacket. "Take this to my house keeper and bring back the mare I received as a payment Lughnasad last."

Ian thought the man looked startled, then smugly amused—

as well he might. It was common knowledge that Ian had turned down a valuable milk cow for the coat. The man took the coat and hurried away. The rest of the onlookers waited for something else to happen, then began to drift back to their various negotiations with the traders. Ian folded his arms over his chest and planted himself next to the painted man to wait for the arrival of the horse. The head trader watched him for a minute, then sidled off to try to interest Gof in the iron blanks he was eyeing.

The sky turned a translucent mix of gray and blue during the wait, like bits of the opaque glass used in Tiffany lamp shades, and though the sun never made an appearance, the clouds exuded light enough to make anemic shade beneath everything. The commons bustled with activity. Coins and jewelry exchanged hands. People came and went, bringing things from their houses, taking things away. Gof scoffed at the iron blanks, but took coins to reset two of the scrawny horses' shoes. Moch delivered two young pigs and took away a length of red cloth. Jemma commandeered Drullwyn's services as translator and after a lengthy conversation with the head trader, Drullwyn's bondsmen and Jemma's neighbors were dispatched to Ty's house to fetch half a wagon load of the goods Jemma had taken in payment for her services.

Drullwyn, subsequently, showed great interest in the negotiations over salt. When Gwen walked toward him with a sack of it she'd just purchased, Drullwyn stopped her and tasted some of it. Ian couldn't hear what they were saying, but Gwen left the salt with him and went quietly among the crowd whispering to each of those who'd also traded for salt. Many of those she spoke with looked at Drullwyn. Some brought him their salt, most simply stopped what they were doing and went back to stand around the salt vendor. Gwen eventually said her piece to Jemma, who stepped unobtrusively to the edge of the crowd. She walked across the commons to her house, returning with a square of the linen she used for bandages.

She gave Drullwyn the cloth. He called his bondsmen and women out of the crowd—five people. He had one of the men fetch a cauldron as large as a washtub from Houel's house. He sent the others for buckets of water. More of the villagers became involved in the preparations. The traders noticed and became uneasy. The cauldron was placed next to the wagon from which the salt was being dispensed. As Drullwyn's people began to fill it with water, all barter ceased.

"Now what're you up to?" the head trader demanded. He pointed to the cauldron. "What's this?"

"A demonstration," Drullwyn said. "Houel, bring me your salt."

Houel handed him a leather pouch—about five pounds, Ian judged. Drullwyn emptied the salt into the cauldron and nodded to the bondsman standing next to it. There was relative silence as the man began mixing the salt. Ian didn't know whether it was standard procedure or if Drullwyn had given instructions beforehand, but the bondsmen began straining the salt solution through Jemma's cloth into the buckets they'd brought the water in. When the liquid was all transferred, they scraped a fine, white residue—no doubt sand—from the bottom of the cauldron and from the linen sieve, back into the salt pouch. The men presented the pouch—now a third full—to Drullwyn, who held it up to the salt trader.

"I believe you owe Houel a refund," Drullwyn said. "Two parts in five of what he paid you."

The trader started to protest, thought about it, looked around.

Twenty men were armed with swords; and at least as many women, as well as Ian, Drullwyn and Gof, were armed with the short knives they customarily wore on their belts. None of them looked happy or forgiving. The young children, the very old people, and the three women whose advanced pregnancies made them vulnerable had all vanished.

Drullwyn spoke again. "...Or you may refund his purchase price and take your salt back. Of course you will have to pay Houel for the water. And for the buckets if you wish to keep them."

Sweat beaded the trader's upper lip. Returning two fifths of a live cow was problematic, and he must have surmised the price of water and buckets would be very high. Finally, he said, "How much? How much to let the deal stand?"

Drullwyn looked at Houel, who said, "Another bag of your three parts salt in five."

The salt trader looked at his leader. The head trader studied the crowd within which his compatriots were enmeshed. He looked furious, but he shrugged and nodded. While Houel waited for the salt man to measure out the salt, Drullwyn's bondsmen carried away the cauldron and the buckets of saline, and the other villagers queued up for their refunds. The process was very slow. The indistinct shadows beneath men and wagons and scrawny horses began to crawl eastward as people haggled over the worth of what would be a waste product in the modern world.

Would be! I've fallen down the Rabbit's hole and ended up behind the looking glass! This is real! Roman Britain!

Ian felt, again, that bewildering sensation of déjà vu. He was thoroughly sick of the mind games, but that was probably the point. The constant, gentle pressure wore one down. Like water dropping on one's forehead. Like water dripping on stone. The more durable material lasted longer, but in the end everything dissolved.

The soft shadows had advanced well across the commons by the time Drullwyn's man arrived with the pregnant horse. Before entering the oppidium, he had rested her long enough to let her catch her breath. And he had oiled her hooves, brushed the dust from her coat and combed her mane and tail. Still, it required no expertise to see the beast was a poor screw.

The head trader was livid as soon as he clapped eyes on her. "It's no deal!" he fairly shouted.

Drullwyn's man presented the mare's lead to Ian.

Ian thanked him and led the mare toward the wagon where the painted man lay watching impassively.

The trader thrust himself between Ian and his destination. "No, by the gods!" His hand fisted around the hilt of his sword, and fist and jaw tightened to white rage.

Simultaneously, five of the village men surged toward him, drawing their swords half out of their scabbards. Ian looked around and caught Gof's eye, but Drullwyn raised a hand before either of them could act.

He spoke to the head trader, so softly that the man had to work to hear, as did Ian, who was even closer. "If you do not remove the chain immediately, we will have to conclude that you're throwing it in." He said something, which was unintelligible to Ian, that the astonished prisoner seemed to understand.

He answered, "Arngwhish."

"His name is Arngwhish," Drullwyn said. It sounded as if he was saying "Angus" with his mouth full. "We're waiting," he added, fixing the trader with a stern look.

Houel, Rolf, Owain and Gof moved closer.

The trader scanned the seeming sea of faces and recognized resolve. He dragged the padlock key from his pocket and yanked the chain to get the painted man out of the wagon. The captive's face remained impassive as the trader opened the lock and the chain fell away. The trader coiled his chain up and backed off.

The painted man seemed stunned; he rubbed his neck. Drullwyn spoke to him again, and he said, "Yes." Drullwyn pulled his knife and held it to the face of the captive. The man kissed it, then turned to Ian to utter paragraphs of gibberish.

"He has sworn on my blade that he will not try to escape," Drullwyn told Ian. "He swears he will serve you as his lord."

Irritated, Ian said, "I don't want him to serve me. I just want him to stay put until Jemma's had a look at his wounds."

The departure was an anticlimax. The traders stowed the remainder of their goods while the villagers watched. Then Houel designated

174

ten men to escort them to the boundary of the clan's territory. "For your protection," he told them, straight-faced.

They left behind a bad taste in the mouth, as if members of the circus had been discovered abusing the dancing bear. And they left behind the old man, the ragged women, the infants, and the teenaged boy.

"Refugees?" Ian asked Jemma.

"Slaves."

"Whose…?"

"Mine." He must have looked shocked, because she added, defensively, "You can't just tell them 'You're free. Go home.' They've no money, no jobs, and they're God knows how far from where they came from. They may even have been sold into servitude by their families."

That made Ian wonder about "Angus." He asked Drullwyn to get his story, and was relieved to hear that the painted man had been kidnapped from his home. It gave them something—besides being strangers here—in common.

26 ebrill

"They clean up rather well, don't you think?"

The clouds had blown east, and the black velvet sky overhead was jeweled with stars. Jemma was sitting before Gwen's cooking fire, combing her damp, golden hair. The fire's light glinted softly from it and from her gold earrings.

As Ian stirred the pot simmering on the fire, he thought Jemma had cleaned up rather well. Bathed and dressed in the dark blue tunic she'd worn for Rolf's brother's funeral, she looked smashing.

Drullwyn and his wife sat across the fire from them. The druid was wearing Ian's suit coat. His wife clung to his arm like a small child. The golden light burned the years from the old man's face, making him seem as young as she. Behind them, in the shadows, Angus squatted on his heels with his arms folded across his chest, elbows on knees. Most of his fabulous tattoos were hidden by Rolf's old tunic and trousers. With his hair and beard washed and combed, he looked almost civilized.

"They all had lice," Jemma continued. "We had to burn their clothes."

"Small loss," Ian said. The aroma emanating from the pot was nearly irresistible. He wished Gwen would soon announce supper.

"Arngwhish believes that you bought him to sacrifice him to our gods," Drullwyn said. "I tried to explain that it was just an eccentric whim of yours, but I'm not sure I've convinced him."

It had been agreed that Angus would stay with Drullwyn until he learned enough of the language to converse with the rest of the clan, or until they could arrange to send him home.

"Why doesn't he run away?"

Drullwyn seemed astonished. "He's given his word. Even among the painted people there are men of integrity." Almost as an aside he added, "Perhaps among the Romans too, though I have yet to meet one..."

Ian felt the same eerie déjà vu that came on whenever he remembered he was out of time and place. He shivered.

"...The others are useful, of course, but his only training is as a warrior, and Houel will never trust him with a man's weapon."

Gwen came out of the house, carrying bowls and spoons that she distributed to her guests. She served them the stew from the simmering pot, then called Rowena before she served herself. The girl came out of the house carrying a huge mug of *corma*. She was trailed by a shy young woman Ian didn't recall having seen before.

"Where's Papa?" Rowena demanded.

"Houel sent him to follow the traders." He indicated Rowena's companion. "Who's this?"

"Una," Jemma said. "If I understood correctly, she's to be my interpreter. She speaks Latin."

"She looks ill."

"She's seriously undernourished. And she has worms."

Worms!

Jemma didn't seem to find it odd. "We'll have to find some *Artemesia*. Or plant some."

Ian gave her a blank look.

"Wormwood. A natural vermifuge."

"I should think you'd have something less primitive in your valise."

"I couldn't bring an entire pharmacy. Chemist's shop," she added, translating from American. "I brought only what I couldn't grow or easily manufacture."

27 ebrill

"You see? It's as I reported." Rolf urged his sweating horse into the clearing as Drullwyn, Ian and the others stared at the devastation. The scene was, indeed, as reported. The shrine of the nameless god had been defiled. Horses had been ridden through the tiny pool that bubbled up beneath the god's ancient oak, and the oak had been girdled. Its leaves hung limp. Flies clouded about piles of human excrement beneath it. The smell of filth and death was as strong as the rage the scene engendered. The ultimate indignity was the bloated body of the horse that had been rolled into the spring to poison the water and mock the custom of gifting the water god.

The corpse was familiar—a skinny, pregnant bay mare whose throat had been cut.

"We wanted you to see this before we cleaned it," Owain told the druid. He nodded to Pyrs and Dyfyd, who dismounted and tied ropes around the legs of the dead horse. They quickly towed it out, at which point, Drullwyn told them, "Drag it away from the water, but leave it in the clearing. Leave everything else as you found it. Let it be a reminder to the god."

He raised his voice and tuned it to the sing-song pitch he used for rituals. "God, grant to all who did this the fate that they deserve."

28 ebrill

"Ian," Jemma said, "I have something for you."

He waited while she ducked into Ty's house and returned with a neatly folded pile of clothing. "These ought to fit."

He took the clothes and put them down, then held up the topmost item—a linen tunic that had a collar and yoke embroidered with vines and animals, and the triskele so favored in Celtic art. He recognized it as the one she'd been stitching the day he'd bested Houel at fidchel, and he blushed, remembering her words: *I pray that the wearer will prosper and be content with his life.* The second shirt was less ornate—a work-day shirt, and folded within it were two pairs of knitted stockings and two pairs of linen pants with drawstrings. Finally, there were two pairs of trousers, conservative by village standards—one dark blue and green plaid with a broad white stripe divided by a thin red one, and the other a blue and green check. He recognized the warp he'd seen Gwen and Jemma setting up on the loom the day he'd heard Jemma's confession of murder.

"I had to guess on the size," Jemma said.

"I can't accept these."

"Why not?"

"They represent several weeks' work, at least."

"You can give me your old trousers. People will pay dearly for scraps as souvenirs. And you can shoe my horses next time they need it." She hooked a finger through one of the holes in his trousers. "In any case, you can't go around like this much longer."

For a moment he forgot they were enemies and smiled. "Very well, I accept."

Then he remembered her past, which would always come

between them, and his smile faded.

Jemma said, "What's the matter?"

"I'd almost forgotten where I am. And by whose agency."

"I didn't ask you to come after me."

"But you did. When you commit murder, you invite pursuit."

Everything fit surprisingly well. After he'd changed into the work shirt and the more conservative trousers, he decided to repay Jemma in kind for her handiwork. To that end, he begged some beeswax from Gwen and borrowed fine chisels and an awl from Ty. He also fetched his reading glasses from the house. The morning was warm, and for the first time in a week unalloyed sunlight gilt the village. Ian took everything to his home from home in the smithy, and sat cross-legged in the shade of the lean-to. He had the place to himself; Gof was away for the day.

He began to fashion a brooch from the wax, starting with the pin, intertwining serpents over its front surface to form a Celticized caduceus, the heads and tails of which would rise over the brooch ring. The ring itself, he covered with the symmetric vine and leaf motif so dear to Celtic art. On either side of the groove into which the pin would slide, he ended the vine with a triskele. And he perched Modron's crows among the vine's branches. He'd nearly finished the design when Gof returned from his errand.

Ian's glasses fascinated him, and he examined them carefully before even glancing at the brooch.

When Ian took back his glasses and resumed working, Gof demanded, "Explain the ritual to me."

"There's no ritual." Ian looked the wax model over carefully. There being no obvious flaws, he began to cover it with clay. Gof watched closely.

When Ian was finished covering both pieces of the brooch, Gof asked, "What next?"

Ian didn't answer until he'd finished and put the clay-covered model out of the way. "We let the clay dry."

29 ebrill

By the next afternoon, the clay had hardened over the model, creating a mold. Ian heated it to melt the wax out.

"Tell me the words you say," Gof demanded.

"There are no words."

"Are you testing me?"

"No."

The smith obviously didn't believe him. "Even the greenest apprentice knows that the proper ritual must accompany the making. If this is not done, with due respect for the spirits and the materials, the object will not be what the buyer pays for, though it be more lovely than a sunrise. And to sell such an imperfect thing would be to cheat the customer and anger the gods. Have I got it right?"

"I couldn't have said it better."

"Well, then?"

"You can see what I'm doing."

"Haven't I shared my secrets with you? Why won't you teach me the ritual?"

"This is just a trinket to pay Jemma for the clothes she made me. The only requirement is that it be beautiful and useful."

"Ah, now we're getting somewhere. And while you're working do you think of the person for whom you're making it?"

"Incessantly…Er, yes."

"What else?"

Ian improvised to please him. "The design must have balance without being boring."

"And numbers?"

"Three and seven."

"What metal will you use? Gold?"

"A more appropriate metal—brass."

Gof was not familiar with "brass." He was amazed when Ian took his car keys from his pocket. "What are these?"

"Where I'm from, we use them to guard property. They're not much use here."

He got a bucket of water ready before he dropped the keys in a clay crucible borrowed from Gof. Then he thrust the crucible into the fire and pumped the bellows.

"Do you make an invocation to the gods," Gof demanded, "for the protection of the user?"

"Jemma's more in need of forgiveness from the gods than protection."

"For what?"

"You might say she's taken two lives."

"You're the most exasperating teacher I've ever had!"

"That's the pot calling the kettle black," Ian said in English.

"Is that part of the ritual?"

"No, just a comment. Look."

The keys were melting. The two men watched them liquefy in silence, then Ian carefully poured the molten brass into the clay mold. He eased the mold into the water, but he was too impatient. With the sudden change of temperature, the mold broke, revealing a lovely circular pin.

30 ebrill

The following morning, the village teemed like an anthill torn open by a badger, with people bustling about in a controlled mania that admitted no pause for explanations. Jemma was nowhere in sight. Ian searched the village for her, then climbed to the ramparts to look down into the surrounding fields. Though he didn't find her, he did notice half the men of the village were using their oxen and horses to haul wood for two great pyres they were building just outside the hill fort entrance. As he kept watching, he noticed a caravan of strangers approaching from the east end of the valley in small chariots, each drawn by two horses and containing a warrior and a charioteer. Ian looked for the ever-present sentries and found them watching the visitors with interest but without alarm. Visitors. Relatives perhaps, or new neighbors seeking clientship with Houel. They were a good half-hour away, and Ian was over-late for work. He decided to see if Gof knew who was coming.

"No one of importance," the smith said, so Ian dismissed them from mind. He'd forgotten them by the time Rolf led them to the smithy.

The newcomers stopped in front of Gof. They were armed with spears, shields and swords, and were painted for war with the blue paint he'd come to know was woad. All of them had hair thickened with lime and teased to stand upright like horses' manes, and most had severed human heads hung from the sides of the chariots, round the necks of their horses, or stuck on top of their spears. Rolf introduced the leader, Dui, as if the smith had forgotten him since his last visit.

Dui was young, not more than nineteen, moderately tall and dark though he'd plastered his hair with so much chalk-wash, to make it stand up, that it looked almost white. He had regular features but his eyebrows turned up slightly at the outer ends, giving him a devilish look. He wore a bright red cloak over red and yellow plaid trousers. The overall effect was comical—that of a punk rocker masquerading as a hippie. But the sword and dagger he wore on his belt looked genuine enough. Ian controlled his urge to laugh.

With Dui, in her own chauffeured chariot, was a woman of the same height, build and general coloring as Jemma. She wore a short tunic over a long skirt, a gilt belt and knife-sheath, and gold armbands, torc and bracelets. She was armed like the men and carried herself like a *diva*.

Dui saluted. "Good day to you, Smith. Will you see to our horses?" Gof nodded.

Ian stopped working to follow the exchange. The severed heads reminded him of what Rolf had said about them, and he found them far less disturbing.

"...For the usual price?" Dui asked. Gof nodded again. Dui noticed Ian taking his measure, and stared at him. He seemed to find Ian's interest amusing. "I see you've acquired an assistant," he said to Gof. Gof grunted. "Who might he be?"

"Calls himself Ian."

"That tells me a lot. I hope you're not as stingy with your materials as your words."

The smith expressed his feeling for this by spitting on the ground in front of Dui.

Rolf grabbed Dui's arm and said, "Leave him alone, Dui. You don't want to get him mad; he might curse you."

Dui laughed, but got out of his chariot and started away with Rolf. "What do I care for a smith's curse?" he said—softly, so the smith couldn't hear. Then he noticed his charioteer was still with the horses. "Here, fellow," he said to Ian. "Come take these horses."

Ian complied slowly enough to let it be known he would not be ordered around by upstart strangers. When he reached for the near horse's bridle, his watch attracted Dui's eye.

He asked, "What is this?"

Ian let him see it, but Dui was less impressed when he had it in his hand. He shook it. He put it to his ear, and when he heard it tick, he was startled and dropped it. Ian's grin seemed to infuriate him. "What is that wicked thing?"

"A device for telling the time of day," Ian said, picking up the watch.

Dui laughed, and the others, including Rolf, joined in. "What sort of fool needs to be told the time of day?" Dui pointed to the sky. "Any *child* can see what time it is."

Ian scowled.

Rolf stepped between them. "C'mon," he said to Dui. "I'll show you where you're staying tonight. Where is it you're off to this time?"

Dui answered loudly enough to be heard by everyone. "We're for Mona. To defend the Sacred Groves from the Romans."

As Ian and Gof watched them go, the smith spat, then went back to work. Ian followed them, unobtrusively. He guessed they were heading for Houel's house, in front of which he spotted Jemma, Gwen and the other women preparing food for the celebration. A cow and a pig had been sacrificed for the occasion, and were being turned on spits over great outdoor fires. Soup bubbled in a huge bronze cauldron, and bread baked at the edges of the hearths. Ian took a position, hidden by the spitted beef, from which he could see and hear without being seen.

Rolf led Dui and the warrior woman past, and Dui stopped when he spotted Jemma. "Who's that?"

Rolf and the woman stopped, too. "That's who I've been telling you about," Rolf said. "That's Epona, though she calls herself Jemma."

"Ah, well. You were right. She *is* a goddess. You'll have to introduce us when I'm cleaned up."

The woman scowled.

They started walking again, and Dui went on, "How is it that a goddess like her has such a jackass for a consort?"

"A mare in heat will stand for anything," the woman said, cattily.

Dui winked at Rolf. "I'll have to insure that if she's ready tonight, she has a decent stallion for her pleasure."

His lady companion obviously wasn't pleased.

"She belongs to Ian," Rolf said, "and you oughtn't mess with a smith."

Dui laughed. "You believe that nonsense if you want to, but I'll lay odds on who spends tonight with her."

Who indeed, Ian thought. He's welcome to her.

But as he walked back to the smithy, he felt a nauseating rage gnawing his insides.

The upcoming party seemed an appropriate occasion for Ian to present Jemma with the brooch he'd made. She seemed genuinely pleased and excused herself to get something from her room. What she'd fetched and gave him was a bar of twentieth century soap, the first he'd seen since they arrived. It was a product so vastly superior to the lye-soap he'd been using, he was almost overcome by emotion. As he walked away, he was aware of Jemma staring after him and at the brooch.

Ian bathed and put on clean clothes. He met Jemma just before sundown. She was wearing a white linen dress with red and gold embroidery. Ian's brooch was prominent on her left shoulder. Loops of gold dangled from her ear lobes. A gold torc encircled her neck and gold bracelets her wrists.

He tried to think of a descriptor, a superlative sufficient to describe her. He felt the familiar pang—the little surge of joy, despair and longing that seemed to grip him when he saw her. Or heard her. Or even thought about her.

Then he felt the usual rage. It made his voice hard as he indicated the general hubbub. "What's this? It can't all be for the benefit of the pirates who've just arrived."

"Cetsamhain. It's a religious festival, though I suppose some would call it an orgy."

Ian waited for her to elaborate.

"After supper, Drullwyn will light the bonfires and sacrifice a white heifer, and the clan will drive the cattle between the fires to insure their fertility and the god's protection from disease."

"Where does the orgy come in?"

She smiled mischievously. "On this night, a man may lie with any woman, a woman with any man, with no disastrous social consequences. In fact, it's the duty of every adult in the community—a sort of religious sacrament—to recreate the union of god and goddess."

"They really believe that?"

"Most of them. For the others, it's a socially sanctioned way to let off steam."

"Everyone's expected to participate?"

"I suppose if the idea repulses you, you could go to bed with the children."

"You have all the answers, don't you?"

"If you were planning to emigrate, wouldn't you bone up on local customs?"

1 mai

I

Houel's house was a much larger version of Rolf's—round, with thatched roof and walls of daub and wattle. Garlands of flowers, and colorful blankets and banners, had been hung from the eaves. Some of the clan's most prized heads were displayed on poles near the door. The surrounding ground was covered with fresh straw.

A whole, half-grown pig was being turned slowly over the fire in a hearth in front of the house by two boys given a dispensation from bedtime in exchange for their services.

Adult villagers sat with their guests on the straw, around the periphery of a circle whose center had been left open for entertainers. Someone was playing a lively tune on a recorder. Dui sat in the place of honor at Houel's right, and next to him were Jemma, Gof and Owain. To his left were Drullwyn, Ian, the woman who'd come with Dui, and Rolf. Everyone else of note was seated a distance from Houel that varied according to rank, while most of the visiting charioteers stood behind their warriors.

The circle was hazy with wood smoke, and amber light from the fire and the oil lamps glinted off the gold or polished bronze around every wrist and neck. As the meal progressed, the men and women of lower rank passed around communal mugs of beer, serving the smith first. Ian thought the stuff was far superior to the *corma* they served everyday and wondered why he hadn't been offered any before. Servers kept the mugs full, and there was much laughter and joking as Houel toasted the visitors, who were beginning to get drunk.

"Houel," Dui asked, "will you contest me for the Hero's

portion?" He was referring to the honored hind leg of the boar.

"Contest you?" Houel laughed and pointed at Ian. "Huh. That gray-beard apprentice could beat you."

Ian leaned around Dui's female companion to ask Rolf, "What's going on?"

"The law prohibits fighting on a feast day, but Dui's spoiling for one anyway. Houel's just volunteered you to fight him."

"I'm not going to fight anyone."

"You have to, or Houel will lose face and you'll be a laughing-stock."

"If I fight him, he'll beat the stuffing out of me, and I'll be a laughing-stock anyway…What *would* happen if he beat me?"

"Then Houel would have to fight him. Houel's counting on you beating him or tiring him out enough so he can beat him."

"What if he beats both of us?"

"Then Dui gets what he wants." Ian raised an eyebrow. "We all go with Dui to fight the Romans."

"Who minds the town while you're away?"

Rolf nodded. "That's just it. Houel likes a fight as well as any man, but he has an obligation to protect his clients. And if the Romans come, as Drullwyn forecasts, there'll be fighting enough for anyone right here."

Dui raised his cup and asked, in a loud voice, "Houel, you want me to challenge that *old* man?" He pointed at Ian. "If he ever knew how to fight, he's so ancient, he's forgotten."

Ian raised his voice just enough to carry across the circle. "You know, Houel, the trouble with these young whippersnappers is they've never learned any manners."

Dui looked at Ian. "Are you impugning my manners, old man?"

Ian nodded. "Also the judgment of your mother. She must have lain with a donkey to have borne such a jackass. Either that or she fostered you with pigs."

The insult was too much. Dui grabbed his sheathed sword from the ground next to him and charged to the center of the circle. "I demand satisfaction!"

There was a roar of approval from the crowd—fights, verbal or otherwise, were a major part of the entertainment.

Ian got up slowly, further enraging Dui by making him wait. Dui drew his sword from its sheath. Ian, who had no sword, turned his back on Dui and extended his hands in an exaggerated now-what-do-I-do? gesture that got laughs. He shook his head from side to side and said, "Oh, no. No swords. Someone might be hurt."

The gambit baffled Dui. In the fraction of a second he spent trying to figure out what sort of idiot would turn his back on an armed opponent, Ian used a karate kick to relieve him of the sword. Dui pulled his dagger, and Ian kicked that out of his hand, too. Then he picked up Dui's weapons and handed them, along with his own dagger, to Houel. "Hold these, will you?" He turned to face Dui and called over his shoulder to Houel, "You'd better keep those until he sobers up."

Outraged, Dui charged; Ian threw him on his back, then said loudly, "Only a woman fights in that position. Get up."

The crowd went wild, whistling and clapping. Dui got up and charged again, and Ian threw him again. He turned his back on Dui and pantomimed that he didn't understand this. Dui stood up silently and jumped him from behind and was thrown again. Finally, he managed to tackle Ian and wrestle him to the ground. They rolled around.

"Your mother wears army boots," Ian gasped in English.

Dui grabbed him by the throat. "You have a very loose tongue, old crow, and I'll soon have it out."

Ian poked at his eyes, forcing him to lean backward, and simultaneously threw his legs up and crossed his ankles over Dui's throat. With a twist, he had Dui in a headlock, requiring only legs and feet to hold him down. Ian rolled on his side and propped his head on one hand. He yawned loudly. "I can wait."

"For what," Dui gasped.

"For you to call off this silly brawl."

Spurred by renewed laughter from the onlookers, Dui struggled harder to get free but was finally forced to capitulate. "All right.

You win."

Ian let him go and rolled to his feet, stepping quickly and neatly out of reach. Then he reached down to offer Dui a hand up. Dui hesitated to take it until Drullwyn intervened.

"Enough, Dui. You've disturbed the peace too much already. Ian's beaten you fairly. That's my decision."

Dui nodded his agreement and accepted Ian's hand.

"When you get to be an old codger like me," Ian told him, "you learn a few tricks." He turned to Rolf. "When do we eat?"

"After you've claimed the winner's share." Rolf pointed to the roast pig the servers had taken down from the spit. "Get your knife. You get the hind leg."

Ian nodded. When he got his knife from Houel, Drullwyn leaned forward to hiss, "You fight like a Roman."

"Is that a compliment?"

"You've noticed I don't urge Houel to make war against the Romans?"

"Now that you mention it."

"That's because I've seen the Romans fight."

Dui retrieved his weapons, and Houel told him, "There's no shame in being bested by your betters."

Amid cheering and joking, Ian walked over to carve a haunch from the pig, which he presented to Houel. "I think the man who wins his battles without fighting is the real winner."

Dui looked ready to kill him, but Houel and his clansmen were delighted. Ian went back for the second haunch, which he presented to Gof. The smith was embarrassed but flattered.

"C'mon, everyone," Ian said, "let's eat."

He sat down, and the servers put the food out on low tables, so everyone could eat comfortably sitting on the ground. Ian took the bowl a servant offered him, and Jemma came up with a silver cup.

"What's this?"

"Wine." He hesitated. "Will you embarrass me in front of this company by refusing?"

"You drink half first."

"Why?"

He didn't answer. She shrugged, drank half the wine and gave him the rest. He noticed the whispering and nudging this caused, though Jemma said nothing, and no one else said anything. He drank the wine down all at once, occasioning laughter and cheers from the crowd, and Jemma took the cup away, looking smug.

"What was that for?" he asked Rolf, indicating the collective reaction.

"They're pleased that we're assured prosperity."

"How's that?"

Rolf seemed to think he was having him on. "You have a great sense of humor." He got up to help himself to some more meat before Ian could pin down his meaning.

They ate. Ian noticed that Dui paid flattering attention to Jemma during the meal, trying to get his goat, Ian was sure, but he didn't succeed because the woman Dui'd come with paid him equal attention. Trying to make Dui jealous, no doubt.

As the meal progressed, it seemed as if every woman in sight was bent upon provocation. Even Mathe had put aside her mourning clothes for a party frock. Ian became acutely aware of the woman at his left. She was much like Jemma in coloring, height and build, but unlike Jemma, she wore no support garment beneath her tunic. Her breasts swelled and swayed provokingly. The wide belt, on which she wore her knife, enhanced the hour-glass curves of her torso, and the way she constantly thrust her pelvis forward—easing the strain, on her back, of sitting cross-legged—led Ian to speculate, in spite of himself, on what she could do with it in bed.

That made him think of Jemma, and he leaned forward so he could see her around the intervening men. Jemma's curves seemed softer, her breasts rounder. She was a magnet for men of mettle to which both Houel and Dui were drawn. To whom Ian was drawn.

A wine mug made the rounds, with each to whom it was passed taking a little sip. And it seemed to pass quite frequently.

When everyone had been served, a red-haired woman, another who'd come with Dui, got up and sang an audience participation song, in which, apparently, anyone was free to join. The audience had heard the song before—everyone seemed to know the cues and their proper order, but that didn't dampen their pleasure. The woman sang:

> "Come gather round, people,
> I've news from all over.
> And I'll tell you of Macha.
> And her shape-shifting lover.
>
> The Goddess went out
> To inspect her fine horses
> The God followed after
> And used all his forces
>
> Of charm and persuasion
> To lay down a dare:
> He said, 'I'll be your stallion
> If you'll be my mare.'"

Someone called out, "HARE," and the woman worked it in.

> "Belinos, the stallion
> Gave good service to the mare,
> Then she changed from Epona
> To a goddess of a hare."

"Rain," one of Dui's warriors called out. Owain said, "Moon."

> "Then she became the good Earth,
> And he became the rain.
> He became water;
> She became the Moon."

"Hedgehog," Ian shouted. He was feeling the wine.
The red-haired woman laughed and blew him a kiss, continuing:

> "The God kept on challenging
> The Goddess most darefully.

When she became a hedgehog,
They made love very carefully.

When Belinos had given her
Pleasure as a stag,
The doe of a goddess
Became an old hag.

It was then that he most truly
Proved himself a treasure,
For he loved the old lady
And gave her such pleasure

That she turned into a maiden
And gave him equal measure.
'It's clear,' said the Maiden,
'That with me, he stays.'

And the Maiden loved Belinos
For all of their days
For he gave her such pleasure
In so many ways."

When the last chord died, a cry of "Bravo!" went up, and the singer bowed, glowing with delight. Houel took off one of his gold armbands to present to her, and—not to be outdone—Dui did likewise.

The lady slipped the bands on her own arms and sang a blatantly flattering song about Houel's courage, cunning and generosity, followed by an equally obsequious ballad in praise of Dui.

The food was cleared away and musicians began to play dance music. When others moved to the center of the circle, Jemma came to Ian and asked, "Would you like to dance?"

"No."

"Are you afraid that if you give this culture half a chance, you'll like it?"

"I like cold milk and hot showers. I *don't* like being manipulated."

Pretending to study the dancers, he watched her return to Dui, who soon had her laughing.

Rowena sidled up and climbed in Jemma's lap. She waited until there was a pause in Jemma's give and take with Dui, then raised her voice to be heard over the music. Ian could clearly hear her ask, "Aren't you going to dance with Ian?"

Jemma glanced at him and shook her head.

Rowena seemed shocked. She got up and ran to Ian. She took his hand and held it until she got his full attention. "Ian, you've *got* to dance!"

"I'm too old."

"You could dance slowly. Plee-ze?"

He saw that for some reason, it was important to her. "Oh, all right. Just one."

She beamed and pulled him to his feet, and led him—not to the dance floor but—to Jemma.

Jemma was still talking to Dui. She seemed startled to find Ian standing over her. He watched his own reaction mirrored on her face—dismay, fading into distrust.

Rowena grabbed her hand and said, "C'mon, Jemma. Dance."

It was obvious that Jemma was unwilling to be publicly humiliated if he refused again. He started to walk away, but Rowena, distressed by his change of mind, kept hold of his hand and planted her feet. Jemma looked at Ian; they both looked at Rowena. And he capitulated. He said to Jemma, "Come on."

She got up, though she was obviously as furious with the situation as he. The smile on her face was as frozen and phony as his. Everyone sober must have noticed, except Rowena, who was happy to see them together.

The dance began formally, with him and Jemma grimly making the best of it. They looked at each other infrequently. They touched no more than was necessary.

Other couples joined them in the circle. The music quickened.

They had to pay more attention to avoiding collisions. Ian's blood began to burn as his body warmed to the exercise. He became aware of the heat of Jemma's fingers through the cloth of his shirt, and the warmth of her body as he held her waist. Her eyes darkened. Her cheeks glowed red with exertion, and a sheen of perspiration glazed her skin, condensed and trickled down the cleft between her breasts. He felt the sweat trickle down his own chest and back and temples. Excitement swelled in him like a huge, deep breath until he felt close to bursting. The dance became a frenzy, an endurance contest, and he and Jemma seemed to be sucked into the spirit of it until, as the music ended, both of them were winded and aroused and staggering with exhaustion. They stood leaning against each other, gasping for breath. He was wondering at the beauty of her, when he noticed what was happening.

Jemma Henderson was a murderess! He felt his joy drain away and disappointment wash the delight from his expression. He let his hands drop to his sides.

Jemma seemed startled, like one slapped or doused with water, though she didn't speak.

He escorted her to her seat, bowed stiffly, and resumed his place.

Ian saw that Houel, Drullwyn and Dui were sober enough to have noticed, for they exchanged knowing glances. Houel and Drullwyn seemed alarmed, Dui delighted.

The wine cup went around again. Jemma began to sing in English *a cappella*. *"Alas, my Love, you do me wrong, to cast me off so discourteously…"*

Greensleeves!

She had a lovely voice, and the musicians immediately joined in. *"…for I have loved you well and long, and delighted in your company."*

The crowd became totally silent. She was singing to him, Ian knew. Everyone could tell. Not understanding the words, they were delighted.

She improvised the chorus:

> "Greensleeves was my delight.
> Greensleeves was my future told.

    Greensleeves was my shining knight,
    My sword and my shield and my torc of gold."

Ian felt as if he'd been slapped.

When Jemma finished, the silence was like another song. No one interrupted it as Jemma got up, wordlessly, and left the hall. Dui followed.

Ian felt insanely jealous. He turned to find Dui's companion watching him, thoughtfully, though her feelings about him were not apparent.

Then Drullwyn made his exit, and everyone began to file out after him. Rolf leaned around the woman—he excused himself, calling her Macha—to tell Ian it was time to go. He stood up, stretching. Ian stood too.

Macha leaned toward him, and he noticed the smoky odor of her hair. She whispered, "See you later," and he had the distinct impression it was an invitation. He nodded. He finished his wine, and followed Rolf outside.

Outside, the air was crystalline and windless, though the odors of wood smoke and manure and fruit blossoms mingled in a fragrant aura that settled among the houses. Torches and cooking fires had been extinguished, and the new moon had not yet risen. Despite the billion points of light overhead, darkness permeated the settlement. Ian felt inebriated—not smashed or sloppy, but well beyond the finer points of discrimination. Bless Bacchus. No. Belinos, wasn't it tonight? Beltaine. May Day. Cetsamhain.

Rolf led the way out the hill fort gates where, in the near darkness, they could just make out people preparing to celebrate the ritual, crowding around the Cetsamhain pyres. Most of the revelers were enveloped in cloaks against the night chill, but here and there a bare leg or naked shoulder protruded, suggesting scanty covering underneath. The collective expirations of the celebrants were strong with the sweet smell of home-brewed antifreeze.

• • •

Unrecognizable in the dim light, two men at the edge of the crowd held the halter of a white heifer between them. Ian could just see Dui standing nearby with his back to them and his arm around a woman—no doubt Jemma—who was hidden by her cloak. She rested her head on Dui's shoulder, and Ian felt a surge of irrational anger.

"This night is almost as uncanny as Samhain," Rolf said, distracting him.

Samhain, he recalled, was the pagan feast that antedated Halloween. An occasion, among the Celts, of ceremony and ritual observance. *Ritual.* The word conjured up a memory of his conversation with Gof on the subject. "*Tell me the ritual.*" Ian repeated the words aloud.

"You know it," Rolf said. "It differs little among all the tribes, even—so Drullwyn claims—those bordering Roman lands."

Ian nodded impatiently. "Tell me anyway."

"After the sacrifice, a man and woman reenact the union of God and Goddess—before everyone disperses to celebrate their own reenactments in private."

Gwen appeared at Rolf's side and smiled shyly at Ian as she pressed her body to Rolf's and put her head against his chest.

Rolf encircled her with his arms, reflexively, and continued. "Tonight, *you* have been accorded the honor of impersonating the God."

Ian felt a little stab of panic. He took stock of the assembled people. All his friends and neighbors were there: Ty and Gof, Houel and Maura and Drullwyn's wife, Llynda. Even Angus was there at the edge of a group of bondsmen. They wouldn't talk him into that! "Oh, no!" he said, in English. He added, for Rolf's and Gwen's enlightenment, "*Un yn Ile arall.*" I want to designate a substitute.

"Why?" Rolf said.

"I'm too old for such shenanigans." Not to mention a command performance of such a sensitive nature. Or the ultimate ignominy—failing to perform. "I'm not *that* drunk." Rolf looked offended, so Ian added, "This is too important a ritual to risk on an old man. How would you like to stand in for me?"

Rolf seemed pleased as well as amazed, but his enthusiasm faded as he considered the proposition. "Ah, but that would be a deadly insult to Houel and Dui. Maybe you'd better ask them first."

"How does one make such a request diplomatically?"

"Leave it to me."

Houel came toward them. "Ian, you're not ready!"

Rolf put a hand on Houel's arm and said, "It'll be all right."

Then Drullwyn came out of the oppidium, wearing a white, full-length tunic, embroidered with gold and red, and a gold torc and dagger. Rolf went to meet him. They argued as they walked toward Houel, Ian and Gwen.

"Rolf tells me you refuse to be honored, to honor the Goddess," Drullwyn said, angrily. "This is unheard of!"

Did they really expect him to make love in public?

"I wish to honor our guest," Ian said, pointing at Dui and wondering why he was bothering to pretend to play the game. "He's much better fitted..." He folded his arms and tried to look adamant. He was *not* going to be *it*.

Drullwyn finally shrugged and nodded, and Rolf hurried off to give Dui the good news. Drullwyn followed.

"Where's Rowena?" Ian asked Gwen. Surely they wouldn't involve so young a child in this?

Gwen's eyes followed Rolf. "Caring for the younger children," she said, dreamily.

Drullwyn led Dui through the parting crowd, to where the fires were laid. He produced a flint and struck it against the blade of his dagger to light the fire, which he then set among the pyres, invoking the Goddess Epona and the God Belinos in a loud voice.

Rolf slipped back through the crowd to envelop Gwen with his arms and cloak. They stood next to Ian as the two men led the heifer to her fate. One of them produced a linen rope that he tied loosely around the animal's neck. He slipped a heavy stick through it and began to twist the rope into a garrote. The second man produced a huge hammer and struck the heifer a resounding blow between the eyes. As the animal sank to its knees, the druid cut its throat with great ceremony and solemnity, again using the gold-hilted dagger. Ian had forgotten the Celts were pagans. How long ago was it, in real time, that he'd been discussing that very subject in the bright, normal sanity of Peter's kitchen?

As if he could read minds, Rolf said, "In the old days, before Drullwyn's grandfather, they would have offered the God a female virgin. Some of the old men still say we should go back to the old ways."

"Not the fathers of virginal daughters, I'll wager."

Rolf grinned. "It's said that Belinos struck the old druid with a sacred fit and spoke through his mouth."

"An epileptic seizure?"

"What's that?"

"Ask Jemma."

Rolf nodded, impatiently. "…Anyway, he told the then chief— Houel's uncle's wife's grandfather—that he had no use for dead women, and he sent a white heifer for the druid to offer him on the feast."

"Very sensible."

"He said," Rolf added with delight, "he liked live women better."

The crowd began to invoke Belinos in a unison chant that began as a whisper and crescendoed to triple *forte*. It sounded to Ian something like Orff's *Carmina Burana*. The chant drew an involuntary shiver from him as the choir had when he was a boy. He found himself swaying in its rhythm. Then the crowd parted and herdsmen drove the cattle between the pyres.

People came forward and laid straw over the mud churned up by the cattle, and threw cloaks and skins over the straw. Resplendent in his scarlet cloak, Dui stepped into the light, drawing his cloaked companion after him. He disrobed dramatically, sweeping the cloak around him like a matador's cape, and sailed it onto the pile of cloaks. He wore nothing except a heavy, ornate torc and armbands that gleamed golden in the firelight. He was as red in its reflected glow as the sun clearing the horizon. *Belinos* personified.

Dui began to dance. The dance was an old one, and he was

well rehearsed. He reminded Ian of Nureyev or Baryshnikov. As he pranced around the woman, he was seducer. Master. God. The woman played her part, letting herself be drawn into the light. She looked, in silhouette, like a Bedouin maiden, all but her eyes covered in the dark cloak, and she moved like the virginal aspect of the goddess she represented—shy, reluctant, innocent.

As Belinos pranced around her, touching her suggestively through the cloak, poking her through the cloth with his priapic organ, she began to move more willingly, even seductively under her covering. Her movements became more definite, more assured, even regal. Suddenly she was the goddess standing in for all the earth in this reenactment of creation.

It seemed obscene to Ian and he looked around at the crowd of voyeurs. But the faces were not those of an X-rated movie audience. The joy and anticipation he read in both men and women were more like the reverence at the offertory of a Mass. However they had been induced to see it, they *were* believers. For them, this *was* the reenactment of the ritual, the actors *were* Belinos and Epona. Dui and Jemma had been eclipsed. Ian felt overwhelmingly jealous, not only of Dui, but also of the people in the crowd. He felt he had no business being here. *He* was the voyeur.

Words without thoughts never to heaven go…

When Dui reached up to remove her cloak, Ian turned away. If he didn't see her face, he could deceive himself that she truly *was* Epona. Or Dui's wife. He couldn't, or wouldn't, identify with the man he'd designated to bed the woman he hated and so dearly wanted.

Another thought struck him. He'd been had again. Either he would have to have her—if he could—as a public spectacle, or watch another take her! Of all diabolical conundrums! But which were behind it? Which victims?

The crowd joined in, driving the phallus of the god earthward with a chant of Belinos! Belinos! Belinos…Someone threw more wood on the fires and sparks flew up. He followed their progress skyward until they merged with the constellations.

He wished, devoutly, that he'd managed to get drunk.

. . .

He didn't stay for the finale. He couldn't bear the thought of watching Dui perform the act he'd secretly longed to. He tried to put it out of mind as he made his way through the darkness to Rolf's house and felt his way inside. The interior was black and silent, and he could barely see as he stumbled around the partitions. A rustle of cloth rubbing cloth made his hair stand up, and he fumbled for the dagger Jemma had given him.

"Who is it?"

"Macha," a woman's whispered voice replied.

His companion at dinner. With his mind's eye, he could see her clearly. He relaxed. "What do you want?"

"You," she said. Her voice came from an intimate proximity. He could smell the wood smoke in her hair. "Belinos."

"You've got the wrong house. I'm not Belinos."

She laughed. "On this night, all men are Belinos." She was so close that he imagined he could feel the heat of her body.

"I think you'd better go."

She leaned lightly against him, and he discovered, when he put his hands out to keep his balance, that she was naked. "Would you refuse the Goddess?" She put her arms around his hips and pressed her body against his.

He couldn't answer. The wine clouded his brain and kept him from thinking of the arguments he knew resided there. Somewhere. The usual excuses—that betrayal of a husband was unacceptable, that disease or inadvertent pregnancy might follow—didn't apply here. He had no wife, and Dui didn't care. Disease was nonexistent—if he could believe Jemma, a dangerous proposition. And children of the god were especially favored among the populace. He shot his last bolt. "I'm too old."

He heard her low laugh. "For this night, I will make you young."

Ian believed her. He thought of Marjory—of how they'd loved. Would she have grudged him this pleasure? He thought not. She'd have urged it. He thought of Jemma—out in the night with Dui.

The woman's hands slid over his buttocks, pulling him closer, until another, older drug began to cloud his thinking. She sank to her knees and rested her face against him. Her breathing came faster. She slid her hands down the backs of his legs, then between his legs.

His hands went to her head; he felt her satin hair between his fingers. "We need a light," he muttered.

"The fire we make will be light enough."

A red glow from the bonfires lightened the patch of sky in the window hole. He tried to draw her into its pale light, but she pulled him bed-ward. And he let himself sink onto the blankets, into the celebration of the feast.

II

Ian awakened smiling, feeling exalted and not the least hung over. The thought—that he had not spent the night with a woman since Marjory's death—passed briefly through his mind. Well, it was time. And Marjory wouldn't have minded under the circumstances. He stretched and looked for Macha, but she was gone, leaving a hollow in the bedding at his side.

Rolf was lounging against the door as Ian came out to look around.

"Where is she?" Rolf obviously didn't know whom he was talking about. "The woman who calls herself Macha?"

Rolf laughed. "Macha? Macha, Maeve, Epona, they're all the same. All the same. All woman are Macha on Cetsamhain, and on Samhain for that matter. You poor boob. You're so ignorant, you don't recognize the names of the Goddess?"

Ian grabbed Rolf's tunic. "That was no goddess I spent the night with! Who was the woman beside me at dinner?"

Rolf was unperturbed. "Dui's wife?"

"Where is she?"

"You don't want to mess with her. Cetsamhain is one thing—

it's all proper and legal on the feast—and you could get away with it on Samhain, but Dui'll kill you if he sees you with her elsewise. Probably just as well she's gone."

"Gone where?"

"Gone to Mona. Gone to fight the Romans. Maybe gone to hell, for all I know. You should forget her. She's a bitch anyway. And you're a crazy man, wanting a slut like that when you could have a beauty like her."

He looked toward Ty's house, and Ian followed his line of sight to where Jemma sat grinding grain with the other women. She looked tired, but very satisfied. "Pretty is as pretty does," he said, sourly. "Jemma kills people."

Rolf's mouth fell open, but he thought about it and grinned. "Not a bad way to go."

"That's not what I meant." Out of habit, Ian looked at his watch. At where his watch should have been. At the bare, white shadow on his naked wrist.

The woman had stolen his watch!

It was the last tangible memento of his former life. His *real* life. He felt terribly disappointed that the woman who'd taken it was a whore—for what else could you call one who exacted payment? He had almost deluded himself that she'd wanted *him*, even if just because the villagers thought him peculiar. He felt cheated. And he was outraged.

"That thieving gypsy, Macha, stole my watch!"

4 mai

"You don't seem as enthusiastic about this," Ian told Drullwyn, "as Dui and his lot." The old man was mounted on his strongest horse, attended by Angus and half the men of the village. Ian was unsure which were going, which staying.

"I've seen the Romans fight," Drullwyn said.

"You could stay here." Ian glanced around the village. A wild rose bush was flowering, white, beside the shrine.

The old man smiled—a little sadly, Ian thought. "Mona is our most sacred place. It must be protected. Our priesthood is the only unifying factor in the land. And the only way to defeat the Romans is for all the tribes to unite against them."

"It'll never happen." Ian wasn't sure whether he was speaking from a knowledge of history or from his personal experience of the Celtic psyche.

"You may be right," Drullwyn said. "It hasn't happened within the collective memory of the Druids. Vercingetorix couldn't do it when the legions of Rome had their swords to the throats of his people. And Caradoc, whom the Romans call Caratacus, couldn't do it." He shook his head. "The Romans will defeat us, one tribe at a time, until all of Britain is Rome's as is all of Gaul. One doesn't require the Sight to know it."

"Then why go?"

"A principle."

Ian wondered if there were any principle he'd die for. He shook his head. "Do me a favor?"

"If it's in my power."

"Take Angus. Let him serve you until you get to Mona, then send him home, *his* home."

"I'll do one better." Ian waited. "If he'll serve me until we get to Mona, I'll give him a horse and spear and a badge of safe conduct."

"Fair enough."

"Will you do me a favor?"

"What?"

"Act as magistrate until I return. Your knowledge of our law is abysmal, but your instincts are good, and you've no special interests to serve."

"I'm honored, but I'd planned to leave soon, myself."

"Then appoint another in your place."

There was a woman among the mounted warriors, conspicuous by her smaller size and hidden head to toe by her black cloak. *Mathe.*

Rolf recognized her about the same time Ian did and hurried to her side. "Where are *you* going?"

"I'm going with Angus."

"You're crazy!"

Mathe let the cloak fall away from her head, so her pale hair shone in the sunlight. She glared at Rolf without deigning to answer.

He put a hand on her horse's reins. "Did you ask Houel?" he persisted.

"Drullwyn said I could go." She glared at the hand.

Rolf kept holding on. "But did you ask Houel?"

"He has no jurisdiction over me. I'm neither wife nor mother, and I'm not his sworn client. I'm a free woman, and I choose to go."

Just for a moment, she reminded Ian of Margaret, in her certainty, and of Marjory in her determination. He fought the little wave of loss he felt and put a hand on Rolf's arm. "Let her go, Rolf. There's no reasoning with a woman in love."

"Love?" Rolf was too stunned to argue. He let his hand drop. The horse shook its head.

Mathe put her hand on Rolf's shoulder and looked down into his face. "No one can replace your brother in my heart, but I deserve a chance for happiness. And Angus loves me."

Rolf and Ian both looked at Angus, armed with a spear and sitting one of Drullwyn's horses a little away from the other men. For a brief moment, he reminded Ian of pictures he'd seen of Native American warriors. There was a reassuring dignity about him that Rolf also must have recognized, because he nodded and patted her knee and said, "Come back if you change your mind." He looked around to see what was delaying the departure.

Ian spotted him first. Gof. The smith was mounted on his best horse and had pressed his second-best horse into service as a pack animal. "Going north," he said, with his usual economy of words, "to try the temper of Roman steel."

7 mai

It was time, and to Ian's surprise, no one raised an objection when he announced he was leaving. After breakfast, he saddled his horse and packed his meager possessions. Most of the villagers came to see him off. Jemma was there too, of course. She hadn't argued in favor of his staying.

"I don't understand why you want to leave," Rolf said. "You could make a very good living here. Out there, without kinsmen, you're liable to get killed."

"I'll manage." He offered Rolf his hand, and shook with the other men, then said good-bye to Gwen and kissed Rowena on the forehead. He nodded stiffly at Jemma, who wished him good luck.

He found he hadn't anything to say to her. It was his gut feeling that she didn't bear him any personal animosity, but he couldn't forgive her for failing to arrange his return to his own world. Not once had she wavered from her claim that they were stranded here. And though he'd considered the possibility of a genuine mania or obsession, he doubted she was impaired enough to believe any of it herself. Whether the others were equal co-conspirators didn't matter as much—he found it easy to think of them as he had found them, part of the milieu. But she was different—she'd brought him to this. And she was different because of the sheer sexual attraction he had for her.

Speaking of obsessions, he hoped that when she was physically out of his life, she'd no longer invade his waking and sleeping thoughts. Their relationship would be finished. Even the word "relationship" bothered him. As if there existed something between them besides antagonism. Or ever could.

He got on the horse; Rolf walked beside it. When Jemma followed at a little distance, Ian stopped to get one last thing off his chest. He spoke to Rolf, though his words were for her.

"You know, the worst of it is how easy it is to fall into believing all this—everyone is so *convincing*, and all the wounds and corpses and severed heads are so convincing. It's like some giant, malignant *god-game*."

Rolf looked perplexed, but Ian could tell by the way Jemma stiffened that she recognized the reference.

"...But I know as soon as I say, 'I give up. This *is* the third century,' someone's going to yell, 'Cut. Pick up your checks at central casting.'"

Rolf seemed totally confused at first, but he must have realized it was Jemma to whom Ian was speaking. She looked ready to cry.

Ian kicked the horse forward.

He stopped it abruptly as a sentry on the rampart above called, "Rider coming." They waited until a horseman clattered in between the ramparts on a lathered horse.

"The Romans are coming!"

People came running to hear the news.

8 mai

I

Farmers and warriors, their families, fosterlings and bondsmen—refugees from the advancing army—poured in from the southeast, swelling the village population to nearly 200 souls, not counting livestock.

The remaining village principals—Houel, Ty, Rolf and Owain—stood on the rampart with Ian and Jemma looking out over the eastern approach. They wore their finest clothes and jewelry. Many were painted and coifed for war, with woad darkening their eyes and a thick wash of lime-water making their hair stand up like horses' manes.

In the meadow below, about one hundred sixty men, two—*centuries*, Ian remembered, wondering that such trivia would surface at a time like this—dressed as Roman soldiers and fully armed with spears, shields, and swords, were ranked below the hill fort ditch, just out of spear-range. Well to the rear, an *ala*—more trivia, and Latin trivia, no less—of cavalry waited with two officers and the baggage train. *Impedimenta.* He couldn't remember the proper terminology for the little carts or baggage handlers, but the whole company looked far removed enough from the standard central casting version of Roman Government Issue to be as authentic as the villagers. While Ian pondered this new turn of events, a rider broke from the Roman ranks and stopped below the gate, just within hailing distance.

Watching him, Houel remarked, with an ironic smile, "They have no honor or they'd send their best warrior to meet me. If I were to ride out and challenge that flunky, I'd soon look like a hedgehog for all the Roman lances I'd have in me."

The rider yelled up at them in their own tongue, "Belgae, surrender!"

Houel answered. "Go to hell!"

The rider turned his horse back to the ranks, and the Roman commander gave a signal. A drummer sounded the attack. The foot soldiers closed ranks and put their shields together over their heads to form a single huge shield. A *testudo*. The word flashed back from another forgotten lesson. It meant "turtle."

As the *testudo* surged forward, with its human components marching in disciplined unison, the Celts rained down spears and rocks and curses. They sounded their *carnyxes*, the ceremonial war trumpets that had vertical stems and mouths shaped like the heads of mystical animals. The Celts, including women and children, shouted and screamed until the awesome din impeded thought.

The *testudo* advanced like a tank. When it came to the protecting ditch, it paused to let individual soldiers form a bucket brigade, filling in the ditch under its protective cover. During the hours it took them to build a walkway over the ditch, a second rank of soldiers, divided into archers and shieldmen, alternately fired arrows and covered each other, returning the defenders' fire. Arrows fell like hard rain on the rampart walk, and the villagers gathered them up and threw them back at their attackers. The young, as yet childless, women pounded the enemy with rocks as fearlessly as did the men.

The invaders brought out scaling ladders, and their archers rained a shower of covering fire on the Celts as the infantry threw ladders up against the palisade. As quickly as the Celts tipped the invaders off, more soldiers surged forward to replace them. Gradually, they scaled the wall, pushing back the less disciplined villagers.

The first invaders inside attacked the defenders at the entrance. People began to fall with serious injuries, and Ian was aware that the blood suddenly flowing wasn't mixed in any special effects lab. The party atmosphere changed, as in a nightmare, to one of terror.

Ian picked up a woman felled by an arrow. Following Jemma, who toted an infant in one arm and a toddler in the other, he carried the woman away from the wall, nearly falling when his foot landed on the calf of Ty.

The carpenter lay with his sword under his hand and a spear in his back, his shoulder half-severed by a deep wound. Ian set the woman down and turned the corpse over, then closed its pale, unseeing eyes.

The woman screamed. Ian grabbed Ty's sword without thinking. Whirling around as he stood up, he swung at the Roman charging him with spear at ready. There was a sickening *thwack* as the sword struck the onrushing body and cut through the man's leather breastplate, a grunt as the man's ribs cracked. He swore a Babel of an oath, and Ian could smell his rage as well as feel it. The man dropped the spear and, as he caught his balance, pulled his long sword from its scabbard.

Ian felt his own rage surging as the man aimed a blow at his head. He parried instinctively. He thrust out in rage, and was astonished to see Ty's sword find the gap it had made in the man's breastplate. There was a little grating sound—or was it a vibration heard only in a mind that comprehended what it signified?

A trick, surely! Like a magician's guillotine. He'd pull the sword out and find it bloodless. The director would yell, "Cut!" The scene would end.

It didn't happen. He seemed to have an eon to ponder it as the sword scraped ribs going in and coming out. Somewhere, between entering and leaving, it pierced the man's heart.

Ian smelled blood. A trickle. An artesian spring. A fountain gushed out around the sword hilt. Surprise, then vacancy replaced rage in the man's face. The vacancy spread downward through his limbs.

Ian caught him before he hit the earth and clutched him as if, by holding tight enough, he could prevent the spirit from departing. But the body seemed to liquefy and flow earthward; he couldn't hold it. He groped for a carotid pulse but felt nothing. For the moment, while he stood and stared at his victim, everything stopped.

"Ian, you idiot. Fight!"

Ian felt the blow as he saw a second soldier swing. Rolf killing the assailant was the last thing he remembered.

• • •

Blood. The dust had the copper taste of it. The sun, overhead, burned its color in his brain through his closed lids. Blood soaked the cotton of his tongue. And was it blood or drool that trickled down his chin?

He opened his eyes cautiously. The village lay flattened beneath the mid-day sun like an over-exposed photo of itself, its usual lively chaos faded. An urgent, orderly activity replaced its *joie de vivre*, as Roman soldiers rounded up survivors and systematically searched the houses, collecting valuables, taking inventory and a census.

He felt his head, cautiously, discovering a great lump, blood stiffening his hair, and a small, oozing cut. A shadow cooled him momentarily as someone eclipsed the sun, then Rolf squatted at his side, restoring noon.

"How are you?"

He had to think about it. His head ached; his whole body felt bruised but, after he'd cautiously moved everything, he decided the worst damage was to his self-esteem.

"I'll live."

"We're dead men," Rolf said, bleakly. "Geldings."

Ian felt a sudden, overwhelming terror—men who'd sever heads wouldn't hesitate to strike off lesser body parts. His groin muscles contracted involuntarily.

"Slaves," Rolf continued, histrionically, glaring at the sentries.

Ian realized he was speaking metaphorically. "Christ!"

His vehemence recaptured Rolf's attention. "You'll get us out of this." The confident tone was a schizophrenic contrast to the gloom and doom of just a moment earlier.

Ian shook his head and looked around. They were in the largest cattle pen, along with those of the male villagers who'd survived the slaughter. Houel was conspicuous by his absence, as was Ty. He remembered seeing Ty killed.

Ty. Not a movie stunt double.

He asked Rolf, "Where's Maura?"

"Dead."

In his mind, Ian multiplied the loss of Ty by the tragedy of all the deaths and wondered why he'd been transported back to this time. Was it just a cosmic accident? Was Ty's death any less poignant for there being no survivors to mourn it? For that matter, was his own life less meaningful for there being no one he could call kin?

He knew his mind turned to such thoughts to avoid the facts. The stupidity and waste were numbing. The Celtic system of warfare—one champion challenging another—was infinitely more civilized than this organized—modern—Roman form of war, though the Romans were infinitely more successful. He wondered how the Roman leader would do against Houel, or even against Houel's chosen champion. He himself—given the opportunity—would fight a dozen Romans.

He asked, "Where's Houel?"

"The bastards dragged him off somewhere."

"What have they done with the women?"

"Nothing. Yet."

Yet!

It was suddenly too much! He didn't want to imagine what they would do, but the probability, given events up to now…

What was it they wanted?

He got unsteadily to his feet and shouted. "I WANT TO TALK TO WHOEVER'S IN CHARGE!"

One of the Roman sentries said something to him, *Shut up*, perhaps. In Latin. Didn't they ever give it up?!

"NO MORE," he shouted, in English. "DO YOU HEAR ME? I'VE HAD ENOUGH!" He repeated himself in Celtic.

Celts and Romans alike stared with the uninvolved curiosity of city dwellers. *The man's mad. Not my problem.*

Moch looked at Rolf and jeered. "You think *he's* a god?!"

This, also, was too much. Ian whirled on Moch with a rage that made him gray and shaky. "I'm not a god! I'm a *man!* An ordinary human who's had enough. *Enough!*"

Simultaneously, Moch stepped back and Rolf stepped between

them. "Moch, are you crazy? Remember what he did to Dui? And he wasn't even angry!"

Ian ignored them. "*Whatever it is you want*," he yelled to the world in general, "*It's yours. I surrender.*"

No one had time to ask him what because, just then, several soldiers marched up with a small anvil mounted on a pedestal, and a brazier filled with glowing coals. A man with the huge arms and hands and leather apron of a smith, and the eyes of an executioner, followed them and was followed in turn by a subordinate carrying a tote full of smithing tools and a sack of jingling metal. The assistant put down the tote and up-ended the sack, dumping curved, hinged iron bands out on the ground near the anvil. The bands were slightly larger in diameter than a man's neck. Ian was temporarily distracted from his tantrum, and he watched as the smith dropped a handful of iron rivets into the brazier. One of the soldiers produced a primitive bellows and fanned the coals until the iron was glowing red.

Three soldiers, armed with spears and clubs, let themselves into the cattle pen and singled out a man at spear point. One of the soldiers twisted his arm behind his back and dragged him out next to the anvil, forcing him to kneel. The second soldier grabbed his hair and held his head still while the third put the collar around his neck. The Roman smith secured it by deftly dropping a red-hot rivet through the holes in the collar's two flanges and striking the rivet flat with a single hammer blow.

Cheaper than a padlock, Ian thought, and a great deal more permanent.

The soldiers shoved the man back in the pen with the others. Their next victim resisted. They clubbed him senseless and collared him, then threw him back in the pen.

Ian was the third to be selected. He didn't fight them, but when he didn't move fast enough, one soldier cuffed him. The second shoved him out of the pen, twisted his arm behind his back, and forced him to his knees beside the anvil. He had to put his free hand on the ground to keep from falling facedown in the dirt. They slapped one of the iron collars around his neck and, grabbing his head like steer-wrestlers in a Wild West show, jerked him into position next to the anvil. The smith's assistant drew a red-hot rivet from the fire and thrust it through holes in the collar. The heat that seared his neck was a further insult, and the ear-shattering blow of the smith's hammer, as he set the rivet, another.

This isn't happening! This isn't possible!

He tried to fight free of the nightmare, and the soldier restraining him sent pain burning into his shoulder. The smith's assistant boxed him on the ear with a well-aimed palm. Ian stopped struggling.

Back in the pen, he watched as the soldiers collared the others. There was an impersonal efficiency about the way they worked—like Wild West cowboys branding cattle, or Aussies shearing sheep—just cut one out of the herd and put your mark on it, let it go, and get another. At some level, Ian was impressed. When they were finished, they packed up the tools and brazier, and departed with the same lack of emotion as tradesmen finishing a job of plumbing.

Slave collars! He thought of the men he'd escorted in irons. But *they'd* deserved it, by God!

What have I done?

The future stretched out ahead like an indeterminate sentence— brutal and dirty—until the most sensible course seemed to be to walk up to one of the spear-bearing cretins and goad him until…

But they wouldn't kill him. He hadn't the luck. They might knock all his teeth loose, and crack his ribs or dislocate a shoulder, but they wouldn't do fatal damage. They would simply try to break him. The only way to defeat them was to refuse to give in. Arguing with them was like trying to herd fog. There was no resistance, and you got nowhere.

He surprised himself. Not even after he'd lost Marjory had he had thoughts like this. He shook himself, and the damned collar reminded him of its existence. Most of his fellow captives gave up after half-hearted attempts to free themselves, but Ian sat against a fence post and worked at getting the collar off, twisting and jerking it, hitting it against the post, venting his rage by cursing Jemma and all her ancestors.

A soft, anguished, "Oh," caused him to pause.

The surviving women, escorted by soldiers, had stopped to stare at them. Ian found himself petrified with shock and reddening with humiliation. Jemma moved out of the group, but was herded back by one of the guards. He didn't try to stop the scabrous child— literally filthy and pocked with oozing, dust-muddied sores—who darted past him and pressed herself against the fence.

The girl had the glassy white skin of one who has suffered terrible burns, and her hair was tangled and matted with filth. When she got close enough, he noticed she smelled strongly of pig manure. This last was too much! Even among the most ill-treated of the village slaves, Ian had never seen such a child. He looked at her more carefully.

"Rowena! What's happened to you?"

She grinned, showing distressing black gaps where her new front teeth had been. She leaned closer, and he could see that the "gaps" were tar covering her incisors. "Hi, Ian," she said, in a stage whisper. "Jemma did this to me so the Romans will leave me alone. She made all the children in the village be lepers."

A game within the game. Rowena was delighted to play, no doubt innocent of the stakes. But Ian had to admire Jemma's ingenuity.

The child suddenly sobered. "She said to tell you she heard the leader tell his officers he doesn't have time to waste being diplomatic. He told them to put slave collars on all the *equites* except the headman, so when Houel sees his alternative, he'll agree to a treaty. She said to tell you she's sorry."

He looked across at Jemma. It was inconceivable that she felt any remorse, but he thought he saw a tear roll down her cheek as the guards hurried them away. He felt almost overwhelmed by his confusion.

The unseasonable heat and lack of water, defeat, captivity, and humiliation took their toll, and by afternoon, the men had all collapsed despondently, sitting or lying—some passed out from blood loss or concussion—in what sparse shade they had.

A woman hidden by a cloak was escorted past them by a soldier. One of the two sentries guarding the men hailed him.

"Junius!"

Junius halted, reaching for the woman's arm to stop her, half-turning her toward them in the process. It was Jemma. Ian took in a deep breath and stood up. Junius let go of her and asked the sentry something, and Jemma used their mutual distraction to move over against the fence. Ian came to the other side of it, but before he could speak, the sentry stepped over and grabbed her breast, laughing as he said something to Junius.

Jemma made a fist and put her shoulder and her whole weight behind it as she let him have it. She kept her wrist straight when the blow landed. It caught him on the right side of the face, just below his nose. Hard. His head snapped backward, and he had to step back to keep from falling. The man was stupefied, though apparently, not seriously hurt. He stared open-mouthed at Jemma, who stood *en garde* with rage blazing in her face and both hands fisted.

Ian could see wheels turning as the sentry calculated how to handle this. Finally he gave an uncertain laugh and said something Junius found amusing. And he grabbed Jemma again.

It was too much for Ian. He reached through the fence and jerked the sentry backwards, throttling him through the bars. The other sentry quickly came to his aid, striking Ian through the fence with his lance end. Ian held on grimly.

Jemma attacked the man Ian had hold of. When Junius tried to pull her off, Rolf and Owain and all the ambulatory captives rushed into the fray. The outnumbered Romans started shouting, and reinforcements hurried up to beat the Celts back from the fence. Suddenly someone shouted, "Publius!" and all the Romans froze.

Publius turned out to be an officer.

He must have asked what happened, because the sentry who'd started the trouble pointed to Ian and babbled an outraged Latin accusation. Jemma countered his charge angrily, making an accusation of her own.

Publius turned and asked Junius a question; he answered in the affirmative. Publius asked him something else, and the sentry paled. Junius looked at him, then at Jemma, and obviously came to a decision, because he answered his superior with a nod and a gesture toward Jemma, without looking at his friend.

Publius pointed to the sentry and said something to Junius about a *centurion*. Junius put a hand on the sentry's neck and they walked away like a felon and his executioner.

Publius turned to Jemma and said something, "Come with me," Ian surmised.

Being Jemma, she stayed where she was and answered him as an equal. Ian didn't understand a word, but Publius did. He didn't seem to know whether to be outraged or amused. He looked Ian over, then glanced appraisingly at the soldiers standing around. The order he gave, finally, was to let Ian out.

"What was that all about?" Ian hurried so they would get where they were going before Publius changed his mind.

"They sent Casanova off to the brig, apparently."

"How'd you get him to let *me* go?"

"I told him I could serve him better if my mind is free of worry for my kinsman's safety." Ian raised a questioning eyebrow, and Jemma gave him a sarcastic laugh. "He said you could come, but since you're probably too old to survive a scourging, you'd better behave."

II

The tent to which they were escorted contained the standards and emblems of the commander's office, a single chair, and a table spread with maps and scrolls. Jemma, Ian and Publius were ushered in by an aide and stood waiting while the commander, who was seated at the table, concluded his business with a man in the dress of a Roman civilian. As the conversation proceeded, Ian gathered that the man's name was Lucius and his business was of a financial nature.

The commander checked the items on his table and held up a scroll. As he spoke and Lucius answered, in Latin, Jemma whispered a translation.

"...pork, wheat, *bracis, corma*, barley, cattle...What *is* this?"

"A payment order, sir, for the supplies your quarter-master had from me last month."

"But what are you doing here?"

"You left Londinium in such haste, sir...if I have to wait for payment until your return, I won't have the capital to replenish my stock."

"Of course I left in haste. I have two legions waiting...you do know how much two legions *eat* in the time it takes to travel from Londinium? Surely you do, to your profit!"

Lucius bowed obsequiously. The commander stamped the scroll, remarking dryly, "At these prices, I expect the next shipment delivered to the front."

Lucius took the scroll and bowed himself out, scarcely concealing his glee.

The aide stepped to the table. "The headman is still awaiting your pleasure, sir."

"I haven't forgotten him. It's my pleasure to make him wait. It will make him more willing to be reasonable. Where's my translator?"

"He's waiting outside, sir, but I understand you won't need him. This woman knows our speech."

"Convenient." He said something else that Jemma hadn't time to translate to Ian, but what must have been, "Come here woman," because she stepped past the aide and bowed deeply before addressing him in Latin. The aide answered. "Suetonius Paulinus."

So the commandant's name was Suetonius. *Suetonius*. The name was familiar but its significance hovered beyond reach. Ian let it go and studied Jemma. She seemed shaken by the announcement, and that appeared to please the commander.

He reminded Ian of the actor, Peter O'Toole. He had the same sort of bemused irony, the same charisma and power.

Then Ian remembered the name. Suetonius Paulinus was the Roman governor of Britain who'd put down the Boudiccan uprising in 60 or 61 A.D. Jemma had told him this was the third century. That was a swingeing mistake. *Wrong century!*

Jemma pulled herself together and answered in the affirmative with composure. Ian didn't understand the Latin, but he studied her body language. Of Suetonius's next speech, he got only, "Deceangli," and surmised that Suetonius was asking if they were of that tribe.

Jemma shook her head.

Suetonius noticed Ian's interest and frowned. He asked a sharp question involving the word *servus*. Slave. Jemma's reaction of alarm at his tone caused the Roman to ask, "*Pater?*" Ian recognized the word "father." Jemma seemed amazed. "*Maritus?*" Husband!

She blushed and stammered, and looked at the floor. "*Necessarius meus est…Et patronus meus est.*"

"*Patronus tuus. Non maritus tuus. Incundus est.*"

Ian leaned forward, fascinated to see Jemma on the spot. He asked her, in English, "What does he want?"

Suetonius slapped his hand down on the table, and Ian didn't need a translation to know he'd spoken out of turn. The Roman impressed him not at all, but he seemed to alarm Jemma. She stepped quickly to the table to plead with the commander.

Suetonius smiled. "*Ergo obseam pro auxilium tuus habeo?*"

Something like, "I have a hostage," Ian surmised when Jemma bowed, though he understood only *obseam* and *habeo*.

Later she translated the rest of the conversation for him:

"My bloody surgeon took a dive from his horse this morning," Suetonius said, "and it seems he broke his neck. With such a small force—only two centuries…To be brief, I have no one left who can stitch flesh. I'm told *you* have some skill in that regard."

"A little."

"If you are half as good as they claim, your kinsman won't have to worry for your safety."

Jemma nodded meekly.

"But I suggest you instruct him in properly servile behavior, or you'll certainly have to worry for his."

She bowed, and he said, "Publius, get her whatever she requires. And when you're done, get that damned headman in here." He dismissed the three of them with a gesture and returned to his documents without giving them another glance.

They followed Publius to the ramparts of the hill fort where the Roman soldiers were dismantling the palisade. Below them, just outside the entrance, the Romans had set up camp with tents in ranks and a protective ditch around the outside. They'd laid out their quick and their dead in neat rows, and were preparing the latter for cremation while the former writhed and moaned. Injured Celts lay where they'd fallen as the Romans dumped the village dead in the hill fort's ditch.

A young man in a tunic and slave collar appeared silently, at Jemma's elbow. He coughed to announce his presence. Jemma jumped. "Who are you?" she asked, in Celtic.

He answered in the same tongue. "Sylvanus, Lady. I was slave to the surgeon, Marcus Apius. I've been ordered to assist you."

She nodded. "Please tell Publius I will need lots of boiling water, and the strongest wine he has—at least a barrel."

Sylvanus nodded and translated, and Publius hurried away.

"My god!" Jemma told Ian. "I didn't plan on sewing up an army. I'll never have enough supplies."

"What do we do?"

"Triage."

Triage, at Jemma's insistence, included the wounded Celts. When Publius refused to gather them up, pleading a shortage of unassigned manpower, Jemma fairly spat at him. "Nonsense! You have three dozen able-bodied captives who'd do it gladly."

Sylvanus translated for Ian.

"You won't waste your time on slaves while a single Roman suffers," Publius insisted.

Jemma crossed her arms over her chest and gave him a thundering scowl. "Since you know my business better than I, you mend them."

He stepped toward her. "Get to work."

"I thought that's what I was doing."

He made a fist and aimed it at her but, at the last minute, diverted the blow toward Ian. Ian saw it coming too late and reeled as it landed.

Jemma didn't move.

Publius's second blow knocked Ian to the ground, and he followed through with a kick aimed to cause maximum punishment with minimum damage. A firestorm of pain immobilized Ian. He curled himself into a fetal position and tried to protect his head with his arms. Publius's toe found his buttocks and ribcage.

"Publius!" Jemma said, "if you injure him further, I will slit my throat with the first sharp object I can put hands on."

There was no question that she meant it—not, Ian thought bitterly, because she cared particularly for him. It was a power play. Another gambit in the game.

Publius hesitated of the moment it took Sylvanus to translate Jemma's threat. Then he stopped.

Check.

Jemma said, "You *will not* force me to serve you against my will." Sylvanus translated.

And mate.

Publius shook with rage a long moment before he whirled and stalked away.

Jemma didn't move until—within five minutes—his soldiers started to collect the wounded Celts.

· · ·

The Romans had lost fifteen men and twenty-three were wounded, and there were seventeen villagers killed, including two infants; twenty-six were in need of medical care.

They operated inside a tent. They rolled the sides up to let in light and air, and two of the least injured soldiers were ordered to shoo away flies. The damages they dealt with were fairly straightforward— internal injuries and terrible cuts from swords and spears, bruises, contusions and concussions from flying fists and falling rocks, one compound fracture from a fall from the ramparts. Several women had been gang raped and severely beaten by soldiers. There was nothing as sophisticated as the crispy aftermath of napalm, or the blood pudding of flesh and shrapnel resulting from antipersonnel bombs. Sylvanus, they discovered quickly, had basic, workman-like surgical skills, and Jemma delegated the minor surgery to him. Publius and several soldiers acted as orderlies, shifting bodies, fetching supplies, now-and-then shoveling sand on the floor to keep the surgical team from slipping in the blood.

Jemma was completely preoccupied with her work, paying attention to the others only when something she demanded was not immediately forthcoming. In between patients, while the crew rinsed the blood off the cart boards that formed her operating table and exchanged a neatly mended victim for one still in shreds, she washed her hands and instruments in a basin, with germicidal soap from her stores. One of the soldier/orderlies had been designated to rinse away the soap with the boiled water Publius had arranged for. Ian had paused to watch her when two soldiers carried in a man, face down, who'd had most of the skin rasped off his back.

Ian felt nauseated for the first time since they'd started. "My god! What happened to him?"

"Publius had him scourged," Sylvanus said, without emotion, "for putting hands on her." He shook his head in Jemma's direction.

Scourged! Ian had been listening to the Scriptures read at Eastertide all his life without ever imagining such devastation. Even Jemma looked a little ill.

Sylvanus seemed not to notice his reaction. "Rumor has it she's a witch. Although I've also heard she's a goddess. Which is right?"

Ian was happy to take his mind off the scourged soldier. "Both."

Sylvanus widened his eyes to mimic being impressed. "Who is she?"

"Circe."

"Oh, ho. Are you, perhaps, one of those she's turned into a beast? Or—you must be Ulysses."

An uncomfortable parallel, Ian thought. But he hadn't twenty years left in which to get home. He said, "No. Gofannon." Sylvanus looked skeptical. "Are you trying to make me angry?" Ian asked him. "Maybe you haven't been warned about a smith's curse?"

Sylvanus laughed. "I've also heard it rumored that *you* have a sense of humor."

8 mai

By sunset, Jemma looked and Ian felt all in, and Publius and Sylvanus were no better off. But all of them kept working.

"It's getting too dark to see, Lady," Sylvanus said, finally. "We'll have to finish in the morning."

Jemma looked down the row of injured and shook her head. "No! Publius, get me lamps and mirrors, all you can find."

Soldiers held oil lamps backed by bronze mirrors—and one of silver, commandeered from Suetonius himself—above the operating tables, and Jemma kept working. Ian stood between her and Sylvanus, helping both. Publius hovered nearby, supervising the lighting crew and awaiting further orders.

Sylvanus was starting to nod off, when Jemma said, "Sylvanus, go to bed. That's an order."

"Yes, Lady," he said, yawning. "May I finish this suture first?"

"Certainly, but hurry."

9 mai

Hours later, the soldiers of the lighting crew had been replaced by others, though Publius was still on duty. Ian found it difficult to make his eyes focus, and it seemed to take forever to decipher Jemma's commands. She was staring as if she didn't understand what she was doing. He shook her awake.

Sylvanus came in yawning. "Why don't you put her to bed?" he asked Ian. "Publius will show you where. I'll finish up."

Ian nodded. He pulled Jemma away from the operating table, wiped her hands on her apron, and removed it. She barely stirred. As he lifted her and carried her out, the sun was just coming up.

Publius led the way to a tent furnished with a small table, a basin and pitcher, and a cot with woolen blankets. A pile of fur rugs stood at its foot. Jemma was still sleeping as he laid her gently on the cot. He removed her sandals, and covered her. He was so tired he could hardly stand long enough to look for somewhere to lie down. The pile of rugs seemed to reach up for him; he was asleep before it caught him.

They were making afternoon rounds in the hospital tent, later that day, he and Jemma and Sylvanus, when Publius made an entry. He ignored the men and saluted Jemma.

"His Excellency wishes you to dine with him, Lady. He has sent what you will need to get ready to your tent."

9 mai

Jemma looked lovely, bathed and dressed for dinner. She was conferring with Sylvanus when Ian barged into her tent. Sylvanus stepped away so Ian could speak with her.

"I can't take any more of this charade!"

She seemed dismayed; she didn't ask *What charade?*

"I've been a police officer for twenty-six years and I've *never* given up on a case, but I *swear* to you—on my *wife's grave*—I'll resign. I won't tell anyone I've seen you! Just send me back."

Her eyes widened, as he spoke, and she clamped her lower lip between her teeth.

"Please," he continued, "I want my life back. I want to see my children again. I want to hold my grandchild."

"You *are* in England. Nineteen hundred years in the past—first century Britain. I can't take you back. I'm sorry. I don't know what else to say…"

He backed away, shaking his head.

Jemma followed. "…It was an accident—you weren't supposed to be there. I'm sorry, but I *can't* undo it."

He shook his head as she spoke, watching her at first, then casting about the room as if the truth might be displayed on the tent wall. His eye caught Sylvanus as he stood transfixed by the drama in the strange tongue. Ian turned on him and began to search him. The astonished slave was too terrified to move or protest.

"Ian!" Jemma demanded. "What are you doing?"

"An operation this big has to be coordinated by radio. Sooner or later, I'll find one."

"You still think this is a conspiracy? What possible purpose...?"

"You tell me."

"There's no conspiracy. There was...there will be a time machine."

Ian was suddenly hopeful. "Where?"

"It stayed in the future. My father was going to blow it up. He believes...will believe we shouldn't be able to tamper with history."

Ian felt suddenly at risk of losing his temper. "*That's mad*," he all but shouted. He clenched his hands to keep them from strangling her, then spread his fingers wide to keep from punching her. He paced back and forth until he felt a measure of composure return, then he strode over and glared down at her.

"You may be able to keep me here against my will, and even force me to play your silly games, but you're *not* going to drive me mad!"

The sentries paid him no attention. Why should they? He was unarmed. And he was Jemma's man. Sylvanus had filled him in on all the gossip. Jemma was the darling of both camps. The proper Goddess. Impartial. Imperious. Ian walked around the Roman camp as if on some important errand. When he judged the sentries weren't looking, he stepped behind Paulinus's tent, slipped beneath the side and hid between the outer tent wall and the arras. He felt like Polonius. An old fool. It was madness, he knew. Paulinus would have him run through faster than you could say "Hamlet."

What mental illness was it that gripped him—this obsession with Jemma, who scarcely noticed him? *Are you so besotted that you're reduced to peeping?*

Not peeping. Surveillance.

He shifted around until he found a vantage point from which he could better see the interior of the tent. The living quarters of Suetonius Paulinus were an amazing contrast to the place where he conducted business. The walls were hung with tapestries, and an oriental rug covered the floor. The bed—a cot covered by linen sheets and wool blankets—was half-hidden behind an embroidered curtain. A table was laid for dinner with silver and bronze bowls that held olives, cheeses, nuts, fresh fruits and meats.

Suetonius was alone when Jemma entered. He rose from his seat and offered her a chair and a silver goblet, then a toast: "You are, undoubtedly, the most beautiful surgeon in the Empire." With no one else present, no one to impress, he spoke Celtic, and spoke it more fluently than she did Latin.

She smiled politely but, as nearly as Ian could tell, the smile didn't reach her eyes.

"Are you hungry?" Suetonius asked. "Publius informs me you did the work of three men yesterday. I have never before heard him speak of a woman with admiration."

"I had the help of two excellent assistants—Sylvanus is a skilled surgeon himself—and your soldiers were most helpful."

"It's a wise commander who gives his men credit."

"I wish I could give them more." Suetonius raised an eyebrow. Jemma added, "Their freedom."

"Ah. I had almost forgotten you are Belgae."

"We are Brythons. *You* call us Belgae."

"We will discuss politics later." He clapped his hands, and the slave who'd been waiting to serve them hurried into the tent.

It was like a good stage play, Ian thought, an exercise for two players.

When Jemma and Suetonius had finished eating, and the slave was clearing the table, Suetonius served the after dinner wine himself. As he handed her the drink, he put a hand on her shoulder and caressed it. She shivered.

"You find me so repulsive?" he asked, coldly. She looked at him without apparent revulsion. "I thought you *liked* older men." She looked down at her hands. "Or is it just older slaves?"

"I'm betrothed."

"Should that make a difference to me?"

"It would to some men."

"*Brython* men?"

"Civilized men."

He laughed. "You have a poor opinion of Romans, Lady. Some of us know how to treat women."

"I spent several hours yesterday sewing up women Roman soldiers *treated*."

"What do you expect from soldiers?"

"Nothing. But they have officers. I expect their officers to be less stupid."

"You know nothing about men. Soldiers kept on too tight a rein turn to mutiny."

"And subject peoples, too badly abused, rebel."

Touché, Ian thought. It seemed that a definite sexual tension had crept into the situation. Jemma and Suetonius stared at each other for a moment, almost angrily, then he smiled. "I like your spirit. Have some more wine."

Was he genuinely entranced? How could he not be? She was so...

Stop it! Ian told himself. Sylvanus had her pegged. She was Circe. Let her turn others into swine.

Suetonius reached for the flagon and flinched, slightly, but continued to pour out the wine despite obvious pain. "You think I'm a fool to let them enjoy the fruits of their labors? They *are* soldiers."

"I think you'll soon discover it's unwise."

When he came near to hand her the glass, she shrank back, subtly.

"You need have no fear of me," he said, dryly. "I have whores enough for my needs." He sat and invited her do likewise with a gesture that evoked another involuntary wince.

She asked, "Were you injured?"

"It's nothing. An old wound that never healed right." He dismissed the subject with a gesture and a laugh. "What I really could use is a decent night's sleep."

"Perhaps I could help."

She got up and stepped toward him. He jumped from his chair and grabbed her, then pinned her arms against her sides with one arm while he felt over her waist and hips with the other.

Ian started to her rescue, but stopped when he realized what was happening. Suetonius was searching her for weapons. Jemma froze, momentarily, which seemed to appease whatever fears the Roman had of her. He lifted her skirt nearly to her crotch, glanced at her naked legs, then dropped it and released her. He sat down again and immediately relaxed. Jemma seemed to relax more slowly, but she approached him again.

"What are you up to?" he said.

"I still think I can help you."

He seemed annoyed. "The best whores and physicians in the province have given up on me. Forget it. Sit down."

"Let me try." She began to massage his shoulders as she spoke.

He leaned into her hands as he discovered how skilled they were. "I haven't felt hands like yours since I left Rome." He finished his wine and poured himself more.

"You drink a lot of that." She kept massaging his shoulders.

"It helps me sleep."

"It helps you *get* to sleep, but you don't stay asleep."

"You're a seeress," he said, dryly.

"…And when you sleep, you don't dream."

"Thank the gods."

"…And you don't awake well rested."

He laughed. "Well, physician, what do you prescribe?"

"You haven't the discipline."

"I?"

"You'd have to limit your wine to three glasses a day."

"Then I would never sleep, not even fitfully."

"For the first month, you wouldn't sleep at all—I don't recommend you start while you're campaigning. In the winter, in the south would be better."

"Then it will be a few years."

"Perhaps fewer than you think."

"A prophecy? And will I prevail at Mona?"

Jemma laughed. "Why don't you send for some oil and take off your tunic. I'll give you a proper massage."

"Why should you want to do that?" He smiled and rang the bell for his slave.

Jemma answered as the slave entered. "A challenge...To see if I can make you sleep without the wine."

He smiled broadly. "I'd give anything for that."

"Anything?"

"Bring the lady some oil," he told the slave.

The man nodded and started to leave.

"One moment, please," Jemma said. The slave paused. "Please prepare spices, for mulled wine but put them instead in equal parts of honey and boiling water."

The slave bowed and left. He returned almost immediately with a small flask of oil for Jemma.

Suetonius moved the curtain away from his bed, as Jemma rolled up her sleeves. Ian could see the glint of something gold around the upper part of her right biceps, but the sleeve prevented him from seeing what it was. She poured a little oil in her palm and rubbed it around to warm it. Suetonius removed his tunic and lay down on the bed. Jemma covered his upper body with a bed cloth and began to massage his feet.

Ian had to step back, momentarily, from the arras to keep the emotion that was shaking him from stirring the tapestry.

Jemma worked her way up, gradually, to Suetonius's thighs by the time the slave returned with the requested drink. He stood in front of Suetonius and drank a third; Suetonius finished it. When the slave left, she continued and asked, "Do you really believe you'd be poisoned?"

"I make him taste everything so he won't be tempted," he said languidly.

"I see." She started to sing in English. "*I gave my love a cherry...*"

Suetonius closed his eyes. "You must teach this magic song to one of my slaves," he said, sleepily.

She answered softly. "There's no magic. Any gentle music will do."

"Hmm."

She continued. "*I gave my love a chicken without a bone...*" Very slowly. Very sadly. She was still massaging Suetonius, but she stared off into space as if singing for someone else.

The hands over Ian's mouth and on his neck caused him to freeze and forced him to back away from the arras. The whispered voice in his ear warned him he'd be killed if he made a sound. Hands and voice proved to belong to a grizzled, one-eyed Roman soldier. "If I didn't have to explain why, I'd run you through," he said, in Celtic, when they were outside. "And if you set a foot closer to that tent before you're sent for, I'll do it yet."

The sentries ignored him.

"She'll be in there all night," Sylvanus said. "You might as well go to bed. Don't worry. You'll get her back in one piece. Suetonius is pretty easy on women. He won't tear her up. And he won't give her any diseases."

Ian whirled around, ready to smash him with his fists. The slave was too astonished to defend himself. When Ian saw he was only trying to be comforting, he dropped his hands. "Sorry." He turned his back. "Thanks."

Sylvanus shrugged and walked away.

Ian could hear Jemma's voice from the tent. "*...Until the twelfth of never, I'll still be loving you...*"

10 mai

Ian was delegated to carry Jemma's medical kit, so he got to go everywhere with her during working hours. Although the slave collar was gone, the Romans saw him as a slave and so didn't see him at all. It was a strange feeling, invisibility, but—if knowledge is power—a powerful situation. Suetonius and Publius spoke as freely in front of him as if they thought him deaf—which, for all intents and purposes, he was when they spoke Latin. But with Jemma, in private, the Roman governor spoke Celtic.

Shortly before his departure for the north, she asked him, "Please leave us our heads."

"Why?"

"Because they mean nothing to you. They have no value to you except as curiosities. But to the people of this village, they're heirlooms. Some of them are ancestors."

"I'll think about it."

After he rode out, the heads reappeared on their poles.

5 mehefin

Publius would be put off no longer, and Jemma could think of no further excuses to stay. The last of the casualties was fit to travel.

The centurion selected ten hostages with a politician's eye. Houel's son, Joess, was the first, then Pyrs and the sons or younger brothers of the clan's best warriors. Suetonius had studied the village well.

Houel's instructions to Joess, before they left, would've done credit to Polonius: "Learn their speech and anything else they can teach you. Never forget who you are."

6 mehefin

As they made their way toward Londinium, one of the things that most impressed Ian was the emptiness of the land. Small farmholds, many devastated by the fighting, were separated by vast tracts of forested wasteland. The inhabited places were connected by fragile tracks that seemed constantly in danger of being overrun by nature. Some places gave him the same feeling of mystery and magic engendered by the Arabian nights. He could easily see why primitive peoples put their cultures at the center of the universe.

He was dismayed to note that he had lost his certainty, the conviction without doubt, that the twentieth century lay just beyond the horizon, that he could return to his own world if only he could convince the right person to permit it. Though he'd never admit it to Jemma, he'd come to accept fully where and when he was.

The convoy stopped on a little rise to rest the horses, and they could see a small community perched at the head of a shallow valley to the north. Jemma dismounted and loosened the girth holding her saddlecloth in place. She yawned and stretched, causing Ian to catch his breath. He hurried off to get water for them and the animals and to get his mind on a less tantalizing subject.

Jemma was watching the village when he returned. "These houses seem to fit the landscape," she said. "Where I came from, the object seemed to be to make them as large as possible. It was obscene. The average garage was larger than the houses here. And in America, they crowded huge buildings onto tiny lots because the land was expensive but everyone still had to show off his wealth with an ostentatious house. I know it's how they kept track of who they were and what they were worth, but if you didn't buy into all that b.s., it looked more as if they had such a terrible fear of the outdoors that they had to close up the open space that we all need for sanity inside their walls."

"Curious," Ian said. He'd found the expression useful when he didn't know how else to respond. Jemma's analysis echoed something Margaret had written after visiting a wealthy friend on Long Island: *They seem to regard their surroundings—the scenery, even the Sound—the same way they do their cars and fur coats and expensive furniture—as possessions, not as things they need for their souls or as anything they're part of.*

When Ian didn't elaborate, Jemma added, "I suppose our biases are wired into our brains with our language. In America, we called undeveloped land empty or vacant. And you referred to it as wasteland, as if it were worthless when humans aren't living on it."

She didn't seem to notice she was using the past tense for events she claimed were in the future. Ian let it go. It was pleasant to converse without arguing, and an intellectual discussion at that. He found, oddly enough, that he agreed with her analysis.

7 mehefin

At a place where the track widened into a small, grassy clearing, several ancient oaks stood in a rough circle. One of them was dead, and a skeleton hung high up on its trunk, white bone against weathered gray wood.

Curiosity drove Ian and Rolf to ride closer. The skeleton's feet were missing; the lower ends of its long bones had been gnawed by animals. The man had been crucified, spikes through the wrist bones fixing his remains in place. As with the heads guarding the oppidium, the head and upper torso were still covered with flesh. Brown hair clung to the skull and to a face vaguely familiar. There was also something about the dead tree that set a memory resonating. Behind the skeleton, incised in the tree trunk, was the legend: *ECCE FUR.* Behold the thief.

Rolf pointed at the base of the tree. "Roman killed."

Ian wasn't sure if he meant the tree, the lower third of which had been relieved of its bark, or to the pile of human bones scattered beneath it.

What *was* certain was that the traders had come to the end Drullwyn predicted.

9 mehefin

Jemma called it Watling Street, and the gravel highway may well have been the road's Roman precursor. Ian and Jemma and Rolf rode together at the head of the convoy. Ian estimated they'd covered nearly twenty miles since breakfast, and guessed it was nearing four in the afternoon. After five days on the road, a hundred miles as the crow flies, men and animals were showing signs of wear. They'd had to travel at a walk to avoid jostling the injured. The slow pace was wearying. The journey brought up memories of that first trip— was it only nine weeks ago?—when he and Jemma had journeyed from the henge. Since then, riding had come to feel as natural as driving, and part of him marveled at how calmly he was taking this new development.

He and Rolf had been allowed to keep their weapons, though the hostages had only their daggers. He felt like a bit player in a local pageant. Any minute, they'd come across the M1 and be as conspicuous as a stagecoach in Piccadilly.

Publius interrupted the reverie, cantering up from the rear of the column. "Something's wrong!" He pointed to a line of trees marking a distant river, above which crows circled. "Londinium," he said. "A bad omen."

As the convoy came within sight of the city, they could see nothing but ruins: there wasn't a living thing in sight except the ubiquitous crows. The convoy fanned out to let everyone in the party get a good view of the devastation.

The Romans soldiers were, for the first time, silent. With shock, no doubt. The Celts were fascinated.

"My God!" Jemma said.

Rolf was awed. "What happened?"

Jemma answered. "Queen Boudicca raised the Iceni in revolt, and the Trinovantes joined them."

"*Hell hath no fury like a woman scorned,*" Ian said. He added, "Think what they could do with napalm and agent orange."

Jemma whirled around on her horse. "They scourged her, for God's sake! And raped her daughters! How *dare* you joke about it!"

She kicked her horse into a canter and rode off, leaving the two men staring after her.

There was no reason to stay. Nothing of value had been left by the city's sackers. What they hadn't taken, they'd destroyed; there wasn't a roof left intact in the town to offer shelter. Nor a soul to offer hospitality. The inhabitants who hadn't fled had been slaughtered, and scavengers had cleaned their bones. The travelers had no desire to associate with the sort of human vermin that remained. The convoy headed away from Londinium immediately.

Just outside of town, Rolf stopped his horse on the riverbank. As Ian and Jemma followed suit, they watched him break his spear in half and throw it in the river.

"What was that for?" Ian demanded.

"Thanksgiving to the Goddess for this victory."

Jemma took off one of her gold bracelets and threw it after Rolf's spear.

"Are you thanking the gods for the carnage too?" Ian asked.

"I'm thanking them we haven't managed to louse up history yet."

13 mehefin

"Calleva," Publius announced, "capital of the Atrebates."

The town to which he referred lay on the high ground before them, surrounded by the ubiquitous bank and ditch, which—even from a distance—they could see was in major disrepair. The informal disarray of the hilltop village had been ordered onto grids of intersecting streets, a formal array of straight lines and precise geometries. Even the market square—the forum, Jemma called it—seemed to be laid out according to a formal plan with everything where it belonged. A few stucco buildings shone whitely under red-tile roofs. And although the daub and wattle architecture still predominated, it had been squared off; there were few circular forms, no circular houses. A fountain. The arch over a garden-wall gate. A small round window high up in a wall. Having never seen such a city before, Rolf gaped.

"This is more like it," Ian told him.

They stopped their horses in front of the grandest of the stucco buildings and waited while Publius went in. He came out with a thin man in a Roman toga, whom he introduced as Constant, Cogidubnus's *major-domo*.

Publius told Jemma, and she translated, "Cogidubnus has invited you and your kinsmen to be his guests. Sylvanus will remain to translate for you. Constant will show you where to go."

Ian was suddenly aware of his rough clothes and primitive tack.

Inside, the "palace" was a typical Roman villa like those diagrammed in books. Jemma, Ian, Rolf and Sylvanus followed Constant to where a slave girl stood. Ian didn't need a translator—Constant asked Jemma to go with the girl, and the men watched them walk away. Then Constant said—Sylvanus translated—"Follow me, gentlemen." They followed; Rolf was awestruck. The suite to which Constant showed them was luxurious, with gilt appointments, mosaic floors, and beds. *Beds!* Sylvanus directed the attendants where to put the luggage, as Ian and Rolf stared like rubes.

"Not the Ritz," Ian said, "but definitely an improvement."

"You'll want to start with a bath," Sylvanus told Ian. "If you'll give me something with which to tip the attendants, I can have your clothes cleaned while you're bathing."

"Splendid idea."

Ian followed Rolf and Sylvanus into the bathhouse and, following the slave's example, disrobed. Rolf, however, refused to give up his dagger. He belted it around his naked waist. When an attendant offered to shave him, Rolf looked at a clean-shaven, shorthaired previous customer and said, "Not on your life!"

The attendant muttered *"Barbarus!"* under his breath as Rolf stalked off.

"Barbarian!" Sylvanus translated. And, "Will you have a shave, sir?"

"Tell him yes, but if he touches my mustache, I'll sic Rolf on him."

They had hot water! Steaming hot water! Rolf's discomfort with the whole situation seemed to preclude any enjoyment of it, but Ian soaked ecstatically. Later, an attendant scraped Ian with a *strigil*, another gave him a massage. He was in ecstasy.

Suddenly one of the slaves became faint and started to fall, spilling the contents of a pail he was carrying and splashing one of the patrons.

"You fool!" the man screamed, "you're finished here! Tomorrow you go to the lead mines."

A second slave hurried up with a towel and tried to make amends. "Please, sir. He meant no harm. He's been stoking the fire under the *caldarium* for two days."

"Take his part, and you'll join him."

As the "facts of life" in the Roman Empire sank in, Ian felt his pleasure drain away.

14 mehefin

The room was palatial and expensively appointed. Servants and musicians hovered about. Two men in togas lounged in the Roman fashion at a table in the center.

Constant led Ian, Jemma, Rolf and Sylvanus into the room and announced, "His Excellency, Cogidubnus, *Rex et legatus*." Sylvanus translated for Ian and Rolf.

The Roman legate and King of the Tribes Regni and Atrebates was a huge man, about fifty, Ian judged, powerfully built and gaudy with torcs and armbands. He had one foot bandaged and propped on a cushion. He motioned the visitors closer and dismissed Constant with a gesture.

The major-domo bowed and departed.

Cogidubnus said, "Welcome. Make yourselves comfortable. May I introduce Julius Classicianus, the new *Procurator* of the province? He's of the Fabian Tribe."

Classicianus was in his fifties or early sixties, and tall.

Ian sat next to Cogidubnus, opposite Jemma. Rolf and Sylvanus stood behind him. It was apparent, from the way she avoided Ian's eyes, that Jemma was still angry with him about something.

Cogidubnus signaled the servants, who began to serve wine and something like *hors d'oeuvres*. "Your accommodations are acceptable?" They were.

Quiet young men, who'd hovered in the background until now, came forward and sampled everything served to the two officials. Tasters. Roman vices; Roman remedies.

"Most luxurious, thank you," Jemma said, in Latin. Sylvanus

translated for Ian.

The king looked at Ian, who nodded. Sylvanus translated, "How was the trip from Londinium? I understand accommodations *there* are poor just now."

Jemma smiled, nodding. Ian followed her lead and nodded.

"It was most inconsiderate of Boudicca's husband," Cogidubnus said, "to take his leave without siring a male heir for the Romans to recognize. I, myself, have fourteen sons, though I plan to live to be ninety." He looked at Classicianus. "That ought to irritate at least six more governors." He noticed that Ian didn't seem to understand his reference, and he looked to Jemma, addressing both of them. Sylvanus translated. "You *do* understand how the Romans operate?"

"They make a treaty with the king," Jemma said, "a client relationship, I believe, and it lasts as long as the king lives." Cogidubnus nodded. "And if, when he dies, his people have been sufficiently enslaved by their love for Roman goods and Roman services—or Roman vices—and for the *Pax Romana*, the treaty is declared void, the kingdom a Roman province, and the tribe Roman subjects—second-class subjects, of course."

Cogidubnus was delighted. "You've obviously studied politics." He asked his companion, "What do you think, Julius?"

Jemma blushed. Sylvanus translated for Ian.

"An excellent summary," Classicianus said, "of an excellent system."

"In spite," Cogidubnus said, "of all that pig-swill they give out about the *Pax Romana*, the Romans love to fight. Our present governor is a sterling example of that—thank the gods for the Ordovices. But as long as we pay our taxes, Rome leaves us alone. And the Roman quartermasters are helping us to pay those taxes."

Classicianus asked Ian, in Celtic, "Did you get all of that?" Sylvanus translated.

Ian chose to misunderstand. "A pox on the Romans, wasn't it?" He spoke English.

Classicianus looked at Jemma, who made some explanation in Latin—no doubt of Ian's linguistic deficits. The Procurator turned and addressed the king in Celtic.

"Then, with your majesty's permission, we can speak Celtic."

Cogidubnus smiled and told Ian, in Celtic, "You can dismiss your men."

Ian shrugged, and Sylvanus started away. At Ian's insistence, Rolf followed reluctantly.

Classicianus continued the discussion where he'd left off, asking Jemma, "Don't you approve of peace?"

"Peace, yes. Enslavement, no."

"Would you say his majesty is enslaved?"

She couldn't contain her smile. "Certainly, he's *immobilized* by his Roman appetites."

The king roared. "You see, Julius? Reports of her are not exaggerated. That quack of a Roman physician couldn't recognize gout when he was staring at my naked foot. Then you'd advise me to renounce my Roman ways?" he asked Jemma.

"At least your Roman cook."

He laughed again. "Is that your best prescription?"

She answered with a smile.

Cogidubnus slapped his leg as he turned to the procurator. "It hurts like the occupation—a sharp, continuous pain."

"If I may be excused to get my medicines," Jemma told him, "I could prepare something that will provide relief."

"By all means."

The conversation seemed to die when she departed. Cogidubnus finally broke the uncomfortable silence. "Ian, have you ever seen such a city?"

"I can honestly say I haven't."

"What do you find most impressive?"

"The plumbing."

The king smiled wryly. "Very Roman."

He lapsed into a silence that the procurator eventually felt obliged to break. "What brought you to Calleva, Ian?"

"A Roman chap named Publius."

"It seems we have a wit on our hands," Classicianus told his host. To Ian, he said, "I meant, what business?"

"I see no reason why you shouldn't know—if you don't already. Jemma killed a man and fled to avoid prison. I have no idea why she brought me. Paulinus captured us and sent us to Londinium, which was sacked, and so we landed here."

"She's not your wife?"

Ian's surprise at this seemed to answer the question, and Jemma's return ended the discussion. She called for wine and, presented with a golden chalice of it, mixed in a tiny amount of a crystalline substance from a cork-stoppered glass vial. Then she presented the chalice to Cogidubnus.

He smiled. "After you."

She was suddenly, subtly alarmed. "I assure you, there is nothing harmful…"

He smiled like a crocodile, showing all his teeth.

Jemma pulled herself together and tried again. "There is nothing that would harm a man."

"Well, that's original, anyway."

Ian could tell from his laugh that he was genuinely amused, but not convinced.

"Julius," Cogidubnus said, "have you ever heard of something poisonous to women but not to men?" Classicianus shook his head. Cogidubnus turned to Ian. "Have you heard this tale before?"

"No, but I've heard of the phenomenon." Cogidubnus raised an eyebrow. Ian got up and walked around the table to stare down at Jemma as he spoke to the king. "There are some things harmless to men which are very dangerous to women…" From the corner of his eye he could see Jemma squirm. Cogidubnus and Classicianus hung on his words. "…who are with child." He turned abruptly to Jemma and asked her, "Are you expecting?" He could see her seething over her options before she answered.

"Yes," she said, tersely.

Ian nodded and picked up the chalice. "And this wouldn't harm Cogidubnus, or even you, but might damage your unborn god-ling? Or is it a baby Roman?"

She gave him a look that might have welded bronze. "Yes."

"Which?"

"A Cetsamhain gift." Her tone was mocking.

He nodded again and held the chalice up for a toast, telling Cogidubnus, "To your very good health, your Majesty." He watched Jemma closely as he drained the medicated drink and, sitting down, felt enormously pleased to be one up on her.

Cogidubnus roared over what must have seemed to be nothing more than a private domestic squabble. He pocketed the medicine vial. "I hope you'll forgive my nasty suspicions, Lady?"

"I understand you haven't remained king all these years by trusting every visitor to your court."

"By the gods!" he roared. "If I'd had a dozen like you fifteen years ago, I could have dictated terms to the Romans. Like you and Boudicca." He signaled, and the servants began to bring the rest of the meal. "What do you think, Julius?"

"I think his majesty has been trying to pry an indiscretion out of me all evening."

"A man's entitled to an opinion, even in the territories."

"Then I'd say our illustrious *governor* is to blame for the recent troubles."

Ian asked, dryly, "How do you conclude that? I thought your predecessor—what was his name...?"

"Catus Decianus."

"...Decianus, set Boudicca off by seizing her property and raping her daughters."

"And why do you suppose he felt he could get away with that?" Ian shrugged.

"The provincial governor," Cogidubnus explained, "and the procurator have powers designed to check one another. Suetonius commands the army, but our friend, here, commands the paymaster, and they report independently to Rome. If Suetonius had been in Londinium, administering to the *whole* of the province, instead of on the frontier harassing the Ordovices, Decianus would never have been so bold."

"That bit of incompetence cost the Empire three cities," Classicianus added.

"Not to mention," Jemma added, "the waste of lives. Or don't you believe in mercy either?"

"Oh, I do," said Classicianus, "but not for the reasons you suppose." Jemma raised an eyebrow. "Dead men can't pay taxes. Besides, oppression breeds rebellion and, Zeus knows, the Belgae are rebellious enough by nature. Just keeping you from one another's throats occupies two legions." He held his glass up to toast Cogidubnus. "As his Majesty pointed out, if you could unite, you could dictate terms to Rome."

Cogidubnus was obviously pleased by the compliment. Ian sat back moodily, not eating, and watched Jemma.

Classicianus also turned his attention to Jemma. "You Belgae are like spirited horses. We could beat you into submission, but of what use would you be? Better to tame you—get you used to the warm stable and full manger. You know the story of Pegasus. When Bellerophon finally slipped the bridle off, he'd lost all his desire to leave."

"Also his immortality," Jemma said, not concealing the irony.

"You should have been born a man, Lady. What a debater you'd have been!"

"I was born a Celtic woman, and in this land, that's at least as good as being born a Roman man."

Both Classicianus and Cogidubnus laughed heartily. Ian, who'd been drinking steadily, held his glass up for a toast and caught Jemma's eye as he peered over it. "*Touché!*"

"What do you think, Ian?" Classicianus asked. "Do you think she should have been born a man?"

Ian leered at her. "*That* would have been a very great pity." Her deep blush was almost compensation.

"Your name wouldn't happen to be Belinos?" Classicianus asked him.

"What?!"

"Never mind."

• • •

Several dozen courses later—Ian stopped counting around seven as he had carefully refrained from noting how often his cup was being refilled—a slave woman began singing to the accompaniment of a lyre. To Ian's admittedly tipsy sensibilities, her song was pallid in comparison with that of a Celtic bard.

Cogidubnus yawned. "I don't want to appear rude, but this foot is killing me. Please continue without me."

He signaled, and servants brought poles that they stuck under his couch to transform it into a litter. He held the medicine vial up and said to Jemma, "Tomorrow you can instruct me in the use of this." He turned to Ian, indicating the singer. "If she pleases you, you may use her as your own."

"Er...no thank you."

"You'd prefer a boy?"

As Ian shook his head, it was obvious, even to him, that Cogidubnus wasn't pleased by his refusals. "I've taken a vow not to lie with a woman—or a boy—until Lughnasad."

Jemma hid her amusement by taking a quick sip of wine. Classicianus stifled a guffaw.

"A very strange vow."

"Nevertheless, I don't wish to offend the gods by breaking it."

Shaking his head, Cogidubnus signaled, and the servants carried him out.

Ian was still slightly drunk when he bumped into Jemma in the corridor, later, and he made an elaborate show of looking to see if she was alone.

"No escort? Impending motherhood's reformed you. Or have you just lost your taste for Roman officials?"

"He loves his wife," Jemma told him flippantly. "What can I do?" She stepped into his personal space and traced a circle on his breastbone with her finger. "Pity you took that vow. I was going to ask *you*."

Before Ian could recover from his astonishment, she closed her bedroom door in his face.

21 mehefin

It was a tribute to Jemma's skill as a physician that Cogidubnus *walked* out to see his houseguests off. Classicianus's escort sorted itself into a tidy column, beside which Jemma, Ian, Rolf and Sylvanus made an untidy clot. Ian noticed that Sylvanus had rid himself of the hated collar. He was Jemma's man, now, though she had given him his freedom.

Cogidubnus turned to the procurator. "Give my regards to Paulinus."

"My informants tell me he's out laying waste to Iceni lands," Classicianus said, dryly. "I doubt I'll see him before fall."

"Then where are you going?"

"To see if anything in Londinium can be salvaged before I report to Rome."

"Good luck to you, then."

The king and the procurator saluted each other, and Classicianus bid farewell to Jemma and Ian.

Then they accompanied Cogidubnus as he *walked* back into his palace.

To the north, thousands of people were killing each other, but the reports seemed scarcely more real than the nightly body counts on the goggle box back home. Millions starved in Bangladesh, thousands drowned in Pakistan, hundreds were massacred in Africa, Bosnia, Croatia, Palestine, Iraq…Only the particular deaths, of the loved ones of those around him, seemed to have any reality. The cook's son slain in St. Albans was a tragedy. The reported death of Boudicca a lifeless fact. Jemma said something similar one afternoon. "It's like hearing about the Civil War—the numbers are meaningless."

Speaking of Jemma, whatever she'd been in her past life, she was here, now, a bloody saint—patient and loving. She reminded him of Marjory, and the resemblance brought his loss constantly to mind. It nearly brought tears to his eyes.

That he had somehow traveled 1,900 years into the past was a fact he'd finally accepted, must accept. What was less easy to comprehend, was that he had not gone mad accepting it.

The month they stayed in Calleva was a looking-glass version of their stay at the oppidium. Life at the palace was pleasant, but not without expense. Living in the palace, as a guest, not a slave, required accepting slavery as the status quo, as well as the regular violation of human beings. Only Jemma, by virtue of her priceless skills, seemed able to set her own terms. Cogidubnus punished Ian for his transgressions by having Rolf whipped.

Ian quickly tired of palace life—lounging about in court, playing dice, and gossiping at the baths were boring, and he soon reestablished his reputation for eccentricity by frequenting the wharves and markets, asking questions of fish-mongers, priests, smiths and potters. The Latin he'd struggled to acquire as a boy returned, and he expanded on it, conquering the argot of the province.

The king was a consummate politician, who balanced the conflicting needs of the Roman occupiers for order and taxes with those of his Celtic constituents for freedom and relief.

In order to silence the criticism of some of the *equites*, Cogidubnus declared Ian an engineer and put him on the payroll. Under this job description, his duties were quite flexible—from supervising work crews to judging torts involving questions of contractors' skill or the quality of their materials.

25 gorffennaf

"What's at this Dubris?" Jemma asked.

"Freedom," Ian said.

"What sort of freedom?"

"As in, 'The truth shall set you free.'"

He could smell the sea long before he saw it, and hear the seabirds crying. And then, beyond the fringe of wind-sculpted brush that screened the horizon, the breakers whispered. They came to the cliff-top and spread out along the edge before dismounting to look down.

Ian knew immediately where they were. There was no mistaking it. Two thousand years couldn't alter it enough to make him mistake it for any other place on earth. One thousand, nine hundred forty-four years, to be precise! Though he had known it for months, he felt the swift metamorphosis of certainty to despair as he stood, staring at the proof. Looking down at the chalk cliffs and channel of Dover was like seeing the body long after the news of death has been received.

My God! Dover!

He felt he was looking backwards. Lot's wife. Turning to salt. His eyes were turning to salt. He'd felt the feeling before, at Eastertide, after Marjory's death, when he'd visited her grave. The finality was overwhelming.

The shock must have showed on his face, because Jemma put a hand on his arm. She said nothing. The gesture seemed appropriate—proper behavior for a wake.

With some peripheral part of his mind, he noticed that Rolf

and Sylvanus were alarmed. Rolf asked, "What's wrong?" but Ian couldn't answer, and Rolf seemed afraid to pursue it further.

After a while, Jemma said, "Let's go."

Ian was immobilized; the others had to lead him to his horse and help him mount. Sylvanus took the reins and led the animal as they turned their backs on the white cliffs.

27 gorffennaf

Ian sat in the inn's common room, at a table with a cup and wine flask in front of him. After two days of drinking, he needed a shave and a bath, but no one in the place had the nerve or desire to mention it. Rolf and Sylvanus sat at a table nearby, eating and drinking. Watching him. The other patrons went about their businesses.

Jemma brought him a mug of soup, which he ignored. She sat down across from him.

He said, "I didn't really believe."

She said nothing.

"…It's not possible…"

"You've seen things these people can't imagine—air travel and lasers, test-tube babies, nuclear reactors…Why is time-travel so difficult?"

He shrugged and shook his head, then took another drink and stared off into space, effectively dismissing her.

And Jemma finally left.

28 gorffennaf

I

Ian refused to leave the common room that evening, so Rolf took it upon himself to stand guard. He sat on the floor at Ian's feet, against the base of the table, nodding off and on until all the other patrons had departed. Ian watched him through a haze of alcohol. Rolf looked around and, finding nothing alarming, made himself comfortable. He was instantly asleep. Ian put his head on the table and wished he could be too.

He didn't raise his head when two men entered. He kept his eyes closed and tried to will the room still and the table solid as he cursed his stupidity and his hangover. The part of his mind that had once functioned in an investigative capacity noted—without interest—that the voice of one of the newcomers sounded familiar. The men seemed surprised to find the room occupied. One of them crossed the room to peer at Ian.

The intruder poked him and grabbed his hair, lifting his head off the table, then letting go. Ian let his head hit the tabletop with a thud. He didn't stir. The man nudged Rolf with his foot; Rolf snored loudly.

"Drunks," the intruder said. He was speaking Latin as he had been when Ian first heard his voice. Where was that? *When* was it? He opened the eye that was close to the tabletop and was just able to see the man help himself to his wine flask. The gesture made a connection in Ian's mind. Wine. "...beer, barley, cattle..." He was Lucius. The provisioner. They'd seen him in Paulinus's tent.

The other man said, "Why don't you take his purse while you're at it?"

Lucius carried the wine flask away, and Ian risked a look at the two from beneath the arm that rested on the table.

"Why don't I just cut his throat," Lucius said, "and really call attention to our presence?" He walked over to a table near the fire and sat down.

The other man followed. "What time did you tell this cattle thief to meet us?"

"Midnight."

"Then he's late already."

Ian could hear the door open, and a gaudy native entered. He started toward the two men, spotted Ian, and detoured. Ian closed his eyes. The raider prodded Ian with something sharp. A knife. Ian kept his eyes closed and didn't move.

"Leave him alone," Lucius demanded in Celtic.

Ian opened his eyes a slit as the raider reluctantly sheathed his knife and joined them. "What's this work you have for me?"

"You know Second?" Lucius asked him. The raider nodded. "We want you to make sure the new procurator doesn't report to Rome."

Ian began to sweat.

"What makes you think he hasn't sent a report already, from Londinium?"

"He has," Lucius said. "But it didn't get there. However, I'm sure he'll send another."

The raider nodded.

"That would not be in our interest."

"What did you have in mind?"

"How many men have you got?"

"Thirty I can count on."

"Good. He'll probably go to Rutupiae to see the messenger safely off. Normally, he'd go by way of Calleva, but an ally of ours is sending word to him in Londinium that malcontents are trying to overthrow Cogidubnus."

Second was surprised. "Are they?"

The raider laughed. "They'd easier overthrow the Emperor."

Lucius nodded impatiently. "But they're sufficient in numbers, if they're stirred up a bit, to impress the procurator's spies, and he knows he's got enemies here. My guess is he'll bypass Calleva and go directly to Rutupiae." He pulled out a map, unrolled it, and started to point out possible ambush sites.

Just then, Rolf started to wake. All three conspirators jumped; the raider whipped out his knife.

Ian rolled off the table, onto Rolf, and whispered, "Play dead or you will be."

Rolf was suddenly wide-awake; Ian could feel him stiffen, but he thought fast enough to obey before the raider got to them. Ian started to snore. When the raider poked his knifepoint in Ian's throat, his snoring didn't miss a beat. The raider kicked him, but he didn't move.

"Damn drunks," the raider said. He spat on them and went back to the table. "Let's get finished here."

II

Tired and hung over, Ian stood with his horse at the top of the cliff, looking down at the Channel. From time to time, he tossed a pebble over.

Was it like this when one died? Was the spirit overwhelmed with longing for what was irretrievably lost? Were hauntings nothing more than souls unable to let go?

But wasn't it better to be a live Celt than a dead Englishman?

That seemed to be a decision. *This* had become his life, *these* his people. He was not sure how such a radical transformation had been accomplished so much against his will, but the thought of never again seeing Rolf or Jemma or Rowena was as wrenching as the notion had once been of never seeing Peter and Margaret again. Now *they* were as faded in his memory as Marjory, as they were truly dead to him, or—more accurately—he to them. And he was powerless to change it.

He patted the horse's shoulder. "I survived Marjory's death," he told her. He mounted and took a last look at the Channel, then shrugged. "Life goes on."

Back at the inn, the landlord was making breakfast for the few patrons who were up. Ian draped himself over the table and tried not to move his head.

Jemma came in. She got a pitcher and clean cups from the landlord, and came to sit next to Ian. She did *not* say good morning.

"Well, getting drunk didn't help," he told her. "Have you anything for a hangover?"

"Have you tried distillate of dog hair?"

He gave her a withering look. She handed him four white tablets and answered his unanswered question. "Aspirin and caffeine. I've been saving them for an emergency." She poured milk from the pitcher for him. "What do you plan to do now?"

He gave her a look intended to say, "Oh, come on!"

"I'm sorry," she said. "I'd change it if I could."

He relaxed. "I suppose what all displaced persons do—find work. Perhaps return to the oppidium." He was shaking from the hangover and from emotion. He paused to get himself in hand. Finally, he said, "I'm too old to start over!"

"What alternative have you?"

He looked at her and saw genuine concern. He said, "You're not like what I thought."

"Is that meant to be a compliment?"

He ignored the sarcasm. "The papers said the man you killed was your lover."

"And the papers are always right."

He said nothing.

Jemma stared into space as she spoke, seeing it all again, and so she spoke with absolute conviction. "I accepted a dinner invitation.

One lousy dinner! I didn't even go up to his apartment. He raped me in his car. Being a doctor, he knew just how much pressure to apply, and where, to produce unconsciousness without producing bruises."

"Did you tell that to the police?"

"How naive you are, Inspector Carreg. Of course I did. Everyone was willing to believe I could be his lover but not his victim. You're a cop. Can you tell me why that is?" He shook his head; he couldn't meet her eyes. "Because he was old enough to be my father, maybe? A rich man? A pillar of the community? A kindly old baby doctor?"

"So you killed him?"

"That wasn't the end of it. Not the worst. He told me afterwards, when the police had let him go—with apologies for the hysterical female, I might add—that I was too old to please him. He liked the young ones. And as a pediatrician, he could pick and choose. *That* was when I shot him. I'd do it again, even more decisively."

Before Ian could say anything, Rolf swarmed into the room. "Ian, you were right! I found where they stable their horses! And Sylvanus had the good fortune to hear the throat-cutter say he'll be leaving in the morning."

Jemma was alarmed. "What's going on?"

"Do you remember if Tacitus mentions a plot to assassinate Classicianus?"

"No. I mean he doesn't mention one. Why?"

"There's one afoot, and we're going to foil it."

"But what if we change history? We might never be born."

"But we were. You're not going to lose your nerve at this late date?"

She looked up sharply, prepared to do battle, then noticed he was having her on. There was a definite sexual tension in the air between them that was too powerful to be newly born. He hadn't acknowledged it to himself before.

Jemma's anger vanished, replaced by a sort of diffidence. "My father was going to destroy his time machine because of the havoc he could foresee, even if it was only used for good."

"We *still* can't foresee the future," Ian said. She started to protest, but he interrupted. "It may be that our being here, doing what we do, is what made our history unfold as we know it. Or we may have changed its course already—we can't know. All those men you saved—one of them may father another Hitler or Caesar or Ivan the Terrible…" She began to be dismayed. "…or Mother Teresa. We can only do what seems right to us *now*. I've been a policeman all my life; I could no more ignore an assassination attempt than you could watch a man bleed to death."

"You're right, of course. I'm out of my field here. But what can only four of us do?"

"We'll have to improvise."

"Even if we die trying?"

"Then that's history. You don't have to come."

"Of course I do. What's the plan…"

"…There isn't much we *can* plan," Ian said.

30 gorffennaf

I

Early morning sunlight filtered through dusty branches overhead, dappling the four travelers and their horses. The sparse grass on the ridge top that formed the track couldn't hold down the dust. It billowed up as they moved, washing track and travelers with the same soft gray.

"We don't know who else we can trust," he continued, "and there are too many of them for us to make a citizens' arrest. We'll just have to follow them until they set up their ambush, then try to slip around it and warn Classicianus."

Jemma rode ahead to ask Rolf something, and Sylvanus dropped back to talk to Ian. "Should we be bringing a woman on such a dangerous mission?"

Ian laughed. "She's a Celtic woman—they laugh at danger, and we're *Cymry*."

"So?"

"She's decided to come. My wife was like her. Once she's made up her mind, there's no point in trying to dissuade her."

"Was? Your wife died?"

"A long time ago."

Sylvanus looked from Ian to Jemma and back, and a light seemed to dawn.

The party dismounted to rest the horses, and Sylvanus held them as Rolf went off to scout ahead.

"There's something I've been wanting to ask you," Ian told Jemma.

"Shoot."

"What made you choose this time?"

"I didn't. I couldn't go forward—there's no statute of limitations on murder. Women were equal to men among the Celts—are equal—in pre-Christian times, so Celtic Britain seemed like an ideal past to flee to. I didn't plan on landing in the middle of the Boudiccan uprising. I meant to come after it was all over—around two hundred. There must have been a glitch. When I heard Paulinus's name, I can't tell you...well, I imagine you know how it feels..." She trailed off as she realized he was staring at her. But how could he not stare? Even coated with dust, she was lovely enough to make him catch his breath. He was debating saying something to that effect when Rolf reappeared.

"They've made camp. Looks like they might be staying for a while."

They heard a loud whistle.

Rolf waved to get Sylvanus's attention, then pointed to the bushes at the side of the road and urgently mouthed, "Get out of sight, quick!"

Sylvanus dived behind the nearest stand of saplings, dragging all four horses. Rolf, Ian and Jemma followed quickly, slipping up to the horses' heads to prevent them from calling to the animals that could be heard approaching.

The whole forest seemed to hold its breath. Insects droning and the far-off call of birds were amplified by the sudden silence. The swishing of the horses' tails sounded loud as whips. The hoof beats of the approaching animals echoed like drum rolls off the green walls of foliage enclosing the trail. Two men rode into sight. Familiar faces. Lucius and Second! Lucius whistled.

Ian drew his sword and stepped out in front of them. "You're under arrest."

Lucius laughed as he dismounted. "I came to warn our associates they were followed. If I'd known it was by drunks, I'd have saved the trip." He drew his sword; he threw Second his horse's reins.

"If your fighting's no better than your planning," Ian said, "I'm safe enough."

"Save your breath, old man. I'm not a stupid Celt, to lose my head over an insult." He charged and, as he got within sword range, simultaneously stabbed with his blade and stepped to the side.

Ian was watching for something of the sort and deflected the blade with his own. When Lucius raised his sword skyward for the *coup de grace*, Ian needed both hands to block it. The impact shook him to his toes and nearly jarred the weapon from his grasp. With his peripheral vision, he saw that Second had dismounted and let the horses go. He ran toward Ian.

"Ian, watch your back!" Rolf's warning was accompanied by his drawing his own sword. Rolf would cope. Ian dismissed Second from mind.

He was beginning to tire. Getting too old for this. And Lucius had murder in his heart. Ian aimed a kick at his knee and heard a gratifying crack as it connected. Lucius swore as he fell, and rolled as he landed. He grabbed a handful of dirt; Ian dodged and buried his face in his sleeve. He could smell the dust as it scattered, could feel it settle on his head. He heard Lucius scrabbling to his feet, breathing hard, and Rolf and Second grunting and swearing. There was a gasp as Rolf's blade found a target in Second's vitals.

Lucius took advantage of the brief distraction to swing at Ian's head. Infuriated, Ian faked a return of the strike and followed with a quick jab at his throat. The point connected, and blood spurted from around the blade to dye his tunic crimson. Lucius looked surprised. His eyes followed the flow earthward and fixed on something immeasurably far beneath his feet. And then they seemed to go unfocused, and Lucius dropped dead on the road.

Ian was not as horrified as he had been when he killed the Roman soldier.

Rolf came up and slapped him on the back. "Ian, now that we are *Cymry*..." He looked at Ian to be sure he was saying it right. "... you have to act like a man and set a good example."

Jemma and Sylvanus dragged the horses out of cover and watched with uneasy fascination as Rolf took Ian's sword and hacked off Lucius's head. Ian flinched as the blow landed, but he didn't dispute the act.

Rolf held up the head. "And since there are no *the-police* in this land, to protect you from evil spirits and bad luck, you *need* this." He lost his grip on the shorthaired, blood-slippery trophy and laughed. "I swear these Romans cut their hair short so we won't want their heads." He quickly constructed a rope sling for the head and charged up to Ian's horse, which rolled her eyes and backed away.

"I don't blame you," Ian told the horse. He asked Rolf, "What about the rest of him?"

Rolf finished tying the bloody talisman around the horse's neck. "It's nothing. Leave it. And the other one's nothing—a back-stabber, food for crows."

"That alone is reason to bury them. Or we might as well send out an announcement we've arrived."

II

The raiders had camped halfway down a broad ravine at the bottom of which a nearly dry stream meandered. Dense forest and great, jagged rocks on the bluff tops made attack on the camp from above improbable; sentries guarded the approaches at either end.

Ian, Jemma, Rolf and Sylvanus had entered the ravine before the sentries were posted and, since the men never looked for intruders between themselves and their camp, the four were undiscovered. The Cymry were watching from a position on a bluff opposite the one above the camp when Rolf pointed to a rock formation on the bluff top above it. "Too bad we can't get up there. We could roll those rocks down on them and wipe them all out."

Sylvanus entered into the spirit, pointing. "That grass is very dry. If we sneak upwind and set it on fire, it would panic their horses."

"I thought the plan was to slip around them and let the authorities deal with them," Jemma said.

"The authorities aren't in a very forgiving mood right now," Ian told her. "If we turn these characters in, they'll all hang. Suppose we just persuade them to go away?"

"We just ride in and show them your bloody trophy," Jemma said, dryly. "And say fun's over guys, go home?"

"Not exactly. They not only chose a great spot for an ambush, they chose a great spot to be ambushed in."

"You're crazy! Four of us?"

"They don't know how many we are."

Rolf was suddenly excited. "What did you have in mind?"

III

The preparations were relatively simple—had to be. They had neither the time nor the equipment to get too creative. They reconnoitered during the afternoon, learning the game trails and streambeds—any path of least resistance through the forest undergrowth. They located and marked the natural drums of several hollow trees, leaving cricket bat-sized sticks nearby to use as drumsticks, and Jemma showed them how to make curious noisemakers. "Bullroarers," she called them, adding, "Too bad we don't have a bagpipe."

At dusk, she and Ian worked their way up the bluff face to the rock formation above the raiders' camp. It was slow work for non-climbers, and they were further handicapped by poor light and the need to stay out of sight. When they reached the jumble of loose slabs and assorted boulders, they carefully loosened the largest of the latter. They wedged it with a branch to which they tied the longest of their three ropes. The rope end was then dropped down the bluff face and *gently* maneuvered into a crack in the rock. One would have to look for it to notice. Getting down without springing their own trap occupied half the night.

Rolf and Sylvanus, meanwhile, cut their non-essential clothing into strips with which they set snares along all the game paths save the two the sentries used. Giant rabbit snares to catch hare-brained conspirators.

31 gorffennaf

I

Jemma was tightly rolled in her blanket when Ian came to wake her, covering her mouth to prevent her crying out. She awoke terrified but relaxed when she recognized him. Ian removed his hand and put his finger over his lips, then moved to awaken Sylvanus as he had Jemma.

Sylvanus yawned and looked around, then whispered, "Where's Rolf?"

Ian answered in a whisper. "I sent him down to keep an eye on things. We should start as soon as Jemma's away."

"You're not sending *Jemma* away!" she whispered fiercely.

"Jemma, listen! Someone has to go, and you're the one who's least likely to be shot on sight."

She saw the logic of this and her annoyance subsided. "Oh, all right."

"Good, then get your horse and lead her over that ridge." He pointed. "...and down the ravine until you're well past the ambush. Then it'll probably be safe to get on and ride like the devil is after you."

She nodded and started away, then returned to thrust a hand at Ian. "Good luck."

She seemed to want to do more than shake hands. God knew, *he* wished for more, but he only shook hands with her and watched as she went resolutely to her horse.

• • •

Ian watched from the ridge above the camp as the mercenaries broke their fast below. From his hiding place, he could just make out the dreamy disturbance in the air above a small, smokeless fire hidden from the raiders. Convection currents. Sylvanus squatted next to the fire and grabbed a torch from among the flames before striding out of sight.

Rolf was painted and coifed for war, his hair stiffened with lime, and strange blue symbols adorning his face, chest and shoulders. As he gave Rolf final instructions, Ian was struck, again, by the resemblance to Native American traditions.

The younger man didn't like the idea of guerrilla warfare, insisting, "It's our custom to challenge their best warrior to individual combat."

"These pirates don't fight fair." He could see Rolf wasn't convinced. "Oh, all right. Go ahead. Challenge them. But be ready to run if they all attack at once." Rolf kept scowling. Ian said, "Running off to fight another day is an old, honorable Celtic tradition. Vercingetorix almost defeated Caesar with it."

Rolf mounted and rode out to challenge the mercenaries, and was nearly impaled by a dozen spears. When he'd high-tailed it back to his own lines, Ian refrained from commenting.

"Rotten bastards! There's not a head in the whole lot worth bloodying your sword to take."

At that moment, Sylvanus set fire to the grass upwind of the mercenary camp. As the fire spread, the mercenaries' horses stampeded. Many of the raiders took off after them.

Ian pulled the rope they'd hidden on the cliff face. The wedged boulder teetered, tipped and bounced, spilling the smaller boulders and loose debris down on the camp.

After that, the three Cymry did a creditable job of picking off their foes. They took turns jumping out of hiding to throw a rock or spear, then dashing for cover to run to another place to attack from, all the while shouting and banging their cooking pots or the hollow trees they'd marked to simulate a larger force.

Individual mercenaries trying to desert got caught by the snares and trip-ropes. Smoke rose from the ambush site as they bailed out in every direction, bumping into each other in their great haste to escape. In no time, all but a handful had fled. Those who remained were near panic because they hadn't seen any of their attackers except Rolf. When Ian, Rolf and Sylvanus charged them, screaming and yelling for their "followers" to join them, the last of the hirelings panicked and broke ranks, leaving only the throat-cutting leader to face the foe. So, Rolf got his chance to fight *mano a mano*. It was a short-lived battle—strike, parry, counterstrike. The throat-cutter was a cornered rat with all to lose, but Rolf was a man whose ancestors had been great warriors, a man who might never get another chance, under the *Pax Romana*, to prove his own prowess. *He* fought like a berserker.

The mercenary suddenly dropped his sword and threw himself at Rolf's feet. "I surrender!"

Rolf swore and kicked the man and kicked his sword beyond his reach. "Get out of my sight, you throat-cutting worm."

Ian, meanwhile, had lost his sword and was chasing a mercenary with a tree branch, when the man ran into the lead rider of a troop of Roman soldiers. Ian skidded to a halt.

"Ah. Reinforcements!" he said. He spoke Celtic. In his excitement, he couldn't remember the Latin.

The mercenary took off. Ian realized he was escaping and started after him, but was cut off by one of the Romans.

"I suppose you're wondering what's going on," Ian said.

The Roman held his ground, scowling.

Ian tried desperately to remember enough Latin to reason with him, but gave it up. "Sylvanus, help!"

Sylvanus came running. Simultaneously, a Roman tribune rode up, and Rolf stepped closer, panting. Rolf dropped his weapons and held his arms out, telling Ian and Sylvanus to do the same.

Breathing heavily, Ian assessed the situation. He spotted a loose horse at the edge of the clearing and said to Sylvanus, "You'd better explain." He raised his arms, then sidled toward the horse as the astonished Romans watched. Suddenly he darted to the animal and grabbed its reins. As he vaulted astride, he called to his friends, "I'm going after Jemma."

One of the soldiers aimed his spear at Ian, but before he could throw it, Classicianus broke from the arms of his escort and deflected the spear.

II

The story in the dust was clear, Ian realized, with as much surprise for the talent he suddenly found himself possessed of as with shock for the event itself. Two men had ambushed Jemma—the huge hoof prints were obviously her horse's. They'd startled her horse. There were signs of it skittering backward. Someone had dragged her from the horse. And one had carried her off—witness the deepened footprints—while the other took the horse away.

Ian followed the man who'd taken Jemma. The tracks stopped in a tiny alcove of grasses among the trees. Flattened grasses, splattered with drops of red, testified to a struggle.

There were no bodies. Ian didn't need to dismount to see that the chase continued. Bent grasses and snapped twigs, and a golden thread of Jemma's hair led him out the far side of the clearing and in a wide arc back to the river, with Jemma fleeing, her ambusher in pursuit. And the odd drop of crimson to show that one of them was hurt.

How long can blood stay so red?

He alternately swore and prayed. If he'd discovered her only to lose her again, he'd surely slit his throat—after he'd cut out the heart of her assassin.

The signs showed that the second ambusher had joined the chase after Jemma regained the path she'd been following before the attack. His feet blurred the footprints of the others and smeared the drops of blood.

Ian almost tripped over the bleeder.

Dressed in Celtic tunic and drawers, but with a Roman's naked face, the body lay face down with its torso pointing the direction of the chase.

Ian dismounted and turned it over.

Flies had discovered the sight-less eyes and immobile mouth. There wasn't much external damage. A trickle of blood marked the spot Jemma's knife entered the belly, but the abdomen bulged—evidence of mortal damage done. There was no sign of the knife. Ian let the body fall face down again.

He remounted, running, and cursed the horse, urging it faster. Trails led off in three directions where no grass grew to point the way, and feet left no traces in the gravel underfoot. He chose the track leading up the side of the ravine, and spurred the horse into a frantic scramble up the wall.

From the rim, he could peer down vertical walls that amplified the hiss and gurgle of tumbling water. Upstream, the channel curled around a corner wall of limestone. Downstream, it widened, allowing a small, alluvial crescent to form where the stream widened in a pool some seven meters in diameter. Above the pool, the ravine rim stretched upward ten meters, in a steep cliff.

Below him, Jemma bent over the pool, kneeling at the water's edge, washing blood from her hands. A bloody dagger lay on the rock next to her.

Before Ian could call to her, a man strode up and dived on top of her. She struggled. She reached for her knife, but her assailant kicked it into the pool. She kicked and scratched and bit, but he gradually overpowered her.

Ian threw himself off the lathered horse and raced to the cliff edge, where he froze, torn between intelligent fear for his life, if he dived, and Jemma's survival if he didn't. It was a higher cliff than the one at Cymry Reservoir, and the depth of the water below it was impossible to judge.

The assassin pulled his knife and tried to stab Jemma. She grabbed his knife-hand with both her hands and twisted, kicking at his crotch. He stumbled. They fell together. He dropped the knife.

She grabbed it. She rolled on her back, pointing it at him. He dove for it and missed, impaling himself, and the momentum of his dive carried him, and Jemma with him, into the pool.

Jemma screamed. Her cry, before she went under, and her violent thrashing as she sank made two things plain to Ian: The water was very deep. And Jemma couldn't swim. He took a deep breath and dived, cutting the water with very little splash. He felt the gravel of the river bottom strike his outstretched hands. His momentum carried him over, backward, pressed him against the gravel. He forced his eyes open and saw green-gold sunlight through grassy pond-weed, a crimson seepage eddying, and the white emptiness of the assassin's face. Jemma's cries came to him transformed, a shimmer of bubbles whipped surface-ward as she thrashed about. He forced himself to be still. Discovered up. Reached for it. Gasped.

And then he went to Jemma's aid, although she nearly drowned him. She was barely conscious when he dragged her ashore and laid her on the grass. The water seemed to have washed most of her glamour away. Lying there, in the pale sunlight, with her hair and clothing awry, she was a life-sized woman. Frightened. Tired. Perhaps in pain. Brave and clever, but human. A woman—he realized—he'd come to love in this new life as he'd loved Marjory in the old.

As he looked her over for injuries, he could see the blood pulsing in her throat and was acutely aware of how her nipples showed darkly, provokingly, through the wet cloth of her tunic. He wanted so much to fondle them it hurt, but he sat back on his feet and grabbed his knees.

He put his palm gently against her cheek. She shivered, but kept her eyes squeezed tight—as if afraid of what she'd see and too exhausted to fight it. She breathed rapidly, through slightly parted lips. Irresistible lips. An opportunity provided by the gods. Perhaps the only chance he'd ever have…

And surely he deserved something for his efforts.

He leaned forward on his hands. He moistened his lips and pressed them gently over hers. Tenderly. Lovingly.

He felt her try to shrink away. Her eyes opened, wide with fear. Then recognition replaced the fear, and puzzlement the recognition. She stopped trying to resist. When he withdrew, she murmured, "What are you doing?"

"CPR."

She was still breathing hard. She smiled and slipped two fingers into the neck of his tunic. She pulled him closer, and they kissed again.

III

After a while, he pulled her to a sitting position and sat beside her. He laced his fingers between hers. They sat catching their breaths, watching the water. Watching the sun disappear below the cliff-top and the silhouette of Ian's grazing horse.

"I think the second thing we ought to do," Ian said, finally, "is teach you to swim."

"What's the first?"

"Get married. This living together is for university students. I'm too old."

"Is that so?" She put her head on his shoulder.

He wasn't yet ready to concede everything. He said, with mock petulance, "I *still* want to see my children."

Jemma took his hand and pressed it against her belly, which was round where it had been flat. As he tried to fathom what she was telling him, she reached up under her sleeve and withdrew a Rolex—his Rolex—she'd been wearing as an armband. She said, "You'll have to wait about six months…"

She gave him the watch, and he let his breath out slowly as he looked at it. It was all too much at once. He put the watch back on her arm.

She said, "You'll have to stick around at least sixteen years for a grandchild."

She put her head back on his shoulder. He put his arm around her, and they watched the water for a while, each thinking his own thoughts.

After a bit, she giggled. "Do you realize we'll die before we're born?"

"What's more frightening—we're at risk of becoming our own ancestors."

August 1

It was a rare, sunny day. The tiny beach on the eastern shore of the reservoir and the grassy, tree-shaded picnic area swarmed with people recreating. The western rim of the reservoir gleamed in the afternoon light, its steep cliff in shadows below.

Margaret Carreg Gwaed and her husband shared a blanket on the grass with Peter—dividing his attention between *National Geographic* magazine, his wife, Susannah, and his toddler-son, Ian. Baby Ian joyously practiced his newly acquired skill of walking, under Peter and Susannah's watchful eyes. And with feet tucked under him and a satisfied smile on his face, Charles the cat sat in the shade of a nearby folding chair and watched.

Margaret stretched and told them, "I wish we could stay a month." She was very pregnant.

Michael gently stroked the bulge of her abdomen. "We'll come back next summer. You know," he told Peter, "it's a mystery to me why you Brits are always complaining about your weather. It isn't this nice in New York at this time of year."

"Huh. If you want a real mystery, tell me who sent this." He waved the magazine at Michael.

"Probably a promotion gimmick," Margaret said. "You'll eventually get a subscription blank in the mail."

"For an American magazine? And it came in a plain wrapper with a London postmark."

"Strange," Michael said.

Peter turned another page and stared at the picture. "Oh my God!" He had the immediate attention of the others. "Look!" He shoved the magazine at his sister and her husband.

Holding tight to young Ian's hand, Susannah looked over their shoulders. "Isn't that the stuff they found up at the henge last year?"

They had all seen the golden Celtic ring depicted in the photo before. On Ian Carreg's finger.

Peter read aloud, "'...found at Cymry Henge with other grave goods in the late first or early second century burial of a Celtic chieftain. Also found were feminine objects that would indicate that the man was buried with his wife.' Oh my God!" He held his hand next to the magazine photo, so they could see that the ring on his finger was identical to the one in the photo. "There's more. Take a look at this!" He turned the page and handed the magazine to Margaret.

The picture showed an ornate, ceramic bowl that had Celtic designs around its base and rim, with figures pictured between them. It required little imagination to see that the figures represented Ian and Jemma with two small children and two oversized gray horses. In the background of the picture, they could see a stylized representation of the Cymry stone circle and the henge.

"Henderson sent it," Michael said, mildly.

And Margaret added, "He said that she'd leave him a sign."

M.I.A.

This gripping novel of suspense is a tale of violent men and violent passions, of missing friends, of loss and love and discovery.

The accidental death of Rhiann Fahey's second husband leaves her paralyzed by grief and has her son Jimmy cutting school and drinking. The widow's problems are compounded by unwanted advances from her dead husband's friend. She does her best to cope, returning to work, dealing patiently with Jimmy's misbehavior, telling Rory Sinter she isn't interested.

Then a mysterious stranger moves next door. John Devlin offers Rhiann beer and sympathy. He offers Jimmy work.

When Sinter tries to discredit John, then beat him to death, Rhiann comes to John's rescue. But she discovers her perfect neighbor isn't what he'd seemed—which leads her to investigate, and to see John in a different light altogether.

A beautifully written story with characters who come to life from the first page, M.I.A. shows one more side of Michael Allen Dymmoch's powerful storytelling ability.

The Fall

How far would you go to save your life and your world?

After a nasty divorce, single mother Joanne Lessing finally has her life together, and she's made a name for herself as a photographer. Then, while on assignment, she witnesses a hit and run. Property damage only. No big deal, she thinks. So she does the right thing—calls the cops. Joanne is dismayed when FBI agents arrive with the local detective. They admit the hit and run driver was a mob killer fleeing the scene of his latest hit. Joanne is relieved to find she can't really identify the hit man.

But when she sees the killer again while on another assignment, she takes his picture and finds her new life and her son's future threatened. Caught between the Mob and the FBI, she's on her own...

Death in West Wheeling

When a local schoolteacher disappears from rural West Wheeling, acting sheriff Homer Deters investigates. Before long he's got three more missing persons, two unidentified bodies, a car theft, a twenty-three-vehicle pile-up in the center of town, a missing tiger, and a squad of agitated ATF agents to deal with.

With no help from the Feds, Homer turns to his buddy, Rye Willis, and West Wheeling's eccentric postmistress, Nina Ross, to locate the missing, identify the bodies, and bring a murderer to justice. Packed with regional charm and Deters' wit, *Death in West Wheeling* shows how wild one case can get.

Caleb & Thinnes Mysteries

The Man Who Understood Cats

Two unlikely partners join forces to solve a murder disguised as suicide and catch a killer ready to strike again.

Gold Coast psychiatrist Jack Caleb is wealthy, cultured, and gay. When one of his clients is found dead in a locked apartment—apparently from a self-inflicted wound—burned-out Chicago detective John Thinnes doesn't believe it was suicide. And Caleb is inclined to agree.

But Thinnes regards a shrink who makes house calls suspicious and starts his murder investigation with the doctor himself. An attack on Caleb that's made to look like an accidental drug overdose starts to change the detective's mind.

Soon, the two men find themselves a whirlwind of theft, scandal, and blackmail. Forced into an unlikely partnership, they'll have to confront not only a killer, but hard truths within themselves that will change them forever.

The Death of Blue Mountain Cat

The art world is the backdrop when a controversial artist reaches the end of his fifteen minutes of fame.

Native American artist Blue Mountain Cat has a style described as "Andy Warhol meets Jonathan Swift in Indian country." When he's murdered at an exclusive showing in a conservative art museum, Detective John Thinnes has no shortage of suspects. Targets of the artist's satire included a greedy developer, a beautiful Navajo woman, and black-market antiquities dealers. Even the victim's wife merits investigation.

Thinnes drafts psychiatrist Jack Caleb to guide him through the terra incognita of the art world, and their investigation turns up a desperate museum director, a savage critic, a married mistress, and shady dealings by the artist's partner. Thinnes and Caleb connect several apparently unrelated deaths as they follow leads from Wisconsin to Chicago's South Side and the mystery's explosive conclusion.

Incendiary Designs

Arson, passion, and religious fanaticism set Chicago ablaze in the deadliest summer on record.

While jogging through Chicago's Lincoln Park, Dr. Jack Caleb runs into murder—a mob setting a police car on fire—with the officer still inside. Caleb rescues the man, but later the cop's partner is found stoned to death. Detective John Thinnes is assigned to investigate.

Evidence points toward members of a charismatic church, but too many of them die in arson fires before the cops can round them up. When arson kills the apparent ring leader, it's too much coincidence. The remaining cop killers plead guilty; the case seems to be closed. But as Chicago heats up in the deadliest summer on record, it becomes clear that a serial arsonist is still at large.

A physician friend of Caleb's is implicated when some of the fire victims are found to have been drugged. To exonerate the man, Caleb sets a trap for the killer, and Thinnes and Caleb are nearly incinerated when the doctor's trap brings the case to a fiery finish.

The Feline Friendship

When a vicious rapist crosses the line into murder, Detective John Thinnes and his prickly new partner draft psychiatrist Jack Caleb to help them track the killer down.

When a young woman is brutally raped in the posh Lincoln Park neighborhood, Chicago Police detective John Thinnes catches the case—even though Thinnes hates working rapes. Worse yet, he has to deal with a new female detective who has a chip on her shoulder the size of a 12 gauge shotgun.

A second victim is murdered, and the rapes become "heater cases." What started as a simple investigation, soon twists around earlier, similar crimes. Tempers flare; the detective squad polarizes across the gender line. Dr. Jack Caleb, a psychiatrist and police consultant, is asked to mediate. But Thinnes's sometime-ally finds himself with conflicts of interest occasioned by their friendship and Caleb's own disturbing case load.

The investigation ranges from Chicago's Lincoln Park to the northern Illinois city of Waukegan. And the explosive climax explores not only the karma of evil but the beginning of a beautiful Feline Friendship.

White Tiger

The murder of a Vietnamese woman in Chicago's Uptown neighborhood brings Caleb and Thinnes together to catch a deadly criminal known only as the White Tiger.

The TV news report of a woman's murder in Uptown flashes psychiatrist Dr. Jack Caleb back to his time in Vietnam.

Assigned to investigate, Chicago detectives John Thinnes and Don Franchi find the victim's son curiously unmoved by his mother's death. Their preliminary canvass of the dead woman's neighborhood reveals that she was well liked and well off, and she had never quarreled with anyone but her "good son."

When Thinnes realizes that he knew the victim when he was stationed in Vietnam—twenty-four years earlier—he is pulled off the case. But Thinnes can't let go. And when a schizophrenic man shows up at Mrs. Lee's wake, connecting the deceased to another Vietnam vet and to an unsolved murder in wartime Saigon, Thinnes starts a retrospective investigation of that crime, soliciting Caleb's help to discover the identity of the White Tiger and set a trap for the elusive killer.